STAR GAZER

A NOVEL OF ONE MILLION YEARS AGO

Steven M. Pitzl

ISBN: 979-8-9905951-0-1

Library of Congress Control Number: 2024908871
Imprint: Steven M. Pitzl, Thomaston, GA USA

—

PROLOGUE

This is a tale of one million years ago. Life evolves slowly and our equipment was essentially the same as today. They must have been the original thinkers and the original lovers, with motivations and daydreams we would easily recognize. We are Nature's first experiment of an advanced thinking species writing its own rules, so why has our recent recorded history been a tale of human upheaval, driven by the actions of empires and regional powers?

I propose that for the longest march of human prehistory, small villages along a trade route that shared genes and language, goods and services, was a very stable unit of human society. And I mean civilized on every scale and over time, where the simple desire of young to start a family and live eventful fulfilling lives in peace is the norm and they had done so.

This tale is in the subtle and expressive language of today and happens in fast-time with a single individual, but consider that the events and astronomical observations could have unfolded on any timescale. Over a lifetime, or even several. The end result being that even ancient people could glimpse their place in the universe, and essential truth about their world.

We had socialized and innovated but had no need for stone monuments to cheat time, and they would not have anyway. If there are, they are buried in the deep sediments of East Africa. You and I are their only legacy.

Darwinian stuffed shirts of the 19th and early 20th century, the men who considered modern Pygmies and ancient humans less than men, would never buy this tale.

This is dedicated to stuffed shirts and petticoats everywhere. Long may they shed stuffing so their minds may take flight, and they might evolve.

STAR RISE I

As a young child he had found the night sky incomprehensibly different sometimes and the same also, a puzzle to be solved later. But if someone pointed to the sky while standing in the river valley looking towards the Rwenzori Mountains to the East, near Rift Valley in equatorial Africa... right after dusk, you would begin to see stars emerging over the mountains. The star field above and around them all rises as one, and the sharp relief of the peaks brings their emergence into the realm of the human attention span.

No one had pointed it out. He had glimpsed it himself. Venturing away from the dying fire watching the sky in wonder at its expanse and looking around, after a time he had become familiar enough with its stillness to notice a light in the corner of his eye where there had been none before. And so it was that he was fixed on the peak long enough to witness a star emerging and rising before his eyes. It was happening more slowly than he had seen anything happen before.

Everyone knew Mr. Sun did just that, but he travels with an entourage of searing light and splendor that obliterates the heavens, and there was much noise in his comings and goings. And Sun was known by everyone. The boy knew some people worshiped Sun and would go on about him and little else, while others worshiped Sun while refraining from mentioning his Name and yet, also went on about that and little else.

And his people did worship the sun in a way. They gave thanks to him and refrained from mentioning him directly, but only when it was daytime. There was no fear of wrath in this, and the whole gods-vs-men thing was safely ensconced in the big baggage of the future. They even told tales about Mr. Sun that were funny and bawdy.

They refrained from mentioning him during the day out of simple politeness, because he did not like to be stared at or mentioned directly.

And there was just one of him. There were so many of these. And they were happening!

———

STORIES

His mother had named him Stargazer, but in common usage it had no direct connection to the night. Its meaning was a cheerful disposition or 'one who looks up near brightness'. It also referred to the planet Venus when it rises with the sun and is visible in the morning sky between thumb and fingers of a shading hand, as it had been on the morning after his birth. It was the custom for women to name boys and men girls, so his mother had suggested it and was given a long kiss of approval.

He had gazed at the night sky before, alone and in the company of others. They always fixed on the bright ones, as he had done. There were names for them and the stories were passed along and the bright stars were people.

Like the one who wants to marry the sun and always lingers near by, but they invariably argue about some silly thing and she runs off, and then she is following him trying to make amends. Their antics play out in evening and early morning. Many wild tales about this couple, detail and drama drawn from their own lives. Adventures in courtship and communal living.

Or the bright orange star with the color of fire who is cast as the hunter. He is known to appear in different places over time, even near the sun where he attempts to woo the bright one. But she spurns his advances and the sun chases him back into the night.

And finally, the great mass that moves with the night is a driven herd of animals spanning the universe, always on the move. It is the only phenomenon in real life they know that resembles it. The tale of so great an animal passing is one of good fortune and prosperous times to a people who are principally hunters, and it always makes a great story line. When ever the bright orange one is near or almost merged with a distant star, children would point and cry, He got one!

The sun always appeared in tales of the bright one who wishes to marry him. They were night tales, since he was barely mentioned during the day. This had resulted from a strange causal loop long before, where the pain of staring had been interpreted as disapproval. Because of this and out of simple respect, it was considered impolite to look at him or speak of him when he was present.

When they admired a sunset their eyes would sweep past the departing sun without seeing. It was an extension of the politeness of not seeing or hearing human activity that was only the business of amorous couples or talking individuals. The moment the first edge of the rising sun peeked over the mountains, people turned away from the East and busied themselves in the luminous morning landscape.

The Moon was the strangest object in the sky, clearly unlike the others. It was also the strangest cultural artifact. It did not mind being looked at and shifting shadows upon it a mystery that begged for explanation and tales.

The Moon was clearly there to make the hunt extend into the night and become more successful, and that could not be denied. The hunt had been the providence of men by tradition, though anyone who demonstrated prowess was welcome to participate. But at all times to the men the Moon was a man and they referred to it that way in speech and story.

And yet the connection between menses and Moon could not be denied. These things were understood by all, and neither menses nor hunt could ever placed into a hierarchy with one above the other. Both sacred, an essential part of life. So it was only natural for women to address the Moon as she, and they had their own stories.

So the Moon was she or he depending on who was speaking. And the tales of the Moon had diverged into two separate worlds. Any tale could have a mix of male and female characters besides the Moon, but it was impolite for a woman to borrow specific characters from a man's tale, and vice versa. But women could build on women's tales and men on men's, so it became a competition that transcended individuals.

And interestingly, the taboo did not extend to event or topic. A man might tell an actual tale of a successful hunt led by the he-Moon and full of characters whose names were hilariously similar to their own, and the next evening a women's tale might re-tell the same hunt in detail with female characters who bested the men in every way. Then a tale of the very same hunt led by the he-Moon and the storyteller, who is always permitted to be a real person in the tale, is trying to teach women to hunt, but they botch the job in funny ways. And then a women's tale where the man-hunt is again incredibly successful, surprising everyone... but it is so successful the she-Moon has to carry the meat home for them because they are too weak (laughter). Then the men insist on doing the cooking and they fall asleep and burn the food.

Moon tales never contained other celestial objects and Moon prefers to associate with mortals. And diddle with them in very explicit ways.

Tales by men and women might contain escapades that the storyteller with a glance and a wink, wishes to happen to themselves.

The Moon's gender depending on the speaker made it a central character of stories of not just the hunt, society and menses but sexuality itself. From teenage love to one night stands to the joys of starting a family while young, which was a joy in the sense that parents are not just privileged to witness their children grown to adulthood as equals, but their children's children, even to the third generation. And also the joy of finding a partner later in life after one's truest love had gone to grave, to banish loneliness and find new life.

So almost half the girls were with child in their teen years with no regrets, whether the father had bonded with them or not, or was even known. There were mother figures and father figures all over, and they shared children and cared for them. Those who wanted to beat the pregnancy odds one way or the other could take herbal supplements, and those were common knowledge shared by all. Some did defer pregnancy until advanced skills were learned, or altogether. And with a total breeding population in the wide area so small, no parents could ever really pay attention to a child's resemblance, for they all resembled not-so-distant relatives anyway.

And contrary to many enduring tales of male intolerance, female fecundity is actually very sexy, and the myth of thinking man's primal urge for strict bloodline children has been hilariously overstated for dramatic purposes. Our ancestors would laugh to hear of it and become concerned for our mental health, and that of our step-children.

Life-bonding was a process of adopting her and her children as one, subject to the same rules as today. We re-wrote the rules as we evolved. The need to seed became the more general need to breed.

And we may have conquered pregnancy, but it seems we must still earnestly pretend we intend to breed. To hit those highest peaks.

And children did not desire to be sexualized or play power or domination games. Sex was all around and it was mostly boring, but great for making fun of adults. Ironically, children did not actually want to breed. They just didn't see a point to it, though they suspected they might some day.

They loved adult role playing along with other games, and an indication every so often that sex had just happened, suddenly, inexplicably and incidentally, just seemed vital to any game's overall credibility. So they made up such an indication. It was any word, gesture or action repeated six times.

It was a joke on the silly repetitiveness of it, like a mysterious 'glitch' they had spotted in adults. Choosing a different action every time made it even funnier. A boy might lift a fruit to his mouth six times when a girl walked by, and she might offer her pretend-infant the breast six times when he passed by. And they would all laugh because it seemed to them like such bizarre and compulsive behavior.

By the time they started to notice strange behavior in their older peers, those peers already had their respect. So they treated them a little more like adults, to whom they were always polite, and gave them more privacy to play their new games. Which did not exempt them from a six-times joke now and then. And they would do a special jig to ward off adult cooties. Doing the dance six times was the funniest joke of all.

Above all, children valued their sanity.

It was a thoroughly civilized society.

As soon as they were mobile, children had the run of the village and knew where and when they were welcome, which was almost

everywhere. They were guests at one's hearth, especially as playmates
for their own children. And parents could ask theirs to go away at
any time in complete assurance for their safety through the night.

That reason might be scorn from misbehavior or a chore not done,
or even because parents wished for 'quiet time' to engage in
strenuous and lengthy exercises away from distracting eyes. It was a
joke among children that parents' desire for 'quiet time' should
always be the reason given to one's adopted family for the night, so
one would never be prompted to explain how they had angered their
parents.

And that is how wandering children not only brought spice to the
sex lives of their parents, but bonded couples in the community as a
whole. For children would always arrive with that particular reason
and the adults would feel a twinge of jealousy, for imagining the
actions of the others fueled their own desires.

So host families always thought others were having fun and they were
not, and then if children from two families arrived at the doorway
the next night, the imagining would grow to fever pitch. If they
inquired with parents during the day, few wished to gossip about
their children's indiscretions if any, and they would usually just smile
and shrug, even more fuel for the imagination.

It brought adults into the children's joke without sharing it. And on
the third night a herd of children might arrive to find the door-
covering shut, which was also a universal sign. It meant they had
probably banished their own children for the night, and they could
be found somewhere else. Perhaps even more children also. And
that would be a fun slumber party!

The young told stories also. In the lull between stories there was
conversation and comments, and anyone who had a story to tell
would raise an arm with fingers pointed at the central fire. Those

who had noticed would call out their name or silently point a finger in their direction as a sign of approval. Then the storyteller would raise arms to the sky and all would become silent. If you were still talking or not paying attention, you might be jostled gently from the side or behind.

When ever they wished, children became storytellers as long as they performed the proper ritual of recognition. Otherwise they would be ignored. With everyone's attention they would articulate as best they could. Their stories tended to be brief, and at any time anyone could rise and step into the stage circle between the crowd and central fire and act it out. The youngest dispensed with language and illustrated their stories with utterances and actions. The audience patient, amused and supportive like school pageants today. But even the young could present astounding ideas.

One night a young girl was recognized and stepped out shakily, under a vista of stars. She adopted the familiar posture of one stalking prey. This was a common theme and one hand grasped an invisible spear, while the other gave hand signals to nearby hunters, a sign that she was leading the hunt. Then she stood suddenly and cast. The crowd muttered as the spear met its mark. They knew it had because she indicated assent.

But then she quickly brushed her waist as if reaching for another, and cast it also. This was a thing, and only the most skilled could pull it off. The muttered encouragement sounded again, louder as she implied it had also met its mark. But now she was reaching again and casting, and then with both arms at once. Now both arms were cartwheeling as she grasped and cast spears constantly from both sides, as if she had an infinite supply. She even swung around on her feet to cast them wide in a slow circle. The crowd laughed with surprise! She paused for a moment and gave a quick nod and pointed forward, a sign by the hunt leader that this stage was over and they must rush in for the kills. But then she was casting again! She had tilted her head back and was casting spears up into the sky. Now she was hunting the great herd! Several dozen imaginary spears met their marks before she lost balance and fell on her back. Even then her hands twitched as if she was still in action.

The crowd jumped up and rushed forward with a roar of laughter, lifting her up to toss her into the air and catch her. It was ultimate sign of audience approval. But as it became obvious that while in the air, she continued to cast furiously into the sky, the roar grew to a crescendo every time she was tossed and caught. Almost a hundred virtual spears took flight. When at last caught and set on her feet, she was surrounded in a group hug. Everyone felt transformed by this. None had ever witnessed such theater, and all who had done the tossing and catching felt the same tinge of satisfaction as a hunt gone well.

A future storyteller began, Let me tell you of the great hunt when animals rained down from the sky. Remembering that evening brought a chorus of laughter. And persons with a name that resembled hers passed into the stories of men and women with new deeds, and as a cautionary tale to never stop practicing spear craft even as one becomes deft. And that girl did indeed grow to become a great hunter, ambidextrous in real life as her own vision had shown. She could cast all the spears she carried with speed and accuracy in the time it took others to cast two or three, and it was something to strive for.

Aging is a gradual process of acting out and becoming, and storytelling itself immersed the young into the world of elders, as elders themselves were regularly subject to episodes of seeing through the eyes of the young, and remembered how they had been.

Such was the power of human society when tradition encouraged all to give their undivided attention to one, even when the one is a small child. There were no 'coming of age' ceremonies in that tribe, not even to celebrate the monster of puberty. Such ceremonies would create schism between friends and siblings who were still essentially children. Or maneuver girls into an uncertain future by becoming chattel to be bartered in the present. Older boys were never subject to rituals as many other tribes did, ceremonies where they were scratched by pretend-predators and emerged as men, ready or not.

Involvement in the real world was gradual and seamless. Children confined to camp would often be engaged in role-playing games, but there was also the firm expectation that everyone must learn everything that had ever needed to be done, and master it to some degree. It may not fit the prejudices of later eras, but boys also learned to gather and prepare food, process skins and cook, girls to carry and cast weapons, and everyone was expected to become a field medic. Young boys watching over infants might fetch a breastfeeding woman to hand over cleaned babies to feed, and take charge of them after with the seriousness of shepherds watching over a flock.

And everyone had to learn the essential skill of weaving with sinew, brambles, grasses and leather-craft, to produce garments and the containers that carried water, and helped heat water and soup with cooking stones. These water baskets and skins took time to create, yet were as essential in their way as food itself. Anyone can imagine famine, but try to imagine a society that cannot easily carry and store water, or cook broth in baskets with hot stones.

Pots would later serve this purpose but there was little workable clay in the valley. Learning tight weaving began even before muscles grew strong and fingers dexterous, and the youngest would braid grasses and straw into cord, or sit next to a post driven into the ground and wrap cords around it, leaning away from the post to pull the weave tight.

Children without the endurance and skill to complete baskets would begin by producing sections of grass weave and soft leather pieces little bigger than potholders. They were used for that purpose to turn shanks and vegetables in the fire and lift them out, and hold meat. There was always a pile of these with thin cords stacked by the cooking hearths. The pile was large and production went on steadily because the pieces were also used for another purpose, women tied them in place under their breech-cloths during the Moon time. A suitor might present hand crafted pads to one he fancied, and if she didn't give them back or he didn't later spot them in one of the piles, a romance was definitely a possibility.

Baskets could become essentially waterproof when treated with boiled tallow, pitch or the unfolded stomachs, bladders and intestines of animals. These organs were useful in their own right and believed to carry unique forms of nutrition. Intestines were strung out beside the carcass and split open with a sharp stone to empty their contents, and given a first cleaning in water as soon as possible. It was not unusual to see a returning hunter, the rope bearer, straggling behind the others festooned with strips of intestine, with hanging stomachs and bladders knotted and dangling from cords.

People would rush to the river to help the rope and hide bearers wash them. Then the bearers would don the cleaned things once more, and the burdened ones ceremoniously strode into camp to the adoration that was the right of any hunter. To an occasional shout, What great ones! But it looks like your prey was already dead. Occasionally hunters did come upon a recent carcass and co-opted it, but the implication they had done so was low-brow humor.

The brighter stars in the great herd who moved with the sky herd were people too, though less often noted. In later times of domestication they might be cast as shepherds, but in the time of the hunt they are the callers, people recruited by hunters to wave things and shout, to divert the herd in circles or in this case, a straight line towards some distant choke point or cul de sac. The moment of engagement by the hunters in the stories was always beyond the sky, which made for tales with no beginning and an ending rooted in the imagination.

The great herd had even infused the language. A hand raised to the sky day or night reminded others of the herd and was a friendly sign of optimism in times of hardship, carrying the meaning, they will come. Hands meeting in the air sealed the prophecy between friend or stranger. Suspicious folk of our age pontificate it had meant one bore no weapons, as if these early people were warlike and always ready to tear one another to shreds. But of course almost everyone had weapons, all the time! Men and women and children, in their hands, their belts, tucked into garments. A young girl was as resolved to attack an advancing hyena with stone, stick or spear as anyone. Such is the world.

People retire to large circular thatched mud huts and there are many on the landscape. The mud comes from a nearby quarry by the river that has been dug for centuries, and it is not quite as dense as clay, but when mixed with water and grasses it will stick in place to seal gaps. After it dries it will shed water without dissolving for awhile. Supporting the shell is a network of many branches interlocked and tied with skill, leaning towards an interior central pole. Near the entrance of each occupied dwelling there is a hearth surrounded by stones, and sleeping skins into the gloom. skins and sealed baskets keep perishables away from insects and mice.

The meeting-place is surrounded by huts, and has a fire fed in the evening for story telling that is permitted to go out at night.

A 'fire kit' is a pouch with twigs and tinder, often dried hair, rolled into a bundle with notch-sticks, twirling sticks and caps. Lighting a fire with these can be almost impossible in rainy conditions. It takes three people to do it in reasonable time, taking up positions around the stick and the first clasps tightly at the top and spins back and forth furiously while applying some downward pressure, so their hands drift downwards. The third holds the cap and presses down firmly. The cap is a piece of stone with an indent so the stick may turn freely underneath. As the first approaches the stick's base the second clasps the top and begins downwards. They all swap tasks so the one holding the cap has a brief respite from the arduous twirling. Smoldering tinder is lifted and blown into flame. There are regular fire-drill-drills to practice this difficult art.

As the community had grown it had been decided to keep two fires burning always in a couple of small dwellings around the common hearth devoted to that purpose, so families were not distracted by constant firelight or the comings and goings of those who need to borrow fire. Torches and spears stand by in these rooms in case predators are sighted and there is need for them. When people retired for the night they had long closed and even barricaded their entrances remembering those times, but the custom of the successful village is to leave them open into late evening to invite conversations and children, unless privacy is desired.

Watchers of the fire are typically adolescents and younger, tending it and keeping vigil over the camp overnight as exhausted adults sleep. Even in these times of peace from predation this is approached with utmost seriousness. Watching is a critical task tied to survival, as they must occupy themselves in the firelight by sharpening things with stones, fire-treating spear tips and the drying, rolling together or weaving of grasses and long stems, softening and stitching of skins, assembling garments. A complement of three, always at least two awake and others welcome, and each watches the others for signs of sleepiness. If one is nudged with a spear point and a smile, it is wise to take a walk to clear the head and shake off sleep.

The fading of a seed-fire to glowing coals was their nightmare, and two might awaken in panic to fumble for tinder and coax from it a tongue of flame to be fed. But the worst of all was to awaken in darkness. Maintaining two seed-fires was a clever idea and kindness saving many young from acute embarrassment and shame. If the other watchers arrived late at night with crazed eyes bearing torches to be lit, those tending the fire would rise and greet them with a long embrace to calm their nerves. They would depart with borrowed fire in complete secrecy. Any who had witnessed it would refrain from mentioning. They might have been awakened by the sharp sound of a well-intentioned stone tossed from outside.

The idea that essential and time-consuming craft work continued 'around the clock' was a great source of pride to the people, for they aggressively traded their manufactured goods. And fire watchers of all ages working in shifts gained status and trade goods for their families in doing so.

The community was on the West side of a small mountain range. The mountains were not volcanic in origin and had been upthrust as recently as some two million years previous, in a series of violent and occasional geologic events. It took only several days to traverse the range on either side but at the time of this tale, migrating animals and humans had approached them from North and South on seasonal journeys from time immemorial, and always had to make the crucial decision which side to veer beside the mountains.

Humans had been migrating North to escape arid lands full of predators. Their communities now extended far beyond to distant lakes and down the headwaters of the Nile, most too distant for regular trade or chance meeting. But the group founding this community had been traveling from the grass plains far in the South, and the gentle highlands and the coolness of the mountains' shadows enticed them, and they had decided to settle there as other groups continued on. This eventually placed them at a confluence of a long corridor of settled peoples, and trade flourished.

They traded for meat to supplement their own hunts, and the skins of animals and plumes of birds to feed an industry of craft, and supplied prepared medicines, sturdy clothing and footwear, or heavily stitched skins for water bearing, and all manner of woven goods from sinew, grass and reed, breechcloths and baskets. Stitched skins and baskets of sturdy reeds with an internal animal lining were prized for carrying food and cooking with heating stones, and were eagerly traded up and down river.

Stories of the days when people were migrants on the grass plains told it was the young vigil and keep of fire-watch that permitted adults to retire into the healing realm of sleep without care. A child who had maintained such a vigil may be greeted formally with a closed-eyes nod which means, 'thank you for the dreams'.

Before pets, fire was the first domesticated animal. It was not unusual to come upon one speaking softly to it, confiding secrets or asking advice, or couples asking favors of it. Some stories even began with the preamble that it is the fire speaking, and these are often cautionary tales of disaster and bad times. One such is the origin of the fire vigil itself, and the pivotal role the eyes of children had played.

The tasking of children to maintain a fire-watch and nightly vigil had a long history stretching into the vagueness of remembered time. Was a time when the people were nomads on the landscape following herds year round with only the crudest of improvised shelter and no generational stone hearths. A task of preparing for the first night in a new camp was to clear a large circle and stocking grasses and wood to feed a fire. Luminous coals had always been carried in the skulls of animals as they wandered, yet all were prepared for the task of stick-twirling when necessary.

On the plains there had been no luxury of idleness for story-time. The adults would collapse around the fire into circles around the children. Elders who attended children during the day when people foraged and hunted were expected to maintain a vigil also and always tried, but diminished faculties and a simple lack of outwardly directed eyes around the circle was a serious vulnerability to all, and it would have been impossible had it not been for the children.

Children would seat themselves around the inner circle with backs to the fire, gazing over sleeping forms into the darkness. Their task was specific and articulated from a young age, and might even have passed into the realm of instinct. In the day they were desirous of close company but at night they would separate around the inner circle, so outward-directed eyes could cover many degrees of arc. There was a 'silent language of children' they taught one another, and each would glance left and right to their peers and converse in gestures and facial expressions through the night. But always attentive to the corner of the eye where night-vision and discernment of movement was sharpest.

They would sleep and awaken by arrangement, but as their number reduced towards three a keen sense of urgency would grow, and they would quietly wake others and reshuffle the circle.

If a fussy infant wiggled away from a sleeping mother, a child would gather it in a wrap to cover its eyes and sit by the fire rocking and murmuring softly. Then it would be returned to the mother who would awaken with a smile, to gather it to her bosom. Children were always rising to tend the fire.

The children had been watching the darkness for eyes reflected in firelight. It was important that the smaller and younger ones did this as soon as they were able, for it was they the eyes would be peering at. This would be the most modern instinct evolved in the human species, for it could never have arisen in animals or before people were gathered around a night time fire. Eyes floating in the darkness is a staple-nightmare of children. Perhaps because some of them remember.

Predators on the Savannah were well aware of humans entering their territory and would creep up on them in the dead of night, when the tallest and most terrifying were prone and still. If only a Moon had illuminated the scene their task would be simple and straightforward as for any predator, to rush in and take the smallest and retreat to darkness. And even with heightened senses the young were helpless and the predators' stealth would serve them well.

Only seen when evasion was impossible, only sounding alarm as they were carried away, soon to be silenced.

But a predator would note that these were different. There was a tongue of flame in the center of the group clearly separate from the calamity of unchecked grass and forest fire. As the predators' eyes swept light in which prey was visible in great detail, hunger would steadily overcome any instinctive aversion to it. It was just a patch of Moon that had fallen to Earth, or sunlight that had lost its way and strayed into night. So they'd dwell on a small objective and plot a bounding path to prey and away into the night. Biding their time. The cover of grass, brush, tree, and darkness had always been absolute.

But then the whole camp woke and burst into motion! Dark shapes swirled in front of the light. Fire breaking into fireflies of fast-lighting torches. This did not panic the boldest predators and they remained still in their hiding places, for they did not fear people at a distance and the noise people were making was not urgently sharp and loud. Confusion presents opportunity also, and their instinct told them that a roused herd is likely to move off in one direction and they can give chase in the dark, culling the young. But these animals brought confusion to the predators. They were fixed in place yet didn't even form a moving circle around their young, as a trapped herd sometimes will.

The predator had been lured into a trap itself, one that had worked for aeons. It did not fear them, but torches were always in motion and commanded attention, obscuring detail in the light. Under cover of confusion a strategy was playing out, organized with quiet hand signals and pointing gestures. Those with spears turned their own eyes away from light, not to glimpse a threat. They were keeping their night vision intact.

Figures and torches formed a V shaped wedge and burst forward, the lead figure headed directly towards the predator's hiding place! But this is impossible! They'd remain rooted in place with rising disbelief, then most predators would break off to the side because their own instinct was to keep a threat or objective in the corner of their eyes. But as their attention had been drawn to the light and noise, dark figures with spears had streamed into the darkness on both sides, flanking in straight lines. When the fire wedge advanced they had already taken positions and the predator would be the only thing moving in the light. Many an intended night ambush ended with a large cat felled by two or more spears and brought back to camp for good eating.

The alarm had been raised by a child calling suddenly and pointing directly at the hiding place, as the predator had first arrived around the fringes and started spotting targets. The child would remain still and never waver from the pointed direction until others noted the position and took up the plan. If the predator hunt was successful the spotter was venerated and given the first bite of meat. Cats are solitary hunters, but if flanking hunters spotted pack animals they'd fall back on a shouted signal and just try to take down as many as they could.

Owls hunt with the Moon at their back to spot a reflection on faces of their prey, and their prey avoid looking at the Moon for that reason. But this played out on ground level.

Children with backs to the fire had a clear and direct line of sight to light reflected from predators' eyes. This was the first time in the whole history of Earth that prey had seized this advantage and turned the tables, and on the timeline of evolution and animal instinct it was as sudden as a thunderclap. The color of eyes reflected in fire is a ruddy orange with flickers of yellow, so that would be the seat of the nightmare.

The fire vigil was a terrifying tale that must be told, they felt, and children especially were glad when it ended. Their backs were no longer to the fire but the fewer people there were, they might begin to feel compelled to turn and take up that position. But even the rising sparks of fire could create brief twinges to make them shudder. Central to the tale was always the message: even as you fear for your life, you must never fear the darkness. And you need not even fear eyes in the darkness so long as you take fate into your own hands and spring into action knowing what needs to be done.

Children would resonate with this idea. Despite any parental effort to spare them from emotional turmoil, there eventually came a time when they would beg their parents to show them what must be done about 'the eyes'. The remedy was to introduce practical defense and weapon techniques and discipline of procedure. Growing skill and poise brought confidence and freedom from anxiety. For a few it actually resulted from nightmares, but for most it was just a rite of passage they themselves initiated.

Humans are a wonder in the world, and their settlement was a modern time of wattle fences bounding the land. Many of the fences were alive and had been planted by previous generations, such as intersecting willows drinking easily from a water table near the surface. Useful plants grew along paths both seeded and harvested with early awareness of agriculture. Fences surrounded human settlements where there was easy river access, fire-on-tap and local predators had long been hunted to extinction. Herds migrated from the North or the South, and the river to the East had long fence lines beside it to create choke-points for animals towards the foot of the mountains. To the West was a broad landscape and a few fence lines useful if humans could drive a herd close enough to them.

Just after sunset the communal fire is stoked and dinner is prepared. Everyone listens intently to stories and there is laughter at hand gestures or things acted out. If the stellar figures mentioned are present, he glances up at them with the rest.

But he has never felt deeply expressive with that type of language and has never stepped forward to tell stories around the fire. The voice in his head is usually a murmuring narration of what is happening, and what do next, as if he lives inside a story without boundaries, hearing it told from without. A stream that would not be intelligible to others but in his mind it is precise and descriptive. He has made up countless 'words' for things that are intricate and unpronounceable in real life, but he remembers them and uses them to himself.

He had been the youngest in recent memory to formally approach his parents about 'the eyes', unusual for one of 4 years. His father had put the word out to acquaintances that they must seek out the boy and busy him in productive activities and skill-building exercises to combat potential anxiety. He associated well with others but tended to be alone.

By the age of 4 children were typically entering a social stage of role playing and occasional busywork, and during that time they would act out everything, and share many stories with one another. This social stage was a period marked by gradual awareness of adult concerns, but also a growing feeling of protectiveness towards everyone, especially the younger. And awareness of vulnerability.

By age 8 they were skilled in many areas and a child might ask about 'the eyes', which at that age was considered to be a tradition expressing personal resolve to learn skills of defense, survival and craft. To signal their readiness to follow a more adult course, and seldom was personal statement of anxiety in those times.

But Stargazer's parents had not been so sure. Nevertheless, once this ancient anxiety had been expressed by a child it could not be denied. To do so was unhealthy and would lead to older ones and adult people who feared the darkness and acted irrationally from a sense of helplessness and dread. Unhappy badly adjusted individuals.

The child's only mental salvation was to build skill and ability to the greatest extent that patient adults could give. His parents gave of their own time and begged others to give it also. They promised favors and gifts to those skilled in survival, craft and hunt who might take the child aside and demonstrate and offer patient instruction, that he might decide the course of his life.

They need not have worried. Thus invited to others' workplaces, this particular child could not just relate to both children and adults, he charmed mentors with a level of dedication and concentration that was extraordinary. He soon had invitations from craft people and cooks, preparers of skins, builders of fences and houses, those who gathered food and herb, water carriers and diggers and maintainers of latrines. He not only charmed them with directed conversation and assistance, but by making 'appointments' for their time in the future. So novel an idea they remarked upon it to others.

Children his age usually rose with the dawn and went to find other children for play, but he was up long before dawn and found his way to those on fire watch, feeding fires and dividing his time between them. Free from the industry and pressure of daylight he was free to watch their craft, then to take over while they watched, stretched their arms and offered advice. His hands moved quickly but not without error, and they'd be amused and impressed when his hands worked furiously and made the same mistake over and over in some difficult process... but without a trace of frustration or anger.

They'd place a hand on his shoulder and tell him to close his eyes and take a deep breath to let his hands catch up, or touch his hands in friendly drama as if imparting magic. Then he'd resume with some muscle or angle slightly changed, and would do it successfully. Then again and again. It seemed he was learning with astounding speed.

It was simpler than that, he just remembered every position and movement with uncanny accuracy. And he always strove to do it without raising envy in others. At the moment he knew something and might be tempted to press on with blazing speed, he would pause and give back the work and let the new skill settle in his mind, just as they had suggested... and he would watch them and give encouragement and praise for their efforts. And then with a polite farewell he'd be off.

His regular presence among latrine diggers had been a novelty at first, for he was a small boy among men while so many other idle boys chose to shadow hunter practice fields. The maintenance of latrines was serious business, for small communities such as this one were the first in human history where these luxuries could be placed around the back of individual dwellings. There were now many dwellings in close proximity, and now only usually only two or three needed to share a latrine.

Large community latrines had always been places of unpleasantness and septic horror, with a constant stream of people using them and some arriving from a distance, and the eventual need for major work to build another and seal the old. But they were much easier to maintain on a smaller scale. And it was a bringer of specialization and local commerce, for it was an early thing those dedicated to the profession could learn to do well and quickly, and the house owners might rather not do.

But they soon learned he was a hard worker doing what ever his small stature permitted, but he was also gifted with a keen mind that was ever on the task at hand and offered good suggestions for improving the work. He could keep an endeavor and the collective purpose in mind and fit them together to refine each.

It was Stargazer who first suggested that every latrine in the village should have three standard plots of ground with one in use, the next being dug over time for future use one layer at a time, so time spent digging was short at each place. And while the third was finally in use, the first could be excavated with less unpleasantness, for nature and time had aged its content.

It was Stargazer who first suggested latrine diggers should take over and organize the regular collection of wood ash from hearths everywhere, leaving the owner only what they desired for fertilizer and craftwork and taking the rest, so they could maintain large central stockpiles of it, and sprinkle it to sweeten latrines and when they were full, help seal them so nature's process could take over.

And finally it was young Stargazer who invented what he called 'hunt and gather digging', which started as his own innovation to the difficult digging of undisturbed earth for deep trenches and graves. Now all used it. Diggers would walk a path in the trench with sharp spears perforating and shifting the earth and loosening it to some depth, always in a line so one's spear had little chance of meeting another's foot. Then they set aside the spears for a time of gathering and excavating loosened dirt with hands and such scooping implements as evolved over time. As little as three cycles of this could be a day's work at any single place, and they could do more or move on to the next.

When he had first arrived among the latrine folk, they were typically called out for dire emergencies to perform rigorous work under pressure because others had too long procrastinated. And they ever had to beg wood ash to do their job well. As his suggestions were implemented they became itinerant workers who roamed through the village between regular appointments of their own, and they worked hard, but there was always time to stretch tired muscles and socialize with those they met.

He focused attention also to a very difficult aspect of craft, the rendering of tough elastic raw strips of dried muscle straight from the animal, into sizes of sinew fibers that ranged down to the tiny, and rolling them over a flat surface into roundness, to eventually stitch skin and toughened leather together and even secure beads and ornaments on all scales of product. Or hold so tightly as make a good seal for water skins and vessels used with cooking stones.

The sight of whole bundles of sinew fibers extracted and rolled from raw materials and each tested for strength, arranged by diameter and ready for use, is a joy to behold. It is very time consuming to do. In a village that had specialized in craft and trade there was now a demand for prepared sinew that was practically industrial in scale. Sinew of all sizes was a necessary component in many supply chains and many stages of production, and raw muscle straight from the animal was now set aside by many villages as a trade good in itself to be received by the craft people, since when dried it was as non-perishable as the final fibers themselves and could be collected over time easily.

Stargazer knew he was somehow boredom-proof, so unlike many acolytes who always strove to become involved in the final stages of production and hold in their hands useful items and take rightful pride in finishing them, he was always content to be part of some invisible support network.

And though he never found a way to dramatically escalate the speed of sinew preparation, he found many small ways to parallelize the task itself and optimize the process for an industrial village. For there had always been a bottleneck in the preparation of the smallest fibers, for only the most skilled could produce them and it took long for them to yield many from a single piece.

But he found that by cutting the edge cleanly and then attacking it at random by stabbing and raking with pointed thorns and keen edged stones for awhile, the subsequent separation of this random attack would yield fibers of all sizes including the smallest, and every one useful somewhere. To be later sorted for size and use.

When he had suggested this might be a good idea he was discouraged, for anyone who worked with sinew would have no use for such an obvious tactic, they could do much better, and they smiled affectionately at his earnest attempt to help. And then he thought about it, and pointed out that a random attack and separation and initial rolling of fibers what ever their size, could also be performed with little teaching by many children at once and those on fire-watch, most adults, and even one whose vision was too impaired to take the next steps. And the whole task was well within any attention span. And they stared at him long and knew it would scale to great usefulness and became excited. And it happened as he had described. He was just glad to help as always, and devoted much time himself to sinew production.

He eventually brought innovations big and small to every place he set to work. They were always delivered as suggestions he demonstrated with his own hands when he could, or posed as ideas to others politely. And he never forgot them, so he could be very persistent over time.

The whole day passed this way and he would keep every appointment he had made. By the end of the day he had done many different things and he would retire early after a self-made meal before sunset. In the afternoon he'd bring ingredients to the fire watchers and prepare a light meal for them, sharing it and bringing some home to present to his family who were full of wonder at this little man who provided for them. Quite the change from his previous nervous and shy self. But that was not challenging. He knew that to others something like a meal carried mystique, but for him it just resulted from a bit of focused deliberate action.

As years passed and aside from a growing interest in weaving and craft, and solitary walking while gathering plants and hunting small game, he had continued to spend time with the most skilled, in a circuit of daily 'appointments'. Every one praised his skill and concentration, indicating that he was savvy enough to make a career of it, and many were confident he'd soon make such an announcement.

He was able to lob a spear with accuracy and force into a distant target. The next step was for him to formally declare an interest to hunt professionally, but he had not done so. But the mentors knew that his skill with targets had a serious weakness. He would gaze for a time in concentration and the first cast was true, but he could not maintain it in speed or motion. As targets were moving he would seriously falter. Younger children soon surpassed him in those areas with furious practice. But also, the shifting landscape as would be experienced during a hunt, seemed to confuse him sometimes.

Ironically by sacrificing a phase of childhood he had gained a head start into the world and by all estimation, had learned to do almost all of the things that must be done, and did many well. But he had not spent child-time among children, or been swayed by the nuance that leads the elder ones into declaring a specialty, and pursuing it with determination. Maybe motivated in part by their desire to seek a mate and begin new chapters of life. He did not socialize for its own sake or specialize. So everyone leaned towards the idea that his path would be one of thoughtful solitude, excelling in a craft.

Adults greeted him as an old friend, children by his name even when he was not the eldest.

Peers drilling as hunters had dubbed him 'he who casts the first spear', which may have begun in jest of accuracy that left when things started moving. But he impressed them with it, and accepted the title and was a star at training camp. He demonstrated helpful techniques of spear making, sighting, posture and stance to others, as golfers seek today.

He served on fire watch often, and while serving in that official capacity he was no longer reluctant to reveal the skill with which his hands moved. In weaving or stitching he was extraordinary. From potholder to spiral weave to completed basket and garment, hands flew in smooth furious motion. He even built a loose man-sized basket from steam-softened branches that was a great curiosity, just so he could see how to do it. He told others, you supply the man.

When others stood by to admire, his fingers and hands would slow to a crawl as he tried to illustrate actions with exaggeration and a bit of narrative was not quite a story. Things like, He runs around the tree and pulls it tight until it leans towards the river. Then he dives in and surfaces next to a log but it keeps spinning and won't let him climb on. When it comes around he snags it and slides to the side, and the log is wrapped round and round, to the end, when he dives down to loop the end and wrap around the other. Then he is off to the next tree, diving under and over the grass. Around the tree and over and under this time into the river, pushing it together on the log and starting a new one. With hands hastening to a blur again.

When he wove or stitched, with little effort he could look at a part of raw material and see the place in the finished product where it would be. It had not proved to be a very useful skill, but it was fun.

One day he arrived to fire-watch with bundles of dyed deep blue and pale grass fibers with an idea in his head for a pad that was to be different from the others. Colors emerged and dived between inner layers until a confusing mass of fibers hung from each surface. To those passing by it looked like a mistake or practicing. But he knew their lengths and destinations, and on the final outer layers a complicated pattern emerged from those underneath that terminated where they were supposed to, as contrasting fibers met right on the very edges of the design and each was tucked under. In little more time than it took anyone to complete a plain one, he had created one that was not so plain. It was an actual white crescent Moon with a dark blue sky around it, with a few white dots suggesting stars. On the opposite side a precise inverse of the image. Day and Night. And the design was embedded in the weave itself.

If anyone involved in the trade network had spotted it they would have been stunned as they grasped its value immediately, and urged him to decorate other things. But he himself was not so aware or inclined, and he just looked at the end product with satisfaction as he remembered the steps to make it. Then he was done with the experiment and casually put it in the pile with plain ones and started making plain ones again. They were later gathered up as a pile for trade.

A few moons later a girl about Stargazer's age sifted through a pile gathering Moon pads. She was of the lake people, and they traded their fish and birds and herd meat and sinew and bone with communities to the North for manufactured goods. The craft people prized the birds for their feathers especially.

Something caught her eye and she reached for it. One of the pads had a pattern so amazing and mesmerizing she had to stare and hold it up to the firelight. She turned it over and was even more surprised. She had also made this type herself and it was very curious. Later she cut a few strands and lifted a corner to see the middle layers and expected to find some easy trick. But the middle was a chaotic mix of the colors and many fibers rose or descended into the outer designs in many places. She could clearly see the outer layer was not painted or dyed, but it was a perfect design in the weave made from many lengths. How do you even plan to make such a thing? Who made this? And why put it with the others? She brought it out to examine many times after, this most amazing thing that had come to her it seemed, by chance alone. It made her think of early childhood and the person she had once been.

Its beauty and mystery would grow on her.

Stargazer already had a place in society, many places actually, but he was different in ways he could never explain. He had seen things and heard things, other people wouldn't believe.

His brain had sung lullabies to him in the womb.

The mountain had sung to him.

And he walks with polygons.

———

INTERMISSION: MUTANT

The drought had altered migration patterns. Grass lands to the South had dried and were now choked with wind swept dust. Lakes to the South were diminishing. Their own river was muddy and barely flowing, and they had dug a circular well into the soft riverbank lined with small stones, so a column of clear water seeped into it and they could dip baskets and skins.

The latest migrations had been spotted East of the mountains in the far distance following greener grasslands towards the North. Fresh meat was now East of the mountains and there was talk of migrating themselves, as they had done long ago. Quiet preparation had begun and if the season did not bring rain, they would set out before they became too weak.

Everyone was gathering what few berries and fruits there were, and some had been foraging in parties along the river both up and down in journeys of several days. As they returned they brought leafy plants and bits of small game, even small birds and the eggs from their nests, honey from hives, slow running rodents. Anything to share and stave off hunger. But gatherers made so much noise, and the hunters were off elsewhere stalking the woods, but so far they reported small game had left or was hiding in the heat. On a long walk North of camp a woman was worried about her child. The little girl was thin with ribs showing but was putting in a great effort to help, packing things she had collected into a basket.

Back at camp everyone dumped their baskets in a row to sort the plants and prepare the meat items. A row of baskets already held hot water and more stones were in the fire, and hopefully there would be some tea-broth by sundown. Behind their backs the young girl was still trying to help with every bit of energy she had.

Suddenly an older woman rose with a cry and ran to a cooking basket and seized the girl's hands. The girl had a collection of distinctive yellow flowers and wax-like leaves. She stepped the girl away and took the items, gesturing to ask where they had come from. The girl proudly showed her cache dumped from the basket. In it were a few more of the same. Taking those too she started walking the piles to spot others. She was agitated and too tired to explain and had no time for a conversation. So the girl never had an opportunity to tell she had already made two trips to the water basket. And had carefully poked them down out of sight with a stick as she had seen others do.

Stargazer's mother was attacked in the womb about 3 weeks past conception. A germinal cell was dividing and a primordial follicle forming around its daughter cell, in a region that would later become an ovary. The follicles would enter a dormant state and might activate during ovulation to produce a mature egg and hopefully, offspring. The ancestral germinal cell was correct but there had been an error in replication. The repair mechanism had been activated, but it had malfunctioned in the presence of some bad molecules floating around.

It was a form of plant alkaloid that poisons in large quantities like many things do, but also has medicinal uses at low doses, and even helps regulate plant growth. Higher concentrations can be part of plant/insect synergies where the plant doesn't want to be eaten, the insect doesn't care, and the insect full of plant and alkaloid becomes unsafe to eat.

But at no time is it safe for pregnant mothers.

Stargazer's mother-mother and several other people felt sick or odd but everyone survived, and the rains returned. And her own daughter was born. His mother was healthy but Stargazer had been the first born after many attempts and a couple miscarries, but even that might have been just a bad start as it is for many women.

So he is a mutant and his genome suffered an uncorrected transcription error near the DCX gene. It was a failed repair affecting the single egg that became him. The part in error is X-linked so a man inherits it from his mother but will not pass it to offspring. So if he had been a she, we all might carry the mutation today. But it will die with him.

In a fetus cells replicate and specialize, and push the resulting mass away and between other things that have started pushing themselves, leading to a human with things attached to things, outside and inside things. But another way of pushing is to push in tandem along a substrate and grow a complex structure, while setting resulting density by inserting gunk and cells that want to become blood-plumbing. Things forming, but a separate mechanism pushing separating material and structure between them cross-ways. So long structures form and we don't wind up looking like a pile of fish eggs. And many things growing in tandem want to curve around into spirals, to form tubes and bundles of nerves.

The human neocortex has gyri structures pushed into the cavity of a skull that grows with them. A distinct outermost layer grows so much faster that it gently warps on the layer underneath, to form deep folds. Neurons live in them, and the surfaces are populated with dendrite and synapse so folding provides more surface area for contact between folds, and evolving circuitry. It is not directly sensory but for a few amazing exceptions. Its primary purpose is to evolve consciousness and a high level of processing from the onset of awareness. To isolate the output side of a neuron's pulses, the long runs to the business end of any neuron have axons and insulating sheaths of myelin, which is superior to yourelin.

The DCX gene expresses the protein doublecortin during corticogenesis and its purpose is to extrude grey matter. Neuronal precursor cells and resulting immature neurons are already being formed and being pushed out. But there is no god dipping a paint brush into doublecortin and giving neurons a swipe as they emerge. Every neuronal cell expresses DCX during that unique brain-extruding period, and the result is a precise amount of protein in the neighborhood that triggers other cells to specialize into a structure that will be interspersed with the maturing neurons. And the resulting 'neuron units' are pushed away.

And it has a time limit. DCX stops being expressed by neurons ~2-3 weeks after they start forming. In the fully formed grey-brain DCX expression grows quiet and the proteins break apart and disappear. Aside from pockets of DCX+ that have mysteriously been sighted in adult brains that might imply new neuron growth.

Brains are pretty well understood now. When neurologists spot something they don't understand, they sometimes brand it a 'lesion' and write a prescription for it. They would have been very curious about Stargazer in the womb.

A lot we know about DCX comes from observing the extreme: what happens if the DCX mechanism is completely broken? Ask sad little 'knockout mice' and they will show you. But one might also ask, what would happen if the separate mechanism of emitting immature neurons does not stop soon enough?

There are many growth processes pushing out into oblivion, which just gives us long stringy babies, but this is happening inside a skull so when they fail it might produce an empty skull with a brain that isn't, or perhaps a brain way past its limit, one that has folded up and squashed itself into dense explody mush that is sure to cause calamity, like Martians buying tickets at a Slim Whitman concert.

When DCX does not happen there is no structure at all, hence a fish-egg brain, a clot of neurons that are too close together to function properly and might even die off from oxygen and sugar starvation. And creepily, there is still function. Lissencephaly or 'smooth brain' people often die before birth or live short frustrating lives, and even if they hold on to age 30 likely die of respiratory complications. There are degrees of Lissencephaly fortunately, thin layers of neurons shouting into the void.

There is no direct candidate for mush-brain, but there is Polymicrogyria, a condition when too many folds form and the structures are too small and too insulated. That is not directly related to DCX and there are other problems, but there is limited connectivity.

But Stargazer's DCX Doublecortin mechanism was obviously intact and extruded 'good brain'... but the mutation was not in DCX, but near its place in the genome. Earlier ZEB2 transition? Something different about the neuron extrusion process? Or things anchor to it? Such as unattached floating interneuron precursor cells and DCX+ in situ, that activate and grow in the fetus? A genetic extension to the infant-to-preadolescent spurt of brain growth and neuron culling, resulting in greater overall neuron density and general connectivity?

Um, no.

Pretend it was all these things. Or just don't. It's kinda sci-fi to imagine some complicated yet functional emergent behavior in genes resulting from a single bit error in DNA. Throughout evolution that most often probably resulted in the organism smelling different to others while hanging around after school, and they never found a mate.

In humans, they find a mate anyway. That's what makes us so cool.

Could something divine have been impressed onto Stargazer's brain as a whole, like God dipped a stamp into his doublecortin hedgehog fluid stamp pad and pressed it into grey matter with the phrase, 'Take me to your leader'. And a neural network formed around the stamped letters. And maybe he might have even started a family whose children spelled out that phrase with their limbs! Do you remember vermicious knids? SCRAM!

It did result in an advanced and unique form of Synesthesia. But the circuits he formed were buffered and gated in the cortex so he was able to carry on a normal life of paranormal ability. And he had an uncanny mechanism of 'continuous ordinal irrationality' and yes, I do sort of mean that in the number line sense, but without numbers. Where he can nail something directly, and also perceive that it is 'above' or 'below' some other thing, without needing to learn and flop around symbols or algebraic transforms.

Something had mesmerized Stargazer in the womb. It had awakened him from dimmest existence to total awareness at a time where most babies are dim thinkers and experiencing gradual awareness of dull sensory input. And not gradually either. He simply existed one day and began to have a series of adventures exploring his inner self.

Imagine that your brain has a long continuous barcode, and by shining a brief synapse-light upon a piece of it, you can know that place's identity and relative position in the whole. You can think directly into the barcode innumerable places along its length.

But when you do, the barcode begins to recite itself forward. It is comprised of a general pathway of short neurons along its length that have branched off one way from the original point of formation. When they become excited a dim flare of activity travels up the pathway... relatively slowly like a burning fuse. The density forces the flare to traverse many of them, and neurons must build up potential to fire. So build-up delay and high density yield slowness. And as the flare passes by occasional portals of thinner insulation, the signal escapes into the main brain and excites circuitry nearby. Just blips it.

So the barcode thinks into you also as it is reciting, over time sequentially. And as the flare traverses the whole cycle you are gently reminded of almost everything you have ever known. But slowly and distinctly, and not quite in a terrifying helpless storm of epilepsy and seizure, the tragic outcome of so many mutated brains. The portals through which you think into the barcode and it thinks into you, are just gaps in the insulation.

Around this time proper nerves are being extruded from other places throughout the body. Bundles grow into long spans connecting things that grow with them. A neuron fires into the tube containing an astounding length of axons end to end, and an impulse appears at the far end. So individual tubular nerve channels are one-way, the paths next to them might go the other way and propagation is quick, so when your toes send an impulse to wiggle your brain it travels quickly.

There is also white matter fused to the grey matter, and the white makes up the portion that fills the space between it and the center line of the brain. It also connects between modern and ancient brains. Andreas Vesalius of the 16th century first noted cortex white matter as he studied humans that were dead when their brains had been removed. The slight difference in color is a consequence of its high fatty content of myelin whipped into a souffle of axons and capillaries, lightly salted with a side of cauliflower.

If grey matter is the decision-making switchyard of the mind, white matter is the network of tracks that carry signals over distance and even routes them between hemispheres. Vesalius correctly identified it as an essential part of the brain, or he would have lesioned it off and wrote a long prescription for it.

The barcode could not exist in white matter, certainly not from any single error. It confers necessary connectivity and proper insulation to the whole in gene-produced extruded structures. There would be little opportunity for the white to electrically 'leak' into the grey from white's long embedded strings of axons. There are no straight lines here, and anything disrupting vital and ancient junctions to the nervous system would produce more of a blob than a brain.

The barcode had to have resided in the highest grey cortex, floating atop its 4mm outer surface, the earliest-grown part. Where it did not perturb the body, just the mind.

Compromising white matter thus would have implied some extraordinary and ugly alien structure that defies belief, like a Mercator map. Ask any planet that has been flayed by one, with its Antarctica bug spanning the whole windshield. Or a creepy Cixin 2-dimensional planetary transformation. And it would surely have resulted in some awful not-brain.

But there are structures in the growing high-brain already, for the senses and born instincts. Nature's sensory gizmos deliver input to neighborhoods in the grey matter from extended axon channels routed through the white. It is the home of the cortical Homunculus, whose body parts are scaled for senses as a heavy-handed grotesque creature, whose tiny penis or clitoris strains credulity and invokes pity, causing neurologists to write prescriptions for them. These things are drawn to terrify students and prepare them for lesions to come.

Fetal nerve bundles are dense only if Nature and gene think they are important. They terminate in general areas, and babies must mostly map them from sensation as they learn. That is why you should always massage babies, and trace along their limbs, fingers, toes and other surfaces, while they are watching if possible.

Hearing deserves mention, for it is used to great advantage by us and in this story, by the 'barcode'.

The cochlea is a hollow fluid filled snail-shaped organ fed sound from the ear canal. It is a winding spiral path that is a continuous low-pass filter, such that the whole range of sound enters its widest end, and along its curved length the highest frequencies are progressively attenuated until at the deepest part only ~25Hz is present. There are tiny hairs of various sizes waving with sound in the fluid, and a membrane at their base supported by hairs that register pressure, such as frequencies where sinusoidal waves combine or null. Its structure is organized for frequency/pitch discrimination, but it also provides clues for amplitude.

Although most humans are capable of discerning ~640 unique frequencies/pitches when they arise as spikes that are tones or musical notes or components of language, you may be surprised to discover there is no direct ear-to-cortex path despite ears being 'close' to it. Nerve bundles leading from the cochlear environs take a long journey from ear to auditory cortex in 4 neuron stages. There are some thirty thousand unique channels. Ears are ancient, nature builds on experience and the cortex only evolved yesterday, so to move along the nerve path from ear to cortex is to move forward in evolutionary time.

Auditory nerves pass through the medulla oblongata, what many call the 'lizard-brain', which is an insult because lizards have modern cerebral cortexes too. Parts of it branch off to other ancient areas.

The medulla oblongata, cerebellum and amygdala once supplied all ear functions necessary for ancient critters. The cochlear nucleus provides front-end processing. You still use the amygdala to locate sounds and jump at unexpected sudden sounds. People with both audio cortexes damaged still jump, though they never 'hear' the sound. Because of two-ear nerve redundancy, people with one cortex damaged can regain binaural hearing over time. And you use the cerebellum to monitor the three fluid filled loops in each ear to maintain balance. These reflexes are not just ancient, they require autonomous attention and quick feedback, so the fewer neurons in those paths the better.

Sound MUST be presented to the brain in a very precise frequency-structure before birth because, if narrow frequency bands were shuffled and presented willy-nilly in the brain, an organism would need lots of high level processing and neuronal adaptive circuitry to make any sense of sound at all. The environment might sound like pink noise. Sounds would be difficult to discern from noise. Developing creatures do not contain sweeping function generators or Moog synthesizers for calibration. And where would the learning cues come from? How long might it take? Quite possibly the creature would just give up trying. Poor creature.

The final terminus for hearing is the auditory cortex in folds along Wernicke's area. There is a tonotomy-map there, nerves arriving in practically the same rank-order to hairs along the distant spiral cochlea. This is astounding! Even if the rank is not strictly precise and musicians must 'fix' things a bit by relearning adjacent notes and reassigning a few neurons, the structure is an amazing thing. There are massive parallel pathways in the system. If you research 'tonotopy' you might learn that "...it is reasonable to expect that the auditory system exhibits a greater degree of precision in its early circuit formation than do other sensory systems."

More precise than even vision? Eyes are hard to build but might be easier to operate. But the real reason eyes are easier is that since the earliest critters, evolution has devoted an incredible amount of cerebellum and occipital lobe circuitry to vision. So the baby sees blobs and hears roars and whistles, but it will learn to spot and track guitars long before it can hear individual notes in a guitar solo. And the baby will soon turn its head towards the sound of a guitar and jump as the guitar solo begins, more ancient circuitry in action.

Extending beyond just seeing things clearly... there is subitizing in the brain, an awesome talent for counting that does not rely on the enumeration of things. Think Rain Man and the toothpicks.

For modern humans this is implicitly suggested with a subitizing range from always 1 to seldom ~8 and no documented further cases. I remember there was a Ripley's Believe It Or Not claim of Rain Man phenomena, but in modern life it is possible that 8 vertices is the limit you would directly train neurons to recognize polygons. And I'm not talking about stop signs. I am sure you have neurons trained for those, but the task of subitizing involves recognizing shapes of irregular polygons, because items to count are seldom presented in a circle. There is a subitizing map in the brain that is linear, so maybe you sweep across the region and stop on the number that 'feels right'.

The whole barcode would have behaved as if was some long slow 'leaky nerve' that had been gene-expressed by the error. If it actually was a nerve it would have been way out of place and very poorly constructed. The barcode has way too many neurons inside, that were originally immature neurons from the precursor site to form a normal brain.

But the idea of any single thing growing 'across' the brain like a tapeworm is sci-fi. There is not enough time for this to happen, especially not to present a spooky result to a growing fetus. And the gyri are 3D folds grown from the center, not extruded 2D noodles. Regular people might be fooled by seeing an endless parade of cross-sections of brains. There is no implicit single path to follow, even if there was enough time for it to happen.

So for Stargazer's brain I am just left with a vague notion that may cause neurologists to write you a long prescription, just for hearing me out.

The mutation was a 'false start' in grey matter corticogenesis, where the early formation of pia mater and laminin basement membrane which will become the outermost layer, and reelin Cajal-Retzius cells are expressed from loose germinal cells, and Stargazer's gray matter neuron expression got under way.

But the error caused a stutter soon into the process, and a layer of reelin was expressed again. Immature neurons are already within the confined space, and their support structures will join with others for blood circulation.

Then fortunately, corticogenesis resumed and completed successfully. A normal brain grew, but there was also a thin layer of 'barcode brain' along the surface of his normal brain. Its neurons matured in the confined space and only the simplest single direction branching occurred, and they grew laterally to join others in the barcode brain. There was no very long axon growth with few connections. So when they cascaded it was like a very slow wave across the surface. Signals were weak and none had the energy budget to fire quickly.

When folds of gyri came together in his later brain development, the extra layer of reelin and its contents were pushed aside, still providing some degree of insulation between the barcode and normal brain but providing a good measure of normal brain cortical connectivity. But there were occasional leaks between the brains because reelin is not meant for the purpose of insulation. But within the vast constellation of quiescent and potential connectivity, was enough separation between for the normal brain to build firing patterns into sentience in the way Nature intended.

So the 'barcode' was a propagation wave relayed and delayed by hundreds of millions of neutrons in his outer brain, the mutant barcode brain. When it was firing at all.

Or some such.

———

LULLABIES

There had always been something creeping through his mind. Most
of the time he was not aware of it. But it was neither self nor other, it
had just kept him awake. It would fade when aggressive sleep finally
took him. But it was always a moving presence through timeless
eternity. It had been the first thing that ever caught his attention.
And it was shaping him, as he remained shaped like himself.

He thought his own thoughts as babies do, during the lulls of its
quieter periods, but something would whisper in his mind that
distracted him. The distractions were not unpleasant in any way, just
curious. And as time passed he began to know what it was. Not
what it actually was of course, but he knew it was THAT thing.
What ever THAT was, it was the first clear concept.

It had always repeated and he had experienced its unique
progressions innumerable times. His mind had been organized by its
whispers into him even before sentience began. Babies are serenaded
by their heartbeats, mother's heartbeats and occasional sensations
within or dull sounds from without. But most of those sounds and
pulsations would only be felt keenly much later. But for now,
THAT was the most intricate and interesting thing there was.

And it wasn't too intrusive. So his first deliberate act of awareness
was to play with THAT, and learn it. As it whispered to him, every
single thing it said was suddenly important and urgent, if he used his
conscious deliberation to fix his attention to it. Even as THAT
moved forward and whispered something else in its constant mutter,
he could hang on to the previous thought and hold it. This brought
a sense of dull satisfaction, to later become wonder and delight, for it
is fun to drive your own universe. Babies in the womb need to know
this, so that is why Nature gave them steering wheels.

As he let go of these delightful deliberate-thoughts, he would once again become aware of THAT's current state, which had cycled past more whispers, but a bit slower? He recognized THAT's new state but was also aware of the states he had passed over while fixing on something, because he knew them all by now. THAT actually had more than a million states and some passed by far more quickly than others.

But literally his mind had formed around them. His knowledge consisted of a thin continuous mesh of lightly exercised young neurons in his normal brain that heard leakage from THAT. They imparted a unique flavor to each state by virtue of their physical place and adjacent states. THAT as a pattern repeated and reinforced. It was no agonizing flare of rapid firing neurons gripping the mind in chaos, like the tragedy of epilepsy.

THAT was for entertainment purposes only. As a grown artifact it was more complicated than anything physical in the standard human brain. But to him it seemed like repeating bits of gobble gook that was all different, a one time pad of the mind. Or his world. And it really did entertain.

Holding on to a thought that occurred during a continuous march of whispers, and knowing their states, he became aware of the clock that drove them. It was no regular clock, just a sequence of things that were also states. And timeless spans of playing the game of fixing on them as they passed by, he blundered into the most amazing discovery of all, one that changed his life and probably saved his sanity. He stopped it.

Maybe he had become bored with pushing into THAT and making things flare up and trying to push THAT into the background by not paying attention to it. But he tried the next logical thing with this ability, to think along the totally predictable states of THAT, but faster than THAT itself was moving. It was an exciting concept! At first THAT was outpacing him because he kept being distracted, then he managed to jump many steps ahead. Then something incredible and completely new happened. And it did not freak him out in the slightest. He not learned that yet.

THAT stopped.

Not for long, and it resumed after a moment with the usual rambling mutter. But the moment was timeless enough for him to experience and revel in something he had never known before.

Silence.

This was not thinking into THAT, this was thought into it along its future path at iterations along that path. Not with the jarring intensity of the wait-for-it thought-fixing-flaring game, but he just noted their identities in a list, back and forth in passing. Like writing, the next ones are this, this, this and this... and quickly scanning up and down what you have written. He had learned to anticipate them but thinking of them was like making a list which was new to him. So he recited the list slowly and THAT responded. But he also realized he should try it more quickly.

Not only could he do it quickly, but with the delicate matrix THAT had eroded into his brain, he could traverse that matrix outside of it in his real brain and the next state was so obvious he could build a list of many of these items in an instant. He did not decide to do this. His brain used these shortest paths to accommodate his urge for speed.

And THAT had stopped. It stopped because it was daisy-chained, captive neurons inside a narrow medium, and thinking into many forward portals made them fire a few times more often and depleted their potential, and delayed their forward neighbors' build up of potential a bit. The depletion was collectively so deep, THAT slowed, faded, and then 'went out' like a burning fuse reaching a gap.

He could slow and stop THAT at will. Then he could do it so deftly, if he wished to think in silence, at the first glimmer of THAT he would hunt and kill the instance. And then, so as not to be distracted by THAT, he learned to suppress THAT as a constant and ever-present notion, so that his subconscious mind kept it at bay, just as he'd later keep his balance without thought.

He moved even a little beyond the subconscious and discovered a way of simply existing that 'leaned' against THAT and shut it up. He even became annoyed if he woke from sleep and THAT was mumbling against his wishes. If you have ever trained yourself not to wet the bed, perhaps you know how this was done.

Focused annoyance is probably rare for a fetus. Nature's glucose and fat firewall surrounds the fetus and it will never know hunger until the mother is ready to drop dead. But who knows how annoying it is to just grow? Maybe that is why some babies are born insane. In the womb there is surely crankiness from disease and developmental discomfort but it probably just trains babies to cry silently and enjoy stopping.

But life was good. He felt, and he was also giving more attention to evolving senses that had taken off suddenly with mental silence. He moved and some other-mother responded, and he heard her speak. When he tumbled or she moved around, his inner ear and cochlear ear was communicating with him. From the games he had played in isolation his brain was more developed than it had any right to be. From his struggle to master THAT he knew the difference between things that you do, things that are happening to you, and mysterious things you don't understand.

But mysteries had their own identities too, which was a way to return to them and ponder them some more. He was already much more than a creature to whom things were just happening.

And when he was awake when his mother was asleep, to pass the time he'd start THAT and let it recite itself, knowing that THAT was THAT and he was Someone Else. And from emotion and sensation he had invented 'intensely', so for the first time he became intensely curious about THAT. And he could commit a state to memory, pause it and let thoughts and ideas tumble around for a while, then resume it where he left off. And yet for all states of which he was aware there was an obvious next and previous one.

He picked a low part of THAT and scanned backwards, which took some extra time but not much, so etched into him THAT's surrounding matrix had become... until he discovered a state that had no antecedent. He would have shouted if he could, it was so novel to find such a thing! He shouted it silently and it responded loudly with its identity. A lot of states only gave their identity but you knew where they were in the whole, before and after were obvious but this one was different!

When he asked himself, what is the VERY Last one? What is the VERY First one? Now the answers came quickly and he tested them, saw the First one was the same state he had discovered by running backwards. That had been a lot of work! He had just never asked that way before. He even jumped between First and Last and sensed the gap between them. The distance was immense, as large a distance as he would ever perceive. But it was known.

But the Last was not the Last! There was another! He thought forward from it.

But the next state felt funny. It was not at all like the clarity and certainty of First and Last and the others. It had an identity he felt was unique and could be committed to memory and remembered and returned to, so he did. He remembered it, and less than a heartbeat later he returned to it.

But wait. It felt different. He brought up the Last and thought forward again. It was not the same! A whole new identity again. These were real identities but they were fuzzy in the middle somehow with a sense of constant changing. The most bizarre thing yet. He thought forward from Last countless times and it was a stream of new ones until he grew weary. It was a real effort despite that his brain hardly ever grew tired. Worse than weariness. And he knew these places were new and unvisited every time he arrived.

So while perceiving the extents of a Last-plus-forward identity, a real state far as he knew, he pushed into it hard, in the way that causes THAT to recite the identity and trudge forward. It didn't work. Something was changing. He pushed into it even harder. Oh...what...?... THAT did not respond. And it had been a mistake. It had been a bad mistake.

He experienced a curious sensation of warmth. But the sensation never arrived, he was just warm. Or hot. Or blazing hot. Hotter than fire. He felt rising panic that something terrible was happening. His vision would occasionally flicker in a chasing pattern of specks while THAT reached certain states. But now it blazed. Awful. Mysterious sound through his mother's belly was a screeching roar. His body clenched in a sudden massive spasm that his mother felt. He felt pain. His fetal mouth opened wide and his throat constricted with his face in silent rictus. He smelled and tasted acrid, searing burning rubber.

Now it may amuse you to think that a fetus in the womb a million years ago is bending over to sniff a tire fresh off the track at the Indy 500. Recall that a smell of burning rubber and dread beyond all measure, is a common thing reported by epileptics at the onset of grand mal seizure. Sometimes the odor is the last thing they remember. Some sensory artifact of smell and taste all firing at once.

Bad things had never really happened to him, but this was all of them at once.

And then it was over, just like that. His brain had forgotten exactly what it had been trying to do and stopped doing it. No THAT or the other things, just silence and paralyzed shock. His mother placed a hand on her belly fearing the worst. She moved it around and he felt it as a movement of liquid and a gentle pressure on his scalp. As thought returned he muttered to himself in tiny tortured loops for awhile and then the True Last state and its identity returned to him.

For an eternal moment he helplessly fixed on the state he knew was the Last, not even daring to dismiss it. He had always been a creature acting on the briefest of impulse, but he noted the way forward from the Last without following it. It was just there to be followed. He decided not to follow it ever again with a determination stronger than anything in the world. Something so awful had happened, he was unlearning it. He had never told himself not to do something before.

But here, and only here he knew, you could go back but the way forward tasted and smelled like burning rubber. Then in an instant, it didn't. He had unlearned it, and didn't perceive it at all. He went back to the Almost Last and everything was normal. He jumped to First and Next was OK. He didn't even look for a way backward from First this time. There was none, but no need either. It just wasn't there.

Why didn't he purge all thought of THAT and his wild explorations in the dark? Because THAT was all there was and what he was, for the most part. And there was no need. The bad thing just wasn't there.

If you catch your balance after almost falling, do not fear the mountain, the fall or the impact. Just step away from the cliff.

Then he went back to First and told THAT to recite itself. This was the elated satisfaction of conscious awareness and deliberation. He lingered at each identity just long enough to push into it slightly, and THAT pushed back with its identity and also illuminated a pathway in is brain that was a thought or idea or sensation. Or nothing, but with new skill of perception he realized it wasn't nothing after all. The identity was there, but it was like you know a light just flashed in the room, but you don't turn in its direction because you know it is not flashing now. There is no need. It just isn't there.

When he felt a hand or other part of his body flare into sensation, he could tune through it to move the invisible sensation and trace its presence in adjacent areas. From touch to pressure to heat to pain was just the strength of mental push, so he didn't push hard. He remembered many places by their identity and his mind was becoming phenomenal at remembering arbitrary things when he could tie them to THAT and the matrix around it.

And there was motor control, without a motor. Fingers twitched and his gut rumbled. Fortunately no glands were activated by this crude stimulation that might cause stress and dangerous dysfunction. He was navigating through the cortex and dangerous things like the heart were behind nature's firewalls, the ancient brains physically isolated in evolutionary time.

As THAT's grand tour progressed and he encountered one of his senses, dense circuits in structures laid out by genes to supply an initial state for learning, he was touched with excitement and extreme thrill. He saw luminous trails that were dots, shapes and arcs. He played with their colors and intensity, jumped between eyes when he discovered the relative identities of both.

He swept from rumble to screech and there was mysterious motor control there too, for some cochleal hairs stiffen on command to help isolate a frequency of interest. He heard a sweep of sounds without recognizing them as such. He was captivated by smell and taste but they were intense and there wasn't as much to experiment with so he moved on. Lots of empty space, identities only, ever forward. He finally reached Last with its dangerous path now unseen.

He turned THAT off and swam in the senses. He would perceive the whole, but by tuning into identities he had learned and remembered, he could create something like zooms for them by pushing into vision and illuminating a dot like a tiny flash, then expanding the push and light up bigger and bigger patches. Sight was still mysterious but sound was great fun.

And he had a yardstick in his brain to measure things with and know their place. Its markings were very small and there were a lot of them. Every mark in THAT was a leakage site between the 'barcode brain' and his real brain, and every leakage site had been grown out with fast neural networks that were his own next to them, that had spread laterally in his 'main brain' against the floor of the other.

But there were many neurons in parallel, going both directions, that had been built and reinforced by not only manifesting unique identities in THAT, but playing with them, and thinking Next and Previous to jump through the sequence. Following these lateral points was slow at first, like sweeping a flashlight in a dark room to find something. But he played this game for eons of thought-time because it was the most interesting thing to do. And Nature responded to his efforts, the rapid firing of neurons along this physical path connected them to others.

THAT and its evolving real-brain circuitry was simply boredom-proof.

For a long time his favorite game had been pressing for speed as he navigated it, forwards or backwards, and it took exhausting days to traverse at first. Chemically induced sleep would overtake him suddenly but he'd awaken knowing where he had been, and he resumed.

The faster he navigated, the briefest touches of brain regions stirred by it in his mind would leave a shimmer as he passed through countless states, like dim moving landscape with buildings and trees and crossroads passing beside the road as you drive, or the sound after the last note of an orchestra in a great hall as it fades slowly.

This incredible moving bubble of persistence was interesting to the point of excitement and elation. It was an artifact he had never noticed before. It was like a gallery of whispers that were previous states, and he felt their identities merging as they faded. It was beautiful and it moved him. But the shimmer only manifested while he maintained highest possible speed between states. To perceive them he had to stop, and when he did they were already fading in distant echoes and then gone. And it broke his heart.

He needed speed. The more states flying behind him the longer it lasted.

There were whole regions where pushing into individual states did not remind him specifically of anything, yet subtly reminded him of everything. Or so it seemed, and this was not actually true, but it was so many things they could not even be discerned individually. And pushing into two adjacent states in this area yielded the same response. Being reminded of too many things to identify in that way was not fun from empty areas. It was actually a place of non-specialized neurons that were casually connected, projecting weak, distant signals to other places and getting jumbled echoes back. They were the empty places.

But it was the perfect place to play A1,A2.

These were two adjacent states in such an empty region. They didn't remind him of anything. He had once asked, could I follow their next and previous links back and forth forever? Direction changing required an effort and if he lost concentration THAT would recite more forward states. He had to tell it to shut up when he noticed, but that was distracting, so it seemed natural when performing the steps to tell it to shut up every cycle. Go forward, shaddap, go previous, go forward, shaddap. It was delightful to follow simple rules that did something!

Perhaps there is such a thing as micro-boredom that makes you try new things, even when you are having fun. Shaddap was hard and took time. So he started ignoring the barcode while playing. Next,previous,next. He pushed harder into it. There is persistence in many things, even inverse persistence, a sudden unawareness of things. He never lost track of the identities. But as he grew faster, and flew back and forth between the identities, they also presented a merged identity that represented the game to him.

He played A1~A2 for uncounted time, never losing interest because he was so busy playing it. Getting better at something was always interesting. He played ceaselessly. Stopping only for sleep, which attacked him suddenly.

It flowed into him like a warm liquid. There was nothing to be done, it was already happening, so he rode it all the way down until the superimposed identity just floated still in his mind and he was only pretending to play. He could feel his resolve fading as pretended actions in the game grew more slow and sporadic. The identity somehow drifted closer and closer, as things do under anesthesia when your consciousness is dissolving. A part of him knew it was going to swallow him, so he resisted and then fought back aggressively and viciously and he was winning! He had thrust it aside, he was playing the game again and doing it faster and better than ever before! He was now doing it so fast, he could even,

But he had been pretending those things also. Sleep swallowed him and taught him humility.

And he would become aware after a long sleep. The game was exhausting. And yet he had a sense that anything was possible, and what next. So he continued. Variations like A2~A3 or A3~A4. Now he was playing A1~A2~A3~A4~A3~A2 which took a great deal of effort. He was slow again, a series of deliberate actions but it was refreshing to try. It puzzled him because the transition between 1,2 was fast as lightning now but the other transitions were so much slower. It was disappointing. He started playing A1~A2 again with more vigor.

He did not realize it, but the transitions he had perceived as 'slow' were actually happening at 10x the fastest rate he had ever surfed THAT before. The A1~A2 identities had superimposed at 50x and his level of prowess had risen to 80x with some conscious awareness of progress.

But he was about to discover what happened at 200x.

He could discern A1~A2 as a separate identity from A1 or A2, and it also now represented the game itself, and the desire for speed. He played the game by pushing into it and giving tiny additional pushes for speed. There was no longer conscious volition of each step. It was just a special kind of push that might have been 'yadda-yadda' which meant, do the next thing. To maintain speed took a small steady push. Harder pushes had not ever had any effect. But micro-boredom had been creeping up lately, so again he'd try to push speed as HARD as he could. So he did.

The world had changed! He had split!

He literally split!

The merged identity had swallowed him!

He was A1. He was A2. He was two.

Perhaps nature's deep circuitry had enabled this on some level, with its duplicity and bilateral symmetry and ancient mechanisms for visual and audio stereo, and thought involvement over two hemispheres. His cortex processing had improved considerably during his obsession with the game, gaining massive parallelism improvements in general and finding many least-distance paths in the 'transitions' that were buildup and teardown segues between every thought-step in THAT manipulation. In a real sense, he had been evolving into a machine specialized to play the game.

While he played the game, excited neurons in his main brain around the A1 and A2 sites had grown towards one another and connected, shoring the quiet links between them into behemoths of connectivity and two way parallelism. This was exclusively an A1~A2 network and the places were nearby in the brain. It had been pulsing quietly back and forth as his attention fixed on each. But when he pushed hard into it, it flared with direct feedback between its neurons that was so intense, the identities for A1 and A2 imprinted him not simultaneously, but alternately in a speed that was incredible for brains, and much faster, smaller and focused than a storm of epilepsy.

He already knew the concept of other, because he already considered THAT something other. But now there was truly another.

Two consciousnesses, superimposed, almost perfectly in phase.

In goofy computer jargon, he had created a high speed context switcher.

He had become they! A neurologist would write two prescriptions.

Each was aware of the other like a vibration in the air. But that feeling was identical too. Each was him, so even their tiniest notions were synchronized. They turned attention away from the game and it kept playing without them. They were both silent, observing.

They were not afraid. They knew they were two. They regarded one another. There was no divergent sense noise as in the real world, so they could do this perfectly in sync and face one another as shapeless entities.

For awhile they did silly things in perfect synchrony. Rambling thoughts and random access to THAT. Each trying to offer a random thought to the other, but so did the other and he reached for the same place. Figuratively glancing at the other who had also had a notion to glance at that moment. It was the first time he had an other to play with, and they were glad for each other, but at what price. It was a boring game. They shared the thought that it was boring. And it grew past micro-boredom into real boredom and that was synchronized too. Which led to the next logical thought for both, could this be a trap that none would ever escape from, unless both did? And how was that even possible? What was the next thing to that?

After another mini-eon of cavorting, like making faces in a mirror, boredom rose to maxi-boredom.

It was no great insight that finally led them both to the compound A1~A2 identity itself. The one that represented the game. The identity was so fixed in their minds they could not even reach A1 or A2 separately anymore. They just weren't there. They were trapped in the game, after all. He/they pushed into A1~A2 and nothing happened. He/they presumed the other was pushing it also.

Then vibration around them changed. It was like a bunch of ticks, things happening so quickly one could only think about the whole, not the little things themselves. It had been steady but now it was rocking slowly. It was not rocking the whole world apart, but they knew it was so elemental, so pervasive, so dangerous, that it could do so. The rocking continued. They heard thoughts that were not their own!

There was Another!

Fits of thought whispers came to them unbidden, every time the vibration rocked. Things not part of their own thought process, which they knew was the same as each other's, though it was like a voice. And they knew the source was not the THAT either. It was Another. They considered that for a micro-eon, listening to the pulsing whispers for clues, and thinking with their synchronized selves.

They decided to push into A1~A2 again, because what else was there to do, and the vibration swelled and the whispers grew almost to shouts! Now they were besieged by it! They could only think in the spaces between throbs. After a time of this, each suggested to the other, perhaps WE could unmake the world if we do it again? And neither wanted to, so that was that. But clues were flooding in now with the screaming throb. There were patterns in the voice that was not theirs, and it was not perfectly clear, but the cadence was unmistakable.

The Another was playing the game.

The idea occurred to both at once of course. Between throbbing cacophony it transformed into another idea, one so incredible it begged to be expressed. And it could only be repeated, as things are often repeated by people who have come to some awful, inescapable conclusion of are overcome by horror. But there was no horror or intent for any drama, those are artifacts that appear later. Just a sense of wonder and awe as big as the world.

"Another is playing the Game."

"We are the Game."

They were still repeating the mantra when Sleep surrounded them all and truly unmade the world. And all three of them accepted it, pretended to do what they had been doing, and then fought it with every possible effort, pretended to resist, and lost.

...

Stargazer... who we should now refer to as A-zero... awoke, startled to awareness. He was being poked! He had felt it as a cry of nerves at a certain place. Then he was being rocked in currents as hands pushed the belly back and forth. Melodious rumbles of sound that was his mother's voice, carried by bone conduction and resonating through her body, a sound that was beautifully sublime, the biggest mystery that had ever begged to be solved. Shouts of the father near the belly were new shapes of delivered sensation, other mysteries. So many! Now a hand pressed to his head, moving it slowly.

He pushed movement hard into his limbs all over with gleeful abandon. It was an expression of his excitement in the mystery. In the real world, he moved. There were more shouts and sounds.

What had happened in the real world was, his mother had gone to seek help because the baby had hardly been moving for days. He had been lost in the game and the constant switching between states made so much noise in his mind he did not respond to his senses, not even his mother shaking him and pushing on him with rising concern. The midwife was also trying to wake him and privately thinking, if something terrible has happened to the baby it must be brought out now. Therefore his sudden awakening and motion was such a relief that she shouted happily with the father.

It was happenstance he had awakened then, after a very long deep chemically induced sleep, for the game had challenged his physiology and depleted him. And it had done so brutally when a brand new beacon had first flared to life in his brain.

THAT was malfunctioning. It was very annoying. It did not pulse perceptibly, or return the single brief pulse that merely conferred its identity. A1 and A2 were constantly shining into his brain like a bright light. Their identities were so well known to him it is perhaps not surprising that he made the next conceptual leap. My mind is still playing the game. He muted them completely, which is to say he didn't flick banks of switches or anything. It just means he ignored them so well, it was as if he had removed the identities of A1 and A2 from his existence. That bright light was still shining in him, but such was his prowess of thought, he nulled it from his own consciousness. Just as he had done before when he had smelled burning rubber.

For you see, the whole human mind is organized around a firm principle of not wanting to smell burning rubber.

And during his game obsession, more cochlear nerves had become available and thickened. Without the noise of game playing and A1-A2's annoying new beacon silent, sound and sensation from the outside world was stronger than ever before.

He had recognized his parents as an other. And they had recognized him! That was exciting, and once he started interacting with them a new whole constellation of games was formed. His mother would tap her belly with each step while walking, and his inner ear sloshed with hers as he noted the taps. And he kicked in sync with her steps. And she felt it. And other things too numerous to mention.

THAT had reached a slow steady state around 5 months in the womb, as many neurons in the thin outer brain had died off from bad support structure. But many had survived to produce the wave of activation he recognized as a 'moving presence'. It had awakened him to full sentience early and given him something to play with.

But now he had some-one to play with!

He embarked on the greatest journey of his life. The phrase is overused but this one really takes the cake.

The beacon was an excited collection of neurons between the A1 and A2 regions of the real brain, not THAT. Call it the 'beacon network'. They had been activated to a high state early in the game, and had pulsed along with his deliberate alternating pushes. In the early days of the game they had sent their pulses outward into the void, which was mostly an unpopulated region at the time but it soon found recurring pathways into the most distant areas of the cortex, because it was connected after all, just in an unused and unspecialized sort of way. These paths pulsed with A1 and A2... and because their roots were singular as were their places of origin, they formed two separate branching networks.

In the final moments of the game he had pushed hard into it, which is to say a neuron firing rate approaching maximum. This surge caused the beacon network to find its least-hop circular feedback paths and the loop became persistent. And for the first time, instead of a mind conducting a series of steps that resulted in them illuminating alternately, they were clocking themselves. And they did so furiously quickly. But nature has chemical tricks to slow the rate, or we'd all light up like a burning bush the first time we had an impure thought. So while the path had burned itself in to become persistent, its rate slowed and became more comfortable, a clock that could endure.

There are multiple short loops in the network. From chemical depletion they may fall silent for awhile as other paths flare to life. The clock is still way beyond the average thinking rate in terms of serial steps. Parallelism helps us to think in many places at once, not necessarily faster. If it had been a context switch, Stargazer would now be a functional multi threaded multi user operating system. To use goofy computer terms.

But I sure you're burning with curiosity to learn what became of the entities A1 and A2, now also known as Thing One and Thing Two. And you cared about them, laughed at their mirror-antics, and a part of you hopes I won't dash off some phrase like, they dissolved into nothingness, so there! like some cheap movie trick, roll credits. They did dissolve with Sleep as everyone does.

But when they awoke, they still knew they were two, but the manner of waking gave them the separation they had long desired. There was no longer a mirror-other, and that was sad, and they mourned. But they eventually found a way to communicate with each other, and Another. The beacon was shining in their eyes too, so they muted it.

But in the end, they had been forked off from one obsessively playing the game. So they were obsessive too for the moment, with free will decided to resume playing the game. So they did.

Then they became bored with the game because there was now an exciting other to play with, so when they established contact, each started making up jokes to tell the other, which they now could, and the other was surprised by the joke and found it very funny! And then the other would tell a joke.

———

BIRTH

Something awful happened! So awful it wrenched his guts! And the sounds! Spasms from outside, spasms within. What does a baby feel when the water breaks and the walls press in? He thought he had mastered awful things, but it happened again and again, and finally a thing happened that was so awful it shriveled his consciousness into a tiny knot of primal distress.

More contractions.

Then he was born and everything was more still, but it was bright, loud and strange. He pealed with surprise and shock and recent memory of torment and did not think about any coherent thing at all, for a long time.

A lot of time had passed before he discovered time. Then he started paying serious attention. He learned things about the world. Language had been easy, but tying words to meanings was hard, and finally understanding was so fun he just liked to listen. Even unfamiliar words, they existed in his mind as mysteries to solve and the nonsense words had their own identities, so he could bring them back later to hear again in his mind and think about them, and quickly connect them to a meaning when enough clues had been presented.

He had mapped sound to idea to motor function to produce those sounds, a dense little package of identities. The ability was tucked away and it even had its own identity, so he could debate with himself whether to use it. But he didn't talk much. By now he had missed some developmental milestones and some thought a he was a little slow.

He was just taking it slow. He would talk when he was ready.

In the confusion and agony of birth and sensory overload he had lost the voice he had thought to himself in the womb, and over time found a new one that sounded like his parents, and sort of like yours too. Maybe the other voice had pushed through and become an identity itself, but what ever the reason, it was no longer a voice. It was a wordless sense of self and some fused ego-id mush. He tallied only his accomplishments in the real world and cataloged them, and scored his prowess.

THAT no longer had a voice of its own. He didn't even remember THAT existing. It never recited itself after he was born, and perhaps its delicate signal had been drowned out by vivid sense information, or his infant brain had simply invaded the barrier and co-opted its circuitry piecemeal. But he had already built his own THAT in the way that towns and cities grow along the coastline of a great river. There was now a busy river in his mind spanning First to Last that he could navigate with ease, and THAT had just been the tiny rivulet that seeded it all.

Phenomenal abilities now rested in the subconscious where they wouldn't distract him. Every game he had played in the womb, even THAT itself, was now just a vague notion of leaning into things or leaning towards things in certain ways, and sensing things leaning back into him. But THAT's places now as 'identities' and its relative positions, he knew in a way that had become implicit.

He walked early because he had already been walking in his dreams and figuring out how, so he just started walking and it required little practice. He not just commanded his muscles, he could silently scream at them to do his bidding with every bit of strength he had, without twitching or shaking. Had he remembered, he would have thanked his mother for her habit of gently slapping and tapping her belly while walking. The sensations had given cadence to the more subtle sounds of footfall and connected with balance signals from his developing inner ear. In modern times walking briskly with thin soles on concrete might yield the same result.

Dreams were vivid and always spanned the world he had seen. In some dreams he was alone, and in others he was with people he was beginning to know, who tended to say things they had already said in real life. But his parents were often there, and in the dream he was just being with them, or setting off from or returning to them, and they were as eloquent and subtle as they were in real life.

But there were also two younger boys in his dreams. Often they'd walk beside him quietly or were felt as a presence, as his own dream world unfolded. They had faces that were his, although he never learned how he knew that.

In dreams he'd be walking and conversing with them only in thought. Whenever he turned to face them they were there. They all played together, he danced with them and he loved walking with them in circles, with ever changing hastily-painted vistas of the world he had committed to memory, and imagined places, spinning by slowly. The boys would point to things and ask questions. He would explain best he could and even made up jokes. They would laugh, and they would tell jokes. They did not relate as people did. He sensed they were his equals, but he had never met anyone like them in real life.

And he would present them with ideas. They would debate. He would listen as they debated each other. They helped him think through life's puzzles. He'd tell them things to ponder until they all met again.

The more people in real life he knew in childhood, the more seldom they appeared in his dreams. He felt their presence even in waking life nevertheless, and he often nudged them in thought and spoke aloud to them when no one else was around. And he welcomed their presence. In some form or another, they remained with him to the end of his days.

———

SENSES

He could push pure identities into his ears, even one ear at a time. Nothing sounded of course, he was firing neurons in the cortex associated with hearing just as they arrived from the cochlea. But to him it sounded as real as the world, and he could even adjust the intensity of either source. He could even 'hear' both the real and imagined sounds distinctly, simultaneously.

He had tried to push directly into vision itself and it was fascinating in the dark but confusing, and in the light things shifted their positions and it was a bit frightening. But if he was looking at something in real life and pushed into the thing quickly and gently, a familiar identity would attach to it, one he recognized from a large collection of 'things he was seeing'. The collection may not have existed all the time, but it was there when he thought of it.

That collection had disturbed him at first. Things often shifted around and reassigned themselves constantly as he moved around and his view shifted. He shook his head vigorously and identities swirled and he could not connect them with anything. Then it settled down and he got their attention, he told them all to go away. And they did. When he brushed one or more things in his sight now, only then would their identities appear.

If he pushed in a certain way in a sequence, lines would appear between the selected objects in his not-vision. They were straighter than straight because he was not seeing them with eyes. He was not even imagining he was seeing them. He was assuming they were there, and they were.

Sound was great. He could remember sounds approximately of course, and play them back in his head, but also project information into sound. He could spread an identity across both ears. It was an incredible, complicated sound and if he ever heard it in real life, he would recognize the identity. He would also know which sound was next, and previous. Even sight could became sound, if you pushed into things you were seeing or things you imagined seeing, and listened to them. But you could not push them directly. It had to be associated with measure.

That was how the mountain had sung to him.

The mountain was the tallest thing ever. He had trained his vision on it since he had first seen it, his mind jumping between features with or without moving his eyes. It was now mid afternoon and every outcropping and every tiny tree had stark reliefs. White shapes with black detail capped the distant peaks and glowed in the daylight. He wondered if he could measure it with his ears. And what it would sound like.

He jumped to First, a vague but precise notion now, and sighted a blade of grass between his feet. Then glanced at the tip of the peak and it became Last, and they were connected with a straighter-than-straight line, as if it had always been there. Following the line was sound, he decided. The line did not represent actual distance to and up the mountain, but a path anchored through his direct field of vision. It remained anchored in place even when he moved or shook his head, and when he lowered his head from sighting the peak.

But the line was so short! First and Last were so far apart! He would have to go through the identities quickly and sound one every so often. He fixed a so-often in his mind. He had played games like this before he was born and rediscovered them after. He positioned the first sound.

It was the familiar sound of First. Then he began to see and hear identity sounds that crept along the line, which was also across the landscape and up the mountain. A very slow straight path. As his sight ascended it traced every so-often identity of distance. The result was a sound as wide as an ocean, and it had parts that were all around him, because he had two ears, all parts of its identity. Even the thought of memorizing such sounds was exhausting, so he just listened to them. It reached crescendos in voices of many pitches, sliding up and down at once. It found harmony occasionally and disharmony crept in like twisting braids. When his focused eyes reached the tip of the peak, the sound was louder than hearing, and he was as elated as he could be. But it didn't hurt.

If you listen to the THX Deep Note and imagine oodles of discrete middle-parts and final parts with more middles growing inside them, going on for almost an hour, that would be a hint of it.

It was exhausting and exhilarating, and it gave him ideas.

——

POLYGONS

Seeing is believing, and walking around is fun.

His eyes would jump between objects on the landscape and draw lines between them that were invisible to other people. While walking he had first been captivated by trees and other things that seemed to march by in the opposite direction, or distant things that drift into and out of alignment with other things as he looked to the side or drifted to the side.

It grew so practiced that the lines from him to things to other things and more things back to him, were there as soon as he looked for them. The lines were as real as the objects themselves to him, and he was seeing both. They made shapes on the ground that would change subtly with every step he took. He could add or subtract them and the shape would snap to become another.

The world was full of wonders when seen this way. Even mundane objects could be points of this shifting puzzle, so he knew no boredom. And every line had intangible properties too that he had invented. As he moved the lines leading from and to him shifted and distant lines between objects would not. He 'knew' how many paces it would take to reach them should he walk directly along the lines. Some distances he knew well, some not so well but those had a feeling of their own. He could feel uncertainty and certainty as a separate measure.

He knew distance this way because he had thought up a game.

He had decided lines had distance but he wanted to know distance by looking at lines, and things. So in deep thought one day he envisioned a game. Children practiced throwing things by throwing things, but this was different. He wanted to cast his thought like a stone and have distance return to him. He would estimate, pace, know, check the estimate against what he had thought, and declare his level of prowess.

This had deeply frustrated him at first because he had decided to do all this as a notion that was vague. Something was left hanging, or missing. There was discomfort in that. He was ill equipped somehow.

He imagined himself playing it well, over and over, better and better, until his prowess was a grinning smile. He was not smiling but the smile shone in his mind all Cheshire Catishly. Something to strive for. Forcing himself to imagine something-anything with repetition and discipline, he began to feel that at least, he would feel certain when the game had taken real shape and he was playing it well.

At no point did he think to himself, this is difficult. The language did have that expression, he had said it himself and heard others say it. But at times like this, the thought seemed like a silly distraction. A declaration for someone else, and there was no one else. He would just think, what to do now. Or next. And there always had to be something to do next.

It seemed appropriate to pantomime the game because he had not done that yet. He set out along one of his imaginary lines, a line of many steps, and arrived. Looking back he saw the line leading back to where he had been. A place was still a place even with no object there. That was another game he played, making up an object on the ground where there was none, connecting it to others, and the lines would still appear.

Having nothing else to do he turned back to pace it again. He paced back and forth. He felt frustration. He stepped onto another line, one leading elsewhere, and paced that. Back and forth. The lines and shapes were clear as ever, but the line he was pacing was becoming clouded, unhappy with growing frustration.

So he stood still and sighed, looked around to spot several objects and some imaginary others into a new mental constellation, a path of vibrant lines leading around back to him with its irregular bounding shape.

Then just for something to feel good about, he performed another trick he had taught himself. He revealed lines between the lines in an instant and each object was now connected to every other object in a web, making a tessellation of shapes between them that were the shape's children. So many lines to walk. He should try walking them all.

When he closed his eyes he could still see the shape-children and their edges. From shouts broken down to a chorus of whispers. Whispers. Or his eyes ascending the mountain hearing that incredible sound. All at once he had it! He made himself breathlessly still for a moment, letting the idea grow. Then examined it.

The more distance a line had, the louder it became! As if it was some level you might have to whisper or shout, to be heard. Or the ascending roar of the mountain. Or the movement of a foot.

So the game had become, he would fix in one ear a guess of how loud the line was. Then pace it, and each step would be louder or more 'forward' than the one before. When he reached the last step he would be hearing its true distance and he'd listen with both ears. And the more they sounded the same, that was his prowess. He could even judge how different the sounds were in paces and know what his mistake had been.

So he played the game ruthlessly and was so focused on the silent noise it made, it was a long while before he noticed while pacing, the line under him grew brighter and flickers of color appeared along its edges with each step. Even the line itself grew thicker and felt heavier. As his prowess grew into a smile he could still see these things, and his 'fixes' were almost true or close to it. But he applied discipline to give most attention to the sound. The multi-sense transformation was his brain trying everything at once, a parallel construction of skill-building inspired by his desperation to succeed in the game.

Stereo vision had always given clues of distance when objects were close by, so his prowess had risen quickly for those on instinct alone. Instinct can be honed with practice. But he was using other traits also. Focusing the eyes extends these clues further until they reach optical 'infinity', but essential clues are also supplied by knowledge of the size of objects or a class of objects, and how much smaller they appeared in the distance.

It was a scale that is irrational in the sense of numbers as we know them, and relies on tricks of thought below the conscious level. Even normal people may be conscious of an 'effort' that yields a quantitative result or qualitative opinion that can be compared to other results in its class, or even memorized. But THAT had honed the skill to a fine edge without numbers.

His gait had changed. Now he always walked in paces, or double-paces, and when he broke into a run it never seemed gradual because it was bounding steps of several paces at once. Even when not performing geometry in his head he could hear the loudness building with each stride and know how many slow paces of distance he had come from somewhere. To others it was seen as an odd, yet athletic grace.

Yet had anyone had asked how far away something was, he would not be able to tell them. But within a broad realm of walkable destinations he could pace that distance in any direction or walk directly to an object, stop and reach out to touch it, with eyes closed. Such a thing was never necessary for survival. But it was fun.

His people had counting words and he knew them well, but they were so few and they took so much time. There was nothing like a scalable cascade of magnitude we have built into a system of endless ordinal numbers. They had no need. He had the intellect to devise such a system, but he just happened to do it another way. And his mind was shaped in such fashion that it helped rather than hindered his effort and yielded a result.

It is true that the 'louder' it was, the more time he spent sliding his eye along the invisible line or glancing quickly between the distant point and a place in front of him. And speed and prowess increased dramatically when there were way point objects adjacent to the path, casting a procession of triangular shape-children into view. This might suggest that the hidden mechanism was based on some form of successive approximations in series-parallel.

But everything to him was anchored to 'loudness', which was his way to reckon the states and paces between objects.

He spent lots of time with moving and changing shapes as he walked between places. They were always visible as soon as he glimpsed or imagined their anchor points. They brought him comfort and satisfaction, as much welcome as the presence of the two young friends in his dreams. He could tell they flanked him while walking, yet in waking life they were never seen when he turned to look. Their seeing was independent from his, yet they all looked through the same eyes. And he could sense their focus of attention as two not-dots that would part from his focus of attention and roam in his vision like fireflies. He could easily ignore them or tell them to go away. Usually though they were present, their focus anchored to his own.

He had once thought of other people living inside his head, but he had brushed away that thought because it was too incredible. Such a simple idea would have so many complications that if it was true, such a fact would have always been known, he decided sternly. When there were not-dots in his vision he could decide to ignore them and they'd disappear before the thought was over. If he told them to go away, they'd drift back into his focus-point or off to the side with slowness, as if dragging their feet in rebellion. This property made them unique in all his visual artifacts. It was a puzzle for sure, but not so unlike the games his own mind sometimes played with him. But he never considered other people in his head. That carried the vague odor of burning rubber.

So he just pretended he had little helpers in his head without expounding on it. It was even a funny idea. And they loved games too. After a thought-eon of tracing lines around and back to him to appear as lines, then a shape... he held back the lines while he swept across two dozen objects in his vision with incredible speed.

Then with the objects shimmering without identifying themselves, he nudged to the left and right, Get Ready. And then stabbed one of the objects in the distance while thinking, Go! And two lines originating from himself at once, met at the distant object and made a shape. It happened in less than double-time but he didn't notice that. He decided to do it that way from now on, and remembered it as a game he had made for himself and won on the first attempt. He had just stated his intentions then expected a result. He loved the feeling of pride and prowess. Perhaps that is the reason we are not all many people inside. The ego-self just benefits from all their efforts and pretends it did all the thinking. King of the hill.

So he walks with polygons. They even lace the walls of the interiors of rooms, if he desires. Interiors are great fun. He can glance all the way round and up and down, with a mix of real and imaginary points, and fill the place with shape-children.

Not every-to-every, which is fun for a few but it becomes a tangled mess that wears him out. Now it is triangles made from nearest neighbors that march along so quickly that they had always been there, like the lines. When he sits down to work and converses with others, the shapes remain in his head. He can be playing mental hop-scotch, while conversing with others, while concentrating on his work.

Hopscotch grows strange when he is mentally hopping along shape-children across the walls and ceiling. He imagines himself looking at himself upside-down or sideways, at himself sitting on the smooth stone he is sitting on, which looks like he is sitting on the wall or the ceiling. With a sideways doorway leading out to sideways-world, or the doorway to upside-down world.

Upside-down world reminds him of the night sky. He should examine it more closely.

Once again he had joined fire-watch and had taken early leave of his parents, as they had been making amorous signs at one another and he knew that his leave-taking would allow that seed to grow until passion took them. They would imagine that divine spirits had rearranged the world to present them with the opportunity, and the spirits commanded them to couple in a wanton and expressive way as they had done as young lovers. They would pretend they could not resist these spirits, and surrender to them and obey the directive given, which just happened to be a command to surrender to one other.

Such were the games played by lovers.

Often kids had a hand in it. Because they loved their parents.

The regular evening migration of children in the village and their temporary adoption at hearths had inspired one of the funniest stories ever told. And it was also the saddest. It was both story and theater. It was told every half-year as the sun swayed to the far ends of its course, as soon as it was seen to be turning back again, and usually by the light of the next full Moon. Alternately told by a woman and a man, each with their own added flair and details.

It was called, Mr. Gatherer and the Children Of The Moon.

——

GATHERER AND THE CHILDREN OF THE MOON: PART I

Gatherer had lost his true love when they were young and had not yet been blessed with child. He had built a hut for his future family on the hill overlooking the camp in times of happiness and promise. But she was taken by sickness and suddenly he was alone at his hearth. And his mourning for her grew into an ornery bitterness that cast dark shadows over his days.

His life became solitary and he did not seek the company of others, for he desired not to see the fruits of the life he had missed, and to spare them his sorrow. He seemed callous and dismissive with children and they never felt welcome at his hearth, which was moot anyways, for his house was usually shut and dark in the evening because he wandered in far places and was away from home for days on end.

His specialty was finding plants. He found plants with food and spice and medicinal value, especially rare ones, even the bark of some trees and mosses and blue-green algae skimmed from the river. He knew which were used in medicine, could identify them at a distance and knew and remembered the land well. And at night when the wind was almost still, he'd find and collect them in the dark by scent alone. He could also scent the spores of mushrooms on the wind and find their places in the night. And in the morning leaves, stems, roots and caps would reveal their kind, edible or inedible, and some inedible were dangerous but had medicinal or recreational uses. All his finds were placed in skins he wore that had stitched pouches and layers when rolled up and tied, to keep everything separated.

He often lit fires in the wild for evening camp. For he had the botanical world mapped in his head, and had made a fire kit with the finest woods and tinders for the purpose, and he had used his solitary time to experiment with them. His kit was scaled down from the one others used with smaller parts and holes, and the twirling stick was straight and slender. Such was the strength of his arms and hands and speed of the twirl, that he could kindle a fire easily in the most ancient way with hands alone, even with a pause to raise them to the top again. He had no need for a capstone.

He would then cook any small game he had caught, and lay specimens he had gathered to dry. And fall asleep without fear or delay.

After a time of wandering he would return to camp at first light and deposit his treasures in the common area where plants were laid out and sorted, a fenced-in place where edibles were covered with skins and mats from birds. He took care to deposit dangerous things in another area where healers looked for them, leaving only common remedies for digestion, inflammation and mild pain. He would often arrive heavily laden, for on his return journey he collected pounds of vegetables and fruits and tubers he had dug. And would always scan other piles gatherers had dumped and sort them by type, on the lookout for more dangerous or poisonous things. As others arrived he would make himself scarce and disappear to the house and sleep. And after a long sleep he would be off again, leaving even in the dead of night.

To reward this effort as best they could, preparers of food from all over camp would bring him cooked meats, broths and soups in late afternoon. Hunters would give to the preparers small game and birds. Sometimes they would share with him, keeping him company for a little while, whether he wished it or not.

He returned with valuable bounty. He was cherished and respected for his skill and they all loved him, but everyone knew it had come at a great price. His heart was broken as could be seen clearly in the passing of years. He was still young but grief had aged him.

Many older girls and women had tried to comfort him. But their actions may have been seeded by a germ of pity, even as genuine desire stirred when they imagined or admired his physique. He seemed to sense this, for he would rebuff their advances so casually and firmly as to even raise their scorn. And the youngest and most prideful of their own attractiveness would feel the deepest scorn, which is only a natural human response for that peculiar hardship. But for his part he felt he was doing them a valuable favor, to avoid even a small entanglement of their precious and beautiful lives, so full of future, with his own dismal existence.

So deep was this funk that even if the living embodiment of his departed wife came to him and she did and said the very things that had captured his heart as young man, she would have been rebuffed with the rest. Life had changed him. He knew he was invaluable and his intelligence and skill may very well be essential for his community's survival. And he truly loved them all, especially the children. The satisfaction he derived from altruism alone, though insufficient to sustain a man indefinitely, would have to suffice. He would toil for as many years as he was physically able, then die alone.

He was held firm in the grip of dark magic that had overthrown his mind. It had left no hope of escape from despair. And the most competent and eager women of his time were unable to help him, and each despaired in her own way. And the men despaired also, to see one among them who should be valued most highly brought low to such a joyless and dangerous life, and they were powerless to stop it. He needed someone he loved to convince him to take others with him, so they might help save each other.

But as it was, some day he would simply fail to return. And all would gaze at the empty house on the hill, and all would despair.

And the storyteller would pause for a long while to wipe tears and take a drink.

Such was the power of this story in their lives that couples embraced tightly and gathered their children into the embrace if they were near. Regardless of age or present status anyone would embrace one flowing in tears, or whose body shook with involuntary sobs. This was not just a ritual story-telling, it was a time for all to celebrate their own deliverance from loneliness and despair, by casting themselves into the story.

Men took pride in control of emotion but might be betrayed as they broke suddenly with some secret fear of their own, or felt a sudden deep communion with the Gatherer and his plight. Women would break in a shapeless but compelling urge to be the one who might have brought comfort to the Gatherer, and their men knew this. Without a hint of jealousy they comforted their lovers and felt new desire surging in themselves, as a most essential and sexy attribute of womanhood was revealed. The men would be brought to tears themselves in grateful thanks for the choice they had made.

The world was a dangerous place and people had gathered to pool their skills and survive, but illness and injury took many in the prime of their lives. Be it from sickness or snakes or an animal in the hunt or a stone by the river striking one on the head as they fell, dire complications of childbirth or bad food. Or even something completely unknown that had claimed a loved one while they were out alone and never returned. And the ones left behind would hold on to hope past all possibility of seeing them again, and sink slowly into helpless and tortured despair.

Adults were keenly aware of danger that screamed and seethed in the subconscious. Children were made aware of much from a young age, yet they were meticulously spared detail, except for careful instruction of actions and situations to avoid. Humans formed increasingly populous communities in great part so those assigned any task in the wild and those left behind could always obey a simple directive known as the hunter's rule: three must go, so one can keep watch as others work or sleep, three can defend, and two can carry one back to heal and survive. Every additional member relieved the burden of this cruel arithmetic and ensured survival of the whole.

The Tale of The Gatherer touched everyone deeply because he was tragic, he was a hero, he traveled alone, traveled freely at night, but his reason for doing so was abject despair. Despair is the most dangerous remaining predator of human kind, for all its ingenuity and resourcefulness. We fight it still.

From the hormonal surge of advanced puberty there was no defense for this tale. Almost all the children were eagerly awaiting the loud part of the story that was great fun, but they scented puberty in others as surely as if it was adrift on the wind. Even if an elder girl or boy had made fun of everyone's reaction to this part of the story in the past, at the first sign of moist eyes or silent brooding attention to it, children would actually rearrange their seating. The younger rose ostensibly to move down the line to converse in whispers with others. There was no insensitivity in this. In fact, in was a game played by the younger conspired in secret, and its purpose was to maneuver specific ones they knew were most deeply affected into compatible pairs so when emotion waxed, they would discover they were seated next to one other.

And such was the wisdom of peers in judging compatibility and readiness, the game played out well even if one or both realized they had been set up. Those who had already begun mutual courtship were excluded from the game and were probably sitting together already. But there could be one who had pined for another and was overheard, or the other who was moody and depressed without seeming to know why, perhaps because they felt pressure to sort themselves out mentally before taking any real next step with anyone. Which could drag on for months and depress everyone.

Those were the most fun to watch from a distance. For one would break and the other would comfort them, and then the embrace would pull stiffer in the excitement of first contact. As the crowd around them became distracted, hands would begin to boldly explore and offer promises, and tears were not just for the story but their own small part in it. Tears of relief that the painful ordeal of loneliness and waiting would soon be over.

Sometimes they would even drift away long before the wildest part of the story began, and their peers would celebrate winning the game louder and longer to wish them well. And further delay adults from returning home.

———

INTERMISSION: OTA BENGA

Consider the plight of one of Stargazer's remote descendants and fellow countrymen, Ota Benga of the Mbuti tribe. It is a modern tale that reveals more about us than about him. Nothing I could imagine could compare to what is known for certain that he endured.

His early life and last day of happiness is not known because an autobiography was never written, though it very well might have been if things had turned out differently. In 1906 he is described as four feet eleven, 103 pounds, and at the age of 23 a photograph shows him boyish in appearance to our eyes, but with the mature face and head of a man. And indeed he had been a grown man in his country with a wife and two small children.

While he was away hunting, slave traders raided the camp and murdered everyone they left behind. In flight from that horror he was captured by an enemy tribe to sell into slavery. He was bought with a pound of salt and a bolt of cloth by American entrepreneur and explorer Samuel Phillips Verner, while en route to a Batwa Pygmy village.

The American was trying to recruit Africans to take part in the Louisiana Purchase Exposition. They were suspicious of Verner until Benga vouched for him and described the purchase-favor the man had done for him, and Benga admitted to them his curiosity to see this strange faraway land. He traveled to the United States with four others from that village and others from neighboring tribes.

The exposition was a success. It was also a masterpiece of kitsch or 'cringe' as we call it now, and these gentlemen tribesmen-hunters were encouraged to 'look warlike', which they achieved only by observing Native Americans who were also commissioned for display. Apache leader Geronimo befriended Benga and gave him one of the chief's arrowheads.

Verner made good on his promise to return them, and after the fair Verner again journeyed to Africa and Benga was once again in the Batwa village where his companions reunited with their families. Benga even found a wife there for a very short time, but that too ended tragically from a poisonous snake. Culture is provincial and his own village had been slaughtered, and despite a warm welcome, with growing trouble in the region Benga decided to return to the US with Verner and hope for a fresh start.

Verner was both friend and benefactor. Amid his own increasing financial difficulties, he found a position for Benga at the American Natural History Museum in New York City. He even demanded a stipend of $175 a month to be paid to Benga, knowing full well the African's potential to draw massive crowds. Average wage at the time was $40 a month. And of course nothing was ever paid to Benga, despite the museum being an endless carnival of kitsch and exploitation that put the St. Louis fair to shame. Benga was miserable there, plagued by dreams of being entombed beyond life as a stuffed museum exhibit. He wanted to walk free, hear birds again. He rebelled against his 'hosts' and Verner found him a much better position at the Bronx Zoo where he could at least be outside and help care for familiar animals.

It is ironic that the zoo got so much consternation for Benga's presence and his 'exhibition' at the monkey house there, for it was the most civilized treatment he had received since his return to the US. He was permitted to roam zoo grounds and care for its charges like any other employee, unpaid of course. He hung his own hammock in the monkey house and befriended them all, because he hated to be inside and monkeys and apes were like children to him. He loved human child visitors and exchanged funny faces with them. As soon as the zoo realized he was more of an attraction than the animals, they were slow learners, there was yet another round of cringe-kitsch. He was in a cage with the primates and the cage was apparently locked during visiting hours, but only to prevent crowd tampering and animal escapees. Because he was in a cage with a gentle gorilla that people didn't understand very well, he was permitted to keep his bow and arrows. These turned out to be more useful for chasing ugly people away.

But it is also ironic that these more favorable conditions lowered his guard and he acted more like himself than ever, playing with crowds, delighting children by staging hunts and showing them how to hold a spear and weave with twine. And drinking soda, of all things. Which sometimes terrified their stuffed parents. When ugly crowds jeered and poked at him he would poke back as surely as any man. And with a hunter's practiced skill and innate kindness, he shot arrows at them without hitting anyone.

Official Consternation erupted over his exhibition at the monkey house, triggering widespread disdain and dialogue by religious peoples on the shameful practice, heralded by the Rev. James H. Gordon... while offering no practical immediate suggestion. Still they were his very own advocates, and their dialogues were published and gained support.

But also period Darwinian Supremacists who swarmed the zoo to prove for themselves, while inciting him to do something primitive, that his race was backwards and inferior. Including an editorial in the New York Times of course. Headpiece filled with straw. Alas! It was those Hollow Men who should have been nailed to the wall by their stuffed shirts, as Ota Benga patiently told them his life story and described all he had endured, right up to that moment by their own hand.

It did not help that his English was still crude and untutored. Many have no flair for languages as adults without patient or loving instruction, and what exactly should have inspired him? Being dressed in suit and tails for the amusement of dinner guests at the History Museum? It also did not help that his teeth had been filed to sharp points as a mature boy, as befitted a man of his stature in Pygmy culture.

So with crowds falling off after the Consternation and his increased rowdiness, Benga was finally dis-invited from the zoo. And Rev. Gordon finally offered a practical suggestion, and that was to put Benga up at the Howard Colored Orphan Asylum in Brooklyn he managed. Considering Benga's love for children and officially uncontested freedom, it is not surprising that he stayed there for four years. Verner, the original advocate who had brought him from Africa had retired to obscurity, perhaps Panama. And then for what ever reason, Gordon fell back to his second practical suggestion.

Benga was off again in 1910, this time to a place with the unlikely name of Lynchburg, Virginia. Founded by John Lynch if you must know, a tobacco trading water town with a population of thirty thousand. He was still officially a man of no means but was sponsored by a kind family there, whose kindness seems to have only been tempered by an idea that he wished to become a seminary student. Nevertheless he was tutored in English by local poet Anne Spencer and attended elementary school.

To help achieve that unlikely goal Gordon stepped up as his newest and greatest advocate, providing Western clothes and most important, paying for Benga's pointed teeth to finally be capped, something that had never occurred to Verner in his attempts to resettle Benga in the US.

Now armed with a winning smile and better English, Benga discontinued school and went to work and received his very first US paycheck at a tobacco factory. Gordon and the good people of Lynchburg collectively deserve the United States' finest recognition for civilized behavior, something at which New York City had miserably failed. His hard earned dollars were being saved to pay his own passage back to Africa, a place he now desperately missed.

But in 1914 Ota Benga's torment was not quite over. World War I put a end to ocean travel. Is it likely he understood how long the condition might last? We do not know.

What we do know is that two years later, his endurance had ended at age 32. Ota Benga was a broken man.

On the Vernal Equinox of 1916 he borrowed a gun from one of his host families, lit a ceremonial fire and burned his clothes, pulled the caps from his teeth, and shot himself in the heart. He had said he wanted to send his soul back to Africa.

Ota Benga died more than a man. But lonely, incomplete.

What of the Gatherer, and the people of his village trying so desperately to save him? I hope my point comes as no surprise.

If one woman in all the United States... and I do mean all, for his story was carried coast to coast in the papers about his stay at the zoo, and maybe over a million people encountered him directly there and in other places.

If one woman of any imaginable cursed 'color', including yours or mine or his own, had recognized in person or from a photograph that he was indeed a man, and she liked his face, and she ventured to meet him. She would have discovered he was a kind and gentle, tortured soul.

But every bit a man, skilled and strong, with endurance and tolerance beyond measure. A playful, intelligent man with a winning smile either way, who adores children, whose own had been taken from him. And who knows what else? If she had offered herself in earnest, and he had accepted. Or she persisted to woo him until her pure motivation was crystal clear.

If one woman had loved him, he would have learned Chaucer's English if that is what she spoke. And he would have called her my dear little one as a joke, for she would always tower over him. They would settle in open country where he could walk in the forest. He would work tirelessly and hard for his family. They would have babies who grew far beyond his height if they were nurtured well. And he would nurture them, teach his language also and every skill he knew, and others he had learned.

And he would return to the land of the living for 50 years or more. His children and grandchildren would love him. And he would love them, and he would love her. The stuffed shirts would not know, because they never deserved the effort to be shown. And the 2017 Lynchburg memorial erected in his honor would not be there. Because he had just lived there.

But only if she liked it. I hope so. Seems like a nice place.

Not one? Seriously??

———

GATHERER AND THE CHILDREN OF THE MOON: PART II

Gatherer was a very complicated and tortured individual. But he needed only simple medicine to break the spell and get on with his life, as he would have years ago had he not been cursed. But the medicine could not be administered by just anyone.

His own intelligence had grown and he had become a master of many disciplines, and not the least of which, survival. His fearlessness alone in the wild was simply a result of mental deliberation in situations many others dared not face alone, and an assessment of the world he lived in, where his people had cleverly stalked and eliminated predators to where they represented a much smaller threat. His solitary life had spared him from hearing the tales that brought them back to life in gruesome splendor.

But he had only witnessed migrating people-predators in the distance, on circuitous tracks that took them far from the encampments of people. How could these know where people were, to avoid them? He knew even with keen senses, discernment of which creature fades with distance, and even if they disliked people they would have to at least approach to inspect and identify for sure. If they in truth feared them.

But then one day he had an idea, and back at camp he had discussed it eagerly with the hunters who visited him. They had also been confused by his reports of big cats making detours around people. What if, he said... it was the people's fires they were avoiding? Burning wood, and even the meats being cooked in the fire? Predators in the wild were always ready to steal fresh kills away from the scene of a hunt, but they never raided hunters' camps any more, and especially did not fancy cooked meat.

They may even have an ancient fear of fire even at distance, for in dry grasslands wind driven fire can outrun even fast cats, if the wind changes and they are trapped by it. Maybe they imagine the smell of burnt flesh on cooking fires as other animals fallen prey to fire itself, a warning of disaster? And we came from the South where they were so numerous, there were always ones down on their luck, overcome by hunger. And it was they who stalked our camps seeking our children, despite the fire. The hunters were very impressed and said he was clever to think of such things, if they could discover a way to prove it is true.

But with the same clarity of mind he rejected women who threw themselves at him, and found he could sense their impending advances easily. And he rationalized his rejection of them in thought alone, and he had created an impenetrable wall around himself.

What he really needed was a woman of course, but someone very special who is not easy to find, and you should consider yourself lucky to be stalked by one. A woman with more intelligence, cunning, patience, and discipline than he. And a natural skill in the hunt and capture of men, whether she knew it or not. She must not only stalk him from a distance, but also challenge him, advance and retreat in ways that confuse his mind. He will know she is his equal, a worthy prize, and that will excite him. She may only casually reveal parts of herself and drive his imagination wild. She might even offer herself in jest, and make him desire to see past her joke and taste her in real life. And when he does taste her and relish her, his dark spell is broken.

And she must make him think it had been his own idea.

And the village was blessed to have one such as this.

Of those who regularly brought food was Baree, who had also lost her lover and companion long ago. From younger days and despite occasional dalliances she had never started her own child, because for some it is very difficult. Later she had even discouraged potential suitors in sadness because she thought she was barren. She had inherited one of her family's huts and lived alone, but she always welcomed children to stay at her hearth. It was a merry place full of beds and mats and she always brought home work to do with them, and over the years she had been a stand-in mother to many and they made things, and talked.

And now she wanted the Gatherer as so many others had wanted him. For years satisfying her own need had been a solitary thing, part of a comfortable existence. But he changed her and set her upon a different course. It had happened quickly. She had seen a line of men carrying large stones from the river, and they had gone past where she was working. She had admired him before from a distance, and had even consoled those who had dashed themselves against him. She was merely curious as they passed by.

They were each carrying a single heavy stone with both hands against their bellies. And Gatherer had two stones, almost as large as the ones the others were carrying. But he had encircled them and drawn them up separately to his shoulders, where each shoulder bore most of the weight of the stone, and the arm was bent to hold it in place and cup it in hand. He walked with a stoop to keep them balanced.

It was a long trip from the river, and his arm muscles caught the sunlight and they were stretched very tight. She had mused to herself, he is a fine gatherer of stones.

Alone in the darkness she usually pleased herself to prepare for sleep. She would place both hands and start with smooth gentle strokes to awaken desire and ride it slowly upwards, and her mind would flash with people and places and things she had to do, but her mind was invariably drawn to a waking dream of picturing some repetitive task that required regular movements of the fingers, and every discrete operation became a stroke against the delicate folds of her vulva. She tried to keep them somewhat genuine, but her mind would become muddled when she brushed against her very center, and a bright flare of satisfaction peaked and settled. Her fingers would be drawn to it and captured by its greediest part, while she is imaging lifting a filament or reed or cord to set into a weave, or pushing it through. Finally the finger actions made no sense, but she is imagining something great being assembled to trick herself into continuing, and pressing harder. And at the last she is consumed by greed until a surge of satisfaction rises and flares. It would release her slowly and drift her to sleep.

When she is working she sometimes remembers these journeys into self, and her working finger movements are at times accompanied by tingles from below. And while she works she clenches deep muscles in a rhythmic habit, and she has made them strong. Now when the heat rises and takes her, the pulses are so vivid the heat stays with her until they are exhausted, and she dissolves into a relaxed state of pretending to squeeze them. Her muscles love her. Love is a warm friend in the dark and always kind.

But on this day, she set herself up with hands in place and glided herself into the usual state, but the repetitive weave became Gatherer's arm and shoulder muscles journeying from the river, and she is tracing them with her fingertips and squeezing them with each step he takes along the path. But it isn't enough, and as his muscles ripple as he shifts his loads, parts of her that usually lie still as she struggles below, are now standing erect and begging to be stroked.

She rolls over and vigorously rubs her chest across the furs and her bottom rises on spread knees to grant access to where her hands need to go. As she strokes with thumbs circling, she is embracing him in her mind with her legs around his lower back as he is still trudging. And rolls over again to take a different journey, this one guided by a finger firmly planted in the center, another hand making desperate visits to her chest and doing other things she has never done before, that are sublimely beautiful because she is imagining he is doing them. And her legs have a mind of their own, lifting her up and dropping her and straining outstretched until they resist, and the resistance itself is a flood of heat and pleasure. Her dexterity makes her bold and she is visiting more places, until her toes stretch and curl as she whimpers and thrashes herself to sweet oblivion and sinks into a buzzing daze.

Finally panting in silence as she lay spread-eagle with arms stretched beyond her head, on a bed wet with sweat and female excitement... she is thinking with sarcasm, I seem to have fallen for this man. I must have this man. But his rejection would break me. I must do this carefully.

In the days to come, she would not touch herself and let tension rise. If she did it would lead to a repeat of this... this... wild thing. On some deep level he would feel her rising tension and desire. And little by little it would draw him to her, and she would be ready for him. There would be nights alone she knew, for this plan involved her casual exit with the words, I will see you tomorrow. And she knew after she left him she would be lying awake struggling to sleep. Lack of sleep would cloud her mind and ruin the plan. What to do? She let this idea float above her like a puzzle to be solved. And felt desire stir again.

Without thinking she brought her arms down and placed hands on her chest, and proved herself a genius with the very first stroke. She deceived herself with thoughts of rationalization, but every touch felt like gentle wisdom. I shall lay down to sleep, and lie still and think about the day and decide what to do tomorrow. Then I shall take these into my hands and say, you will bring me the peace and rest I need, for you love me still. You have awakened after a long dream, or what ever you do when there is no lover to excite you or baby to keep you busy.

So she stroked their surfaces lightly and squeezed them gently against one another and then apart, lifting from below and pressing with her palms and making lazy circles that got smaller until she was grasping herself like two suckling infants, fingers and thumbs pulling and twirling and pinching softly. And felt herself drifting towards sleep in total relaxation, and her movements grew more quieter until the fingers only moved very slightly, and it carried her mind away. Time passed without thought and she was almost asleep, and now just his quiet face floated in her mind. His face and the sensation of the two faceless infants she had always wanted, precious little embers of life.

The embers merged and grew into a smooth quiet flame that infused her entire body and passed over her in a slow, delicate wave. It was beautiful beyond belief and she remained completely still as it swelled, and as it faded it made no further demands of her, fingers relaxed as she passed into restful sleep in complete contentment.

She had never had a baby of her own, and yet she had discovered one of the secret joys of motherhood.

She awoke in a wonderful mood and made it known that she would be the one to bring dinner up the hill. Others who did this thought, here we go again.

But the joke they were thinking of remained untold. And they agreed of course, because it felt good for them to agree, and it would be pointless to refuse. Such was the awesome power she exerted on people she met.

For she had completely got it wrong. It was not rising tension that was called for, and that was in fact what he sensed easily in others which triggered his gallant defenses. And her wild erotic adventure had brought her great joy and release, more than anything in her life, but it also encouraged a sureness of rapidly escalating tension when she actually sighted the object of desire.

What she needed to win this game was a quiet confidence, poise and grace, things she already had in great measure. And the golden warmth that had thrilled her and put her to sleep was not the same phenomenon as the culmination of her wildcat escapade. That had just set more firmly in her mind the objective, and raised her hunger.

It is the purest love of all, a rising heat that takes new mothers by surprise, and helps their bodies recover from childbirth. Muscles clench to contract where the baby has been and reduce it to normal size. And the rhythm and place in the mind is so similar to the final thrill of love, it triggers that also if there is even a dormant seed of salacious desire. And it passes over a woman as a gentle and beautiful happening that is not by her own direct action, not the culmination of some desperate struggle. It makes her feel unconditionally loved in a way her mind cannot resist or debate, and eases tension completely.

Its glow and associated hormonal surges beautifies new mothers and fascinates men. They sense it and it will stir secret desire in them, just to see her calm face and vivacious movement. And in everyone it curries a subconscious yearning to please her and accede to her wishes, and leaves them with a warm feeling that they are participating in her success.

So Baree became the one who visited, and the food she brought was diverse and satisfying. To those who prepared it her beaming smile in asking was reward enough to give extra attention to it, and their own families who ate the major portion thanked them also. She always set aside time to prepare something special, small bites of meat, fruit or vegetable that had been marinated or sprinkled from the spices he brought them all. And yet it was the first time he had tasted some of them in another's dish. He would remark on this and identify the source, and she would say yes, you were wise to bring it, and smile. And she never betrayed her own effort to lavish attention on the dish.

Days passed and he was still at home, she noted with secret joy. She was too stubborn and brilliant to admit it, or give any direct voice or hint to her desire. Or even tackle, subdue and take him as one had suggested. So they would sit and share food and conversation. She often carried a bundle of grass stalks and reeds with her to do as they talked. Eventually she would take her leave, and yet he had grown to enjoy her company, and found more odd jobs to do in the village, and he would note her presence at a distance. Still when they talked he seldom met her eyes because he did not feel desirable himself, and his home was full of memories.

But sometimes in comfortable silence he would turn and she would
be looking at him steadily with a tiny smile, as if they had been
sharing a secret joke. He could not help smiling himself. And as he
looked her gaze would never waver. And she welcomed his gaze with
nothing else passing between them, as her hands kept steadily busy.
He marveled that her work needed no eyes upon it very often. But
he had some such work too. And he realized that his whole life he
always sat with others as if he was a nervous dinner host, hands
unoccupied and fidgeting. Funny to think that after so many years.

The next time she visited she found a small work surface in front of
him, and various stone and wooden bowls of plant matter laid out
on the floor. Their surfaces were rough but insides very smooth and
rounded from meticulous and steady chipping, and he had round
river stones to rock within them. Grinding spices and medicines was
something he often left to others now, but he had a large stock of
bowls and stones for cutting and grinding, and soft square skins to
bind mashes and powders to wrap them. He had even gone to the
common store and gathered some whole plants he had left there, and
there were many tough seeds he needed to dry and crack, some to
mash. His effort would let the healers rest their own hands a bit.

After dinner and usual conversation he gathered the work surface on
his lap. She was weaving something large in pieces but dense with
many crosses in it, and without looking she would pull several reeds
out of the bundle from behind her as if she was reaching for spears to
cast, and merge them into the weave. Her eyes settled on his. He set
to grinding seeds and set aside a pile of them to grab at need, and laid
some along the inside of the bowl.

He looked at her with his own tiny smile, and from that moment
their eyes never strayed from one another. He ground dry hard seeds
in stages, and the first was to crack the outer husks by bearing down
hard on the bowl in his lap until the sounds of cracking were heard.

She used her knuckles to track and identify individual strands, and would push unwoven groups into an arch by sliding them forward under knuckles along her thigh.

He kept one bowl underneath the other and its top was sturdy and flat, so he could nudge it aside with his knee while his hand grasped the other, with a smooth motion and fingers fluttering, slide the seeds from one bowl to the other.

She guided individual reeds with one hand in and out of the arch raised by her knuckles, fingers stretching and flexing as one hand did the work of two.

He gathered more seeds from the pile and sprinkled them to be cracked. He used night vision often and had trained himself to walk around looking to the side, to see with the corners of his eyes. So he hardly ever needed to gaze aside when reaching for things. And that was fortunate... for he might have missed that she had half-completed the row and spun the work, dipping one thigh and lifting the other to set it down on the corner of the competed portion to pin it in place. He started cracking again, bearing down a little harder than he needed to.

She remembered her mother cracking individual seeds between her teeth with great effort, spitting pieces into a bowl with a tiny puff of air, and filling the bowl very slowly. How amazing these curved bowls and round stones are. She noted the rounded motion in the bowl, and also how the muscles near his shoulders tightened as he leaned into the stone.

She had turned the work, and to his amazement, she was now performing every tiny motion in reverse at the same speed, as if she had just flipped her mind over and hands simply obeyed. And the work slipped, and the thigh lifted a bit to set it deeper, and now pressed down firmer than before.

She watched him lift the cracking bowl and poured the other at the place where the whole seeds had been, now a pile of tiny pieces, and set them up again and gathered a pile and dropped it in, and reached at his feet for a smaller curved stone with a narrower rounded edge. All without looking away from her.

He saw her lift the whole rectangle from between her thighs and her hands worked their way around its edges, tucking in loose strands between others, pulling and squeezing tightly as the open loops of reeds shrunk and collapsed. She was doing it with both hands, but force was applied alternately and her wrists and arms were tensing and relaxing, revealing stretched tendons. He almost shifted his gaze to examine them closer.

He is now pressing harder in the second stage, holding the bowl steady with almost as much strength as he is pushing the stone, she realized. Of course. Otherwise something would drift sideways and the whole thing would suddenly flip over. He seems to be blinking more often. But most enthralling is the way his muscles flex when pressing on the stone.

He saw her set aside the bit of work she had finished and was about to reach for another row of strands, but as she reached behind she did not count them with fingers. She pulled out just one. Then slowly reached for another. And another. He stopped working, and stopped counting. Every reach was slower still, a graceful swivel of the arm and a sustained view of the tense area around her open armpit, with a short tuft of hair. And her loose skin jacket revealed a curve of ample breast from the side. When she had a dozen of them in a row she relaxed and rested both hands in her lap. And her smile widened a bit as if to say, what now?

He couldn't break eye contact or he would lose the game. But he could break the silence.

I have to pass water, he said. And in a moment of unaccustomed boldness he added, how about you rise and follow me for a moment, and we gaze at one other by the light of the Moon?

She answered without delay while resuming her work and looking down at it.

She said, Or how about we both move over to stand by the fire where we can see one another more clearly? And then lean together until your nose touches mine and your water joins with mine and we put the fire out? Then in the dark you can guide me to another place and twirl me between your hands, and I will start a new fire. I promise not to close my eyes.

Confound this woman! he thought. She is on me like a predator! He turned and went outside.

He stood outside for awhile in the moonlight, pondering the strange game with the locked eyes. He had never heard of such a thing. Had she made the first move, or had he? When he closed his eyes he could still see her looking at him, reaching ever so slowly back, to grasp another piece. One at a time. And a part of him wondered if when he returned, she would be stretched out on his furs, all of her in view, open and inviting. He felt a surge of elation mixed with stage fright mixed with confusion, and it was a messy emotion. Confound this woman.

But the world seemed a bit lighter on his shoulders.

He returned to find her weaving with eyes closed. Probably resting them he thought. There was that little smile again and she faced him again. She brushed hair away and asked him questions about his work. Her mother had been a healer and she had seen many setups such as his, and even knew some of the medicines. And he asked her questions about the techniques he had witnessed, and how the pieces were joined together. And they ate some more, and he brewed some tea to show how rich it tasted when plants were ground small. And he resumed grinding seeds and he watched as she weaved, glancing at each other only occasionally this time. She told him of her mother and gathering adventures in the wild they had shared. And time passed slowly and more comfortably than it ever had before.

He felt a jolt in his heart when she said within the stream of conversation, I'll be getting home now. And started collecting things into bundles that hung from her shoulders.

But in the doorway she turned and said silently in slow, expressive gesture, I. will. see. you. tomorrow.

He reflected as he lay down. So playful, so strange. Demure, not timid.

And he was still at home after several days now, which was also strange. Why have I not awakened in the night and just said, time to go, as I have always done? And he remembered her standing and gesturing, as if commanding him. Every night she had said it in words near the end before she arose, as if it was just a polite way to end conversation. And yet he knew he definitely would be here tomorrow, for he could see her gesturing slowly over and over in his mind. His last thought before sleep was, Confound this woman.

And she was not timid. She confided to a female friend next morning in mounting frustration, one of these days I will bring a spicy warm broth to his house and pour it all over him, and put his surprise and rising indignation to good use! Her friend had laughed at this bold plan, and they began to swap recipes for preparing and tenderizing men.

The next night she arrived at his house after sundown, fed the fire and opened the doorway to let out the smoke, and warmed the dinner she had brought. The bright full Moon shone through the doorway, and they admired it while eating. And nothing had been poured on him, for she knew it would be a waste of good food, and she was a practical woman who always did the right thing.

And the right thing to do right now was set down her work and rise, approach and bend over him and start setting his things aside, with her long hair dangling near his face, as if she was just helping him do a few routine tasks. She glanced at him before doing each thing, with a warm smile that seemed to ask, would you just do me this one small favor? As she turned back to the task without waiting.

It riveted him, his silence and stillness in that moment was all she was asking, and he granted her these small favors without question, even without seeing any possible end, for her warm scent was in his nostrils, and her firm movements while slowly lifting and carefully setting aside even heavy things was a joy to behold. It seemed that every small favor he granted her was also a favor to him.

And then the rearranging of things was over. She stood straight and brushed hair from her face and her eyes were wide with gratitude as if to say, thank you. And in that moment she asked silently with a smile, could you do me one more small favor? And his eyes said yes in silence and stillness. Her very nearness was a gift, and he reveled in it.

And such was her power over him and complete triumph, her success as a woman filled with desire, that she could very well have offered her hand and pulled him upright, to lead him to a place of final conquest. His defenses would flare briefly and then dissolve in confusion as she drew him against her, and asked him to remove her garments, as the next small favor.

If that might not be enough, she could also pull him upright and squat slightly to encircle arms around his upper legs, lock fingers together and lift him off the ground, his chest against her face as she found balance, and stood. And with slow deliberate steps, carry this large stone from the river to the place she needed it to be. For her mind had been conquered by the sight of his strength, but she was capable of her own feats.

And that would have obliterated his defenses without contest. Gatherer was strong and he praised strength in men to encourage them, but he had a deep fetish for strength in women, a fetish he had never realized or discovered. His state as she bore him would be so amazed and thrilled that she would feel his rising need pressing against her, as his thoughts were drawn to her beautiful sturdy legs vibrating with tension, and what wonders he might find between them. When she set him down he would already be ablaze and unthinking, and he would reach for her.

But she did none of those things. She sat in his lap and stretched her arms luxuriously with a sigh as if she was just getting comfortable, embraced him and whispered with her breath in his ear, Tell me a story.

If he had circled an arm beneath her legs and placed the other on her bottom and lifted her, bearing the weight easily as he stood and each step brought her closer to bliss, she would have cried out in surrender to him. It would seem her life's greatest fulfillment, to become the stone he carried, and her body would be aflame.

But he remained there, sitting still. So she danced upon him slowly.

Her arms were restless, and she was restless all over, as if every part of her was having difficulty to find a comfortable position, and she almost carelessly brushed his lips and swayed slowly, and pressed her bottom and chest sinuously and firmly in the way that prepares men. It was the best thing that had ever happened to him, moment by moment. He felt a stirring and it was his body that finally surrendered to her.

They locked gazes again, and they both began to enjoy her undulating restlessness. It was a delicious recipe that needed to be stirred slowly. Strong hands gathered inside her animal skins against her skin, fingers that delicately traced her spine and back in waves until she shuddered. Then stroked as they descended and started heading where she wanted them to go, then suddenly veered off and squeezed the sides of her bottom tightly and guided her against him, and she gasped suddenly and knew she needed him as he kneaded her.

That is actually how the story went. And the storyteller would pause at this point as if thirst had gotten the better of him. And would sip slowly to whispered comments and long periods of quiet. He knew the story was going on in the minds of adults, and even children knew what was happening and what the elders were thinking. The young glanced at one another and found it hilarious to know. But their part in the story was about to begin.

A shrill voice in the night called out her name. She grew still in Gatherer's lap but did not startle or turn, for she knew the voice well. The hands strayed from her. A boy stood in the doorway, a bit nervous. He had approached the house and was glad to recognize her. He started to speak but trailed off uncomfortably, and it was to be the standard greeting of children seeking refuge for the night, may I?

Gatherer's face was still locked in a smile because her eyes were upon him, and he dared not betray the real emotions that crossed him. Not even as she turned and said without delay, Of course! Come in, sweetheart! For she had never refused. The boy sighed with relief and entered.

She sat poised on his lap and turned back to face him, and she slowly and firmly pressed her chest tightly against his, and he could feel she was very erect. She swayed back and forth slowly, dragging herself against him. Then with open eyes very close to his, she announced loudly and sensuously, He is going to tell me a story. Then with a beaming smile full of promise she rose to her feet and looked around for soft things to lay out by the fire.

But there were more voices on the hillside and as she looked out, three girls and a boy were approaching. They had their sleeping furs in hand and as tradition required, as soon as they saw her they all stood politely and asked in unison, may I? Of course! Come in! she said softly, and her smile was as genuine as it was amused by the turn of events. Gatherer took her hint and gathered himself, then rose to delve into packed-away things and gather his mats and soft tents, hats and loose furs, to lay out on the dirt floor in front of the fire.

So we're going to have a little party tonight, are we? She said to the four little ones now sitting by the fire. Yes, Ms. Baree! One of the girls said loudly. Just a little party! Such a teeny tiny party! And she laughed, and the laughter was echoed from down below. There were whispers and more laughter. It continued in waves. Surprise at the sound brought Gatherer and Baree to the doorway and outside.

Torches were ascending the hill. Children were marching up the hill in groups, and others in the distance. Some children saw them standing outside and shouted, MAY I?

Yes you are all welcome! Baree shouted, mindful of ritual. Many were bringing outdoor sleeping gear, fire kits, bundles of food. They had evidently gathered somewhere and returned for supplies as it was evident this would be a mass convergence. At this point it all seemed like an elaborate joke, and she wondered if the friend she had shared recipes with was involved. That would be mean, but also funny. Then she looked around the scene and thought, no that's impossible. What is happening?

Almost all had organized their furs and makeshift tents outside on the lawn in front of the hut. Some older boys and girls were directing placement and had even kept a straight path from the hut down the hill so the hosts would not be inconvenienced. Older children with torches were taking younger to the latrine around the back, and staying with them until they returned. And they lit little fires all over, for many had brought wood.

Baree and Gatherer were repeatedly approached by boys and girls who had been delegated to formally ask by others, may I? And what else could anyone say now? It was a regular jamboree. At least those clouds will not bring rain tonight, she noted with a practiced eye. Then another arriving group, some carrying younger friends or siblings. And another chorus of May I?

Instead of the usual lights of fires through doorways here and there, the entire village was dark. It was bizarre.

And the stories she got from individual children when approached were surprising. / They didn't tell me not to watch, but no one fed me so I left. / They're rutting like rabbits! It's funny! / Mom says she needs a lot of quiet time with Dad. / Daddy is making Mommy happy / and variations of those. Children who just jerked back and forth and made gestures or spoke nonsense. Oh right, that six-times thing. / They were knocking things over and I couldn't sleep. / Don't worry, I put the fire out before I left because they were busy. / They're making me a little brother/sister. / They're rocking each other to sleep but I don't need that, I'm older now. / They're doing, you know. / Mom's on top again! / Why do they ask for quiet time when they won't be quiet? /

But the most impressive was a smart young girl who told stories around the fire, and she was good at it. She walked up and introduced herself. Ms. Baree, In case you didn't know, Lady Moon has cast a spell on our parents. We walked around for a while but all the places had doorways shut and dark, and there were other kids coming out of them anyway. We passed by your place but it was dark and we thought, you know. You're a pretty lady and should do it more and kick the kids out. We understand. So we just wandered around and saw the fire in Mr. Gatherer's doorway. Are you doing it with him? Not now I mean. He's a grumpy man. How many times do you have to do it, anyway? Well aaanywayyyy... she gathered her breath and shouted, Everybody's making babies tonight! All babies! All night! Babies! Babies! Babies! Babies! Babies! Babies!

And she laughed and skipped down the hill shouting, Babies! Babies! Babies! Others took up the chant. Then she turned back to them and shouted, We are the lost children of the MOOOON!

Gatherer was doing chores for the guests like he was in a dream. The strangest story ever told had arrived at his house. He had interviewed individual children with similar results. Then he had started preparing what food he had left but the kids shooed him away and finished the work. Many had brought water and food and were cooking outside and handing it around.

The last group to arrive were older ones, heavily laden with camping gear used for extended hunts and bad weather. They were followed by a line of children carrying bundles in their arms. It was an elaborate and coordinated effort. They were gravely serious as they set about erecting tents and laying out furs in them. The children carried their bundles inside. Baree approached the tents with a single burning question in her mind, and it was soon answered.

A young mother stood before her cradling and nursing two infants. A boy stood behind her, one hand rubbing a shoulder gently and stroking her hair lovingly, and kissing the other shoulder, with another arm stretched around her front to help her support the weight.

Three of us have milk, she said, and Moon has spared us to care for the little ones. She was sweating heavily in the cool night. Or I think we have been spared. It is a wild time! We work at the nursery and know where the smallest ones are, and when we realized the spell was so strong we entered places with torches. Most were already holding little ones to the breast as they loved, but some were so carried away they were only able to focus on us as we stood before them with babe in arms. We gestured a sign of safekeeping, and there were happy tears and stuttered words of gratitude, which were seized by Moon and turned into passion. So we left them, and were never pursued. Um… may we all?

Baree felt a surge of affection and awe for this amazing young woman, and embraced her and her little charges tightly as one. Baree then turned to the boy. He was also sweating, and she was in awe of him also. She felt the need to encourage them. She said to him, I can read the signs plainly. She is not spared, she is fighting it with every bit of strength she has, and she needs yours also. When this need is over and all is quiet, you must present her to the Moon and fill one another with two full nights of joy, to reward her efforts and yours. The boy nodded and smiled in surprise. It was the most exciting directive he had ever been given by an elder, and he would obey.

Gatherer was off with others to the river and fill skins with water. Later as things settled down, he and Baree were once again standing outside the doorway looking down on the scene. And since there was too much to say about the night already, she just turned to him smiling and shrugged.

Then she felt he deserved a little hug and gave him one. But it just wasn't enough. She gathered him in her arms and pressed him tight against her, parted her lips and began to plant little breaths and kisses on his face with her tongue stroking him. Now it was she who felt the stirring, and with eyes closed her arms slipped down around his back and she squeezed the breath out of him. And then drew him in even tighter. He is thinking to himself, this woman is incredibly strong. And he wondered if she was that strong all over and his excitement started to rise.

She almost had to fight her own self off of him when the kids around them started shouting, Oh no! Oh no! It's happening again! Where will we go now? Oh no! Please stop! And some young ones who didn't understand all that was happening just started screaming, because screaming is fun. They encouraged one another and shrill screams swept the hillside.

They parted reluctantly, in haste. Baree was practically panting with arousal, and they stood apart because they dared not move closer. Then they turned and looked down the hill and the screaming faded but anxious little voices were pleading with them to calm down.

Then they noticed story-teller girl moving through the ranks of children shouting, Quiet! Please, quiet! I need everybody's attention! Please! Quiet! She had a very authoritative voice and they loved her, so soon there almost was silence.

Everybody! We've been making too much noise. This is so funny, get ready to hear something, but please don't laugh. I want you all to stand and look down the hill and LISTEN QUIETLY! Okay?

Just listen! Okay, go!

Silence filled the night. Or so it seemed. The Moon had passed behind a fast moving cloud, and as they grew quiet and listened, it passed over the edge and flared, casting bright silver on the village below. The spell was carried by moonlight, for they heard a man shout wordlessly and a moan. More silence.

Suddenly a long, pealing wolf howl.

And a young girl shouted, That's Mom! She's on top!

Energy was pouring into the village below and they greedily let it build.

———

INTERMISSION: HOW IT WORKS, WHEN IT WORKS

Imagine that everything is poised and trembling, and perfectly aligned.

Or imagine it is not quite aligned, and women make the final adjustments with their hips and many muscles that are glad to be of service. They guide their portals using signals from the delicate folds and petals that make their hips such beautiful places. They do it with precision and ladylike grace, and can even do it in the dark with eyes closed. Thus the portal is offered, and if the offer is not accepted soon enough a greedy woman can thrust her hips forward and completely surround a man, holding him prisoner with few options.

For the least imaginative IT begins with the usual thud into one's partner and elicits moans and cries of joy, if both are lucky. This is repeated until something important happens. Nature's basic strategy in human breeding is that the man becomes interested and involved, and the woman becomes accepting and committed.

Nature's plan is, what ever you are thinking and feeling as you willfully and eagerly complete the task of breeding, it will flare up and become indescribably delicious. Simple animal satisfaction will always be sufficient. But Nature will also deliver rewards for any subtle action or behavior that has in the past contributed to success. Even specific to-do items for humans.

Not just the obvious, like his sudden elation when he feels seed rising and the desire to thrust deep and hold himself in for as long as he delivers. But her surprise as she feels it, even as she has been expecting it, and the way her mind fixes on the thought of it as excitement

108

hopefully propels her to completion also. And she receives a final reward as she circles him with her legs and lies completely still with him inside her, till sleep do them part. It's just good breeding. And a serene 'glow' over several days of lovemaking as a surge of actual testosterone passes into her bloodstream. That is what reproductive success feels like.

Then along comes the bloated human cortex in a split-second of evolution, and now there are complicated concepts and vivid memories floating in the mind. The ancient cerebellum helps with arousal and that feeling of rising excitement, and the transactional pleasure of thrusts, squeezes, squishes and slides in the right places.

But if one's cortex is occupied with the conquest of every one of another's erogenous zones, to the lucky recipient any unexpected stroke, squeeze or pinch is an exclamation of surprise like a bolt of lightning that dissolves into a wave of pleasure and heat. And if any sharp sensation of the zones drifts into sync with the animal act itself, that erogeny builds into blissful orogeny. It escalates the psyche to a whole-body state of submissive greed for more, and any pretense that stands in the way of rising and completion is ignored, or more likely, is itself is transformed into bliss with no regrets.

And the best part of the human conquest of erogenous zones and submissive greed, is that the fortunate one is aware at all times that their lover has done this, is doing this. What is happening is not some simple rollout of animal love they could easily reproduce themselves or expect any other lover to replicate exactly. And when combined with a heartfelt joy of witnessing another's build and climax, lovers can and do imprint on each other for life.

They can even plant an idea in the final moments of sex, so they will be sharing it when the end comes. Even if the idea is some complicated modern construct like, I am going to have your baby, then the modern mind fires in complete sync with the ancient mind and all of Nature's sweet rewards will be bestowed in sustained, mind-blowing waves. As each does every little thing they must. He will deliver, she will stretch wide and receive.

That is the game young lovers play.

He may think he is expressing true love or starting a family or doing a heroic deed or sword fighting with his phallus or stroking a kitten, and all of that works because every idea he has, even the stupid ones, is incredibly yummy as long as he is also doing Nature one small favor. And that favor is to thud himself into a woman and glide forever, or how ever long it takes. With every glide he clenches a muscle that gathers stuff important to Nature and shoves it down a tube.

He always does this, even though it could lead to serious trouble. And Nature laughs, for it has already trapped him inside a woman and is now just toying with him. Will you do this thing and clench this tiny muscle for me, please? Nature asks as it pours infinitely sweet goodness over them. And he begins thrusting and clenching harder because every time he does he gets a taste, and to do otherwise is unthinkable. Life becomes slides and clenches. So Nature just leaves him alone in boredom, and waits for the bell.

There is a tiny chamber at the very center of his being that desperately wants to be suddenly full of something. It is very sensitive and yearning for the onset of heat and fullness. The buzzing turbulence of warm liquid passing through makes it howl with delirium. But it is a wicked smart chamber that cannot be fooled by piss, and that is good, or men would develop vulgar habits.

The little chamber waits patiently and when its destiny is fulfilled, or filled full, the bell clangs and rouses Nature and it closes the circuit to flood his mind with helpless happy perpetual astonishment. Nature grabs his loins by the tail and thrusts them forward and holds that position, while he delivers pulsing squirts to his very last in attentive syncopation, like a scratching DJ.

The fool thinks he is the one dong it all of course, and some men imagine that the woman is compelling each squirt and he would be powerless to stop her, which is very cute and romantic, but he doesn't even try, and the truth is that Nature has taken him out of the loop. The elation is to keep him occupied and imprint her upon him. The act is too important to be left to chance, and he'd probably foul it up. Nature retreats and slumbers, leaving him with fading incandescent thoughts and warm emotions.

Hopefully the woman is still there, and he has not just filled an empty elevator. But regardless, a small part of him will imagine he is still squirting the next day. And every time he clenches his secret muscle, he recalls the woman or the elevator fondly.

And fortunately for them... men are generally useful. They are serviceable in family settings for the every day care and protection of children. If they help children stay safe and sane and grow past reproductive age, that is all Nature really cares about. Human children are a difficult hands-on experience. Not just the simple rearing of them, but all the mental instruction and supplement to pure instinct we have developed to harness technology and society, and subdue the environment to our will. Of all animals we alone have this ability. And Nature patiently awaits the result of that experiment.

We are trapped in a vicious circle of post-instinct progress that men and women have built over time, where the feeding of the brain itself with intricate information is crucial to child development. That is an equation that formed long ago with some eggs and then gestating mammals, producing young ill-equipped to survive on their own. Complicated, needy young. Courtship dances and mating rituals are fought with urges and sublime rewards, but for this new challenge Nature needed something more long-term. So it invented love and pair-bonding. And because Nature is a low budget operation, it merged the urge to couple with an urge to remain coupled and couple often.

That is why humans remain sexually active throughout the year. It is an ancient reward for caring for our children and their mothers effectively in all seasons and all situations. She goes into oestrus once a month, instead of some longer or shorter span to balance a boost in population with the disruption of caring for young. In place of our females occasionally going into incendiary heat and its scent driving males crazy and disrupting train schedules, we are in heat all the time and bonkers all the time.

Nature has rewarded other classes of animal with short ovulation periods not tied to the season, such as rodents and rabbits. Subterranean burrows are also fine places to raise young from changing climate conditions. Large litters are also Nature's way to produce enough young to carry on the population, despite high mortality and small fierce predators that stalk the burrows.

But the power of thinking, teaching and learning raised humans out of the physio-instinctual loop. They formed larger social groups and began to directly target predators and natural threats with determined, coordinated action. Such an action may even have originated in a single non-breeding individual with a good idea, and persisted over the generations as customs and tradition that gifted the species both quality of life, and avoidance of death.

One of the most intriguing coincidences of our solar system is that the moon and sun have equal shapes in our sky, despite relative size and distance.

But another enigma that blows it away in my opinion, is the magnificent and eerie synchronicity between female oestrus cycles and the visible synodic period of moon phases. The flat-fact today is that the moon's period is ~29.5 days, give or take a few hours during the year. And her current period is an average of 28 (~23 to 35 days normal). This places it firmly in the realm of an extraordinary coincidence, for moon phases are a phenomenon witnessed by eyes and a calculating mind. Theories about the effect of light on the landscape and predation and prey do not really work, even in the supportable case of owls and hunted rodents. It does not need to be disproved that there MAY be causation, it speaks for itself, and we should be free to indulge wild and delicious theories on how this originated, free of the constant whining of fuss-budgets.

A fuss-budget is among other things, someone who feels the need to point out that something has not been conclusively proven by revealing its precise mechanism during the Golden Age of Science, which seems to have begun with the invention of the typewriter. The guests one tolerates at Thanksgiving. They will point out outliers and exceptions by framing their arguments deviously, such as proudly announcing that women begin their cycles at different days of the lunar month, though that is not the main point of your observation at all. Or so-and-so is different, or she varies, ignoring the concept of average that is part of it. They are the score keepers and will always win, for they don't stop playing until after you do.

Fuss-budgets scolded school children drawing maps with pencil and crayon, for noticing that the continents really do seem to fit together, and what are the chances of that? For which they later received no apology. Or anyone trying to reconcile the chaotic conditions within the sun with the eerie clockwork of its sunspot cycle, and committing intellectual sin by noticing the elephant in the living room, the orbital period of Jupiter. Or anyone in early history trying to reconcile celestial events without plugging in the ordained orthodoxy that Earth is the center of everything. To guarantee personal safety.

So anyway, we can all sex each other up any day of the year. Even the reddest time of the month, for which Nature only endorses the shower, and never the douche. Beware advertising claims. A woman's own blood is the only substance that will not seriously risk infection, alter her delicate internal chemistry, remove helpful bacteria, or subject her to the horrors of flooding with soap or the chlorinated disaster that is tap water. And besides, even if she irrigates to an awful and alarming extent, it will not remove all evidence of blood.

So women can help Nature out a bit here, by simply not breeding with men who cannot stand the sight of healthy, wholesome blood. It really is, all things considered. Before, after, and during. This period avoidance scourge has lasted for millennia now and has hampered her health and well-being by striking days from the calendar, and placing an arbitrary barrier between lovers who should be completely accepting of one another and desire to please, even then. If he cannot stand the taste of salt or superior lubrication, he should get out of her kitchen.

The demand for clean bed linens has really screwed us over in this regard. As has the bed itself. So find somewhere else. A hacksaw and sturdy wooden stool that aligns her with him perfectly when she is sitting, can be the second greatest sex toy a man could buy. He can perform well standing as she discovers the delicious delight of sex anywhere anyhow with fewer challenges, or bracing her legs ever so tightly against the shower stall. Measure carefully to account for squashed buttocks and take two measurements, stools for him and her. She can perform standing and tease him and herself to great length while avoiding the exhausting demands of assumed patriarchy. And he can discover the role reversal Nature intended.

Human fathers and lovers of mothers in general, have this important role. From gestation through adulthood of offspring, all mothers doing the right thing operate at a constant high level of stress. Animal mothers are driven by instinct and hormone into new behavior patterns that optimize the care of young. Well good for them.

But human mothers have inherited a higher brain that overlays a cloud of intricate thought patterns on everything, including uninvited and unhealthy ones. A man's suggestive overture or caress of his woman should unleash such a warm memory and delightful promise to her, that she can easily brush aside what ever mental demons she is fighting that day, and submit to a drawn out erotic massage with benefits. And a shoulder rub is not enough, she must be drawn up and over the top.

Every release brings fresh joy and relaxation to her, and even helps keep her in good health. Generic men are generally suitable for this every day use. But a man with imagination, discipline and kindness can become the coach of a record-breaking female athlete, in the greatest sports of all, sex and parenting. Only he can tease and urge her on with the slow surprise, delicious wonder, full body stroking, pelvic contact joy, mammary squeezing, pinching and rubbing, that results from being loved completely by another.

And as she finally crosses over the edge, or you have pushed her over with a grin of mischief as she is dealt a merciless sensation that kindles her greed to surrender, as her mind is flaring brightly and she is about to embrace ecstasy... by all means, tell her she is a good mother.

Happy Mother's Day!

Two of Nature's greatest gifts to humans are strong and nimble hands that can reach our own genitals. Where ever we go, there they

are, so one thing leads to another. But even if completion is assured
there is a jarring split-brain duality to the act. Lovers give and receive
all the time, and not just in a mechanical sense of moving or stroking.
Thinking individuals vary their technique, or it is varied for them by a
streak of dominance by the other. Sensations become a spectrum of
sounds or subtle responses. The other's movement in response to
one's own action is exciting, even more so if it is the result of a spasm of
joy. The face of a lover becomes more beautiful and fascinating when
they are aroused, and riveting as joy is building, and expressive with
release.

Inevitably children will explore themselves because the dense nerve
endings are already there, but even after puberty, manual solo activity
simply does not suffice. We need each other. The success of the
species over at least a million years up to the availability of battery
devices proves this empirically.

But now there is some impressive love technology. This is possibly
dangerous, because its effectiveness is unexplored territory in
evolution. With vibration, throbbing or shiatsu massage gearing that
attempts to mimic a human, one can bear down and race over the top.
Or tease oneself by one's own hand, in subtle analytic equations of
thought and sensation, and an ascension guided by personal
discipline. But of what is being done there is only pretended surprise.
There are no others, just pictures in the mind.

The danger of pure mechanical stimulation arises because Nature's
implicit and evolved ultimate dissatisfaction with self-activity, no
longer strictly applies. The action is being performed by electricity
and the sensation is now just being 'applied'. And surrender is more of
a smooth convolution of an equation with a pre-ordained outcome.
Males discover seed is nigh and Nature pilots him to the end. Females
can play with fingers or buzzing for a long time, but she may finally
tire of the dreamy meditative state that gradual, self-teased love

delivers. And she might bear down with the device on her most sensitive place, causing a sudden firestorm of sensation in the brain that freezes the hands in place for she cannot resist it, as she is compelled to rise quickly and shoot over the edge like a pop-gun.

Adults who remember and pine for good lovers will use mechanical devices to obtain temporary relief. Lovers will use them when the other is not available, and their fantasies are still based on real memories and there will be aroused speculation of what unexpected things may happen in the next encounter. Even in advanced puberty the desire to explore love with others has already been established, and even if the devices deliver an awesome experience for them, they at least remain open to the advances and attempts of others.

But my fear is that mechanical love devices for all would enslave children and impair their development. They will receive an awesome and extreme reward that transcends Nature's firewalls around masturbation. They will receive it regardless, whether they are prepubescent or barely pubescent. And they will be imprinted by the device as the most satisfying and dedicated lover would. It becomes a regular and obsessive habit. Their interaction with others is curtailed by time spent alone with it. They may even share it with others, who immediately desire their own as it imprints on them, or engage in device-sharing with others. Not even mutual masturbation such as older ones might do to explore the concept of love, where hands and fingers deliver pleasant surprises to another while enjoying the expressions on their faces, and taking pride in having done it. But a sham-parody of it, where individuals see others rendered helpless in the throes of the device, and they will not desire the others, just the device.

Device worship may create children with no natural curiosity to explore others, or even touch others. And Nature's hints and nudges that encourage one to find a lover and start a traditional family might be flatly ignored. Bringing us one step closer to a Brave New World of solitary individuals who claim fulfillment. A very different world, and a social upheaval that is not to be taken lightly. And if some critical mass is reached over time as children become rare as a result of their choices, a threat of extinction.

Conversely, the safest place for such a female-pleasing device is in the hands of you, her lover. You can tease with ease, apply earth shaking cataclysmic vibration and stillness to her alternately, until she is floating on dense waves of pleasure, less vulnerable to a desperate rise to the top, as might happen by her own hand. Or fill her with throbbing vibration while your tongue and lips glide over her clitoris and hands massage her breasts. Or get to witness the astonished face of a woman who feels for the very first time, a gentle vibration against her cervix. A place you might never hope to reach, the place through which life begins. Or find a G-spot if you can, with your longer reach and ability to position a vibrating member precisely at any angle. Hold it within her firmly and explore and apply pressure. If it suddenly fills her with waves of heat and launches a happy ending with spasms and orgasmic clenches, that might be it.

So by the time you enter her, she has already peaked several times by your own hand and with what devices are available, and in the unpredictable teasing way that makes being loved so exciting. She is already rippling and floating on orgasmic energy, and after a brief period of quiet she will be ready again. And if she feels something warm pressing her open slowly and entering, she will look at you as shivers run down her spine and her back will arch as her legs encircle yours. Because she knows it is you, and she loves you. And as you glide, taking care to give attention to the most amazing part of her which is also the smallest, her heat should rise with yours. And when she sees you take leave of your senses, she will step off the edge that becomes more attainable when she has been there before, and ride with you in ecstasy and abandon all the way down.

Men must never forget they are bounded in time, and squirting mentally depletes them. They must often rouse themselves to please her in other ways, or eventually begin again, hopefully, maybe.

And a freshly satiated man is not the most imaginative creature in the universe.

For the female it is a long process of ascension, and a woman being teased in delicious and unexpected ways by a partner can actually re-tune her whole body slowly until it becomes one big erogenous zone. And Nature has given man two hands, so that during her long ascension one can be assigned pelvic duty. It involves a thumb on the tiny pea, three fingers to spread her wide and explore, and a pinky that wanders as it pleases.

The excited woman whose man has begun to spend, if she is not fortunate to be driven over the brink herself by the sensation of it, becomes a truly desperate woman. He is still while she needs movement. Female erogenous zones might send her over and tumbling into the sweet abyss, if he only had the presence of mind to squeeze them tightly in the same rhythm as his deliverance. For her ultimate finish has muscular contractions also, and those sharp signals from his pinches would cross over in her eager brain to convince her that the most beautiful thing is happening to her also, and then it would be so. But so often it does not, and she fails to grasp her waning pleasure as it slips away, to be replaced with the noble altruism of seeing his vacant eyes and suspended self. Nature has taken him out of the loop.

Resigning oneself away from imminent orgasm while witnessing it in another, is one of the most challenging and courageous things, and the saddest, that a woman might endure. The world's worst letdown, an invading chill to what should have been a celebration of peak warmth and white-hot fire. It should bring you to tears to think of it. And so many do it every day, and survive. They are strong.

Good men want to please their women completely and love them very slowly. And though they are clever and dexterous, some are even ambidextrous and play the trumpet... like fools they will choose the accessory that is most dear to them, to tease. And the excuses! Because it is already down there, it will leave my hands free, she really likes this, it was made for this... and the most hilarious of them all, only for a minute. The dearer the woman is to him, the more likely it is that a brief venture inside to massage and tease her softly, will go awry.

So he will enter hands-free suddenly and linger, applying unpredictable motions of gentle pressure all around, and her body will writhe slowly. Perhaps he even finds a good place and tickles it, and her wide eyes and lips parting in a surprised gasp remind him, this is a very good idea. Clenched hands and fingernails tighten on his back as her hips move sensuously, eyes half-lidded. Maybe I can find these places with the tips of my fingers, and experiment with real pressure. How long will she last? How long can I make her last? And Nature taps him on the shoulder and whispers, or... how about you do THIS? She will like it. You can DO this. Try it. The first thrust is free.

And ten seconds later he is sliding and thrusting. Maybe she opened her eyes suddenly in delicious surprise and thrill at the first sliding thrust. And the next was great also. Great. Wonderful! Great. But he has not actually found something better to do, just something he cannot refrain from doing because it keeps getting better. And she is not some instinct driven primeval woman, to whom things are just happening. She is homo sapiens thinking woman, and she can take charge of her own destiny. She does not need magnetic resonant imaging to show her how hard he is clenching his secret muscle with each thrust, and how soon the squirt will begin. His face says it all.

And now he has leaned slightly away from her, because his addled mind has convinced itself that leaning away with his stiffly erect member sliding with a bit more pressure along the top of her well, and these long horizontal strokes, will please her even more. And for many it does, sort of. He even imagines he is pushing deeper, and Nature gives him a sweet pat on the head for thinking of the idea. But the sad truth in real life is, the friction just pleases him more.

But what did she feel when he leaned away? What happened?

Imagine a warm sunny day and a tornado of leaves that are rising towards the sun, and she is rising in the air with them, and each brush against a leaf brings a spike of happiness, warmth and a delicious shiver. But she can also swim upward in bold strokes and push leaves down along her body, and what was a series of pleasures becomes a torrent of shuddering, ascending delight. And she knows when she reaches the sun all will melt together into blazing final rapture.

She can even hover just below the sun with the torrent tightly encircling her, and every one of them is touching her, and she feels a timeless gladness to be alive. And all she has to do is reach up to touch the sun and it will flow into her. Perhaps she can not quite reach it. Perhaps she is drifting slowly towards it. But she is a few strokes away.

But Nature is not commanding her to swim into the sun, as it does men when their seed rises into the tiny little chamber. The one they are all forced to love in the end, as it bestows waves of love upon them.

She is a free woman. Nature has given her the gift to delay her final pleasure, if her will is strong, and she practices with herself and a patient lover. Until her lover or Nature finally pushes her into the sun. Or greed overtakes her and she subdues her own will, and surrenders. It is a powerful gift.

What she felt when he leaned away was a sudden total eclipse, twilight and the leaves falling away from her. Floating in semidarkness, where there had been a timeless light of elation and satisfying excitement, now there is just the dull comfort of lovemaking, pleasant and nice, but the contrast also brings a flash of sadness. And frustration, urgency. Just as unpleasant in its way as if he was nearing his peak, and strong hands grabbed him from behind and pulled him out of her.

He had leaned away from her clitoris. It is a small thing no bigger than a pea on the outside. It is a very big thing to her on the inside.

He was nearing his final peak. She had to act quickly or face the sad, slow decay of coitus interruptus.

She knew exactly what to do, and proceeded to do it with the intelligence and skill of woman. Songs should be sung of her desperate quest and ultimate triumph. She lifted and threw her arms around his upper back to support herself, stretched her legs wide to spread her center folds, and lifted and angled her pelvis, slightly, precisely. His next thud against her and deep into her brought his taut pelvis into contact with her folds, spreading them even wider. And she thrust back at him, crushing him against her clitoris, which was squished and pushed gently to the side. She cried for joy as the sun shone brightly in her mind again. She shook her hips in what seemed like a shudder, but was actually a maneuver to rock the tiny pea back and forth under pressure, as it rubbed across his pubic hairs.

He started to glide back and she followed him for a moment, still rubbing. And she felt everything from her effort in slow motion, as a delicious waterfall breaking over her. She clenched a secret muscle of her own and it flared, and even his sliding within her was a source of growing excitement. He thudded against her again, and she vigorously rocked the little pea side to side against him, and she climbed higher in blazing heat. Now he bellowed, for he felt sap rising, and with a full body shudder Nature took over and he held himself tightly to her. There was river of warmth within that made her tingle in a helpless moan, for Nature had touched her mind sweetly because that is a sign of good breeding. He squeezed and she even felt the strength of the spurt and its delicate impact inside, and the heat within her mind turned to raging fire at the thought of it. Another sign of good breeding, and she was a very proper lady. She tightened her arms and brought her chest into contact with his, whimpering in joy as her taut nipples slid across it.

And as he was nearing his last, she shook her hips again and pressed the pea so tightly, she howled with delight and elated certainty and rode her man all the way into the sun, and they danced together in the realm of sweetness for a long while.

A far better outcome than, oh, oh, Ohhh. I'm sorry. That's okay, it was nice.

The clitoris and its little accessories are an incredibly urgent matter.

It is literally the woman's penis, the whole business end of it. Some 8-10 thousand nerves head from it to the brain. They are the very same nerves, the very same for both of them. Some 5 weeks after conception there is a bundle of nerves and precursor cells that will solely determine whether a girl or boy will ever enjoy sex, and very likely life itself. Gender genes are expressed and whole different systems form, but the 'pleasure system' remains the same, with portions changing shape, size or orientation.

That is an incredible amount of nerves devoted to pleasure alone! It is probably an embarrassment in the animal kingdom. But it delivers motivation. If nerves were foot paces... when a man's tongue explores her tiny clitoris and the area surrounding it, her pleasure is 5 miles wide. When she takes the tip of him into her mouth, his pleasure is 5 miles wide also.

So what is beneath the tongue and inside the mouth is most of it. These things are crucial and without them our world would be a joyless place. There are no other bundles of pure-pleasure nerves elsewhere. Think of it as a 'barcode' of pleasure that speaks into the minds of happy humans. For the areas spanned are so small with so many connections, especially in a woman, that when a man talks to her in this way he will never repeat himself. Every flick of the tongue is a new hash pattern of pleasure for her, and fills her mind with delicious surprise because it really is new.

There are plenty of places where sensations contribute to enjoyment. Some of them in surprising ways. The most celebrated by men and women who love themselves, is the female areola and the nipple. Breastfeeding releases oxytocin to promote uterine contractions after pregnancy. But during sex they are very erogenous, because their nerves terminate in the genital cerebral cortex of the brain, adjacent to signals from the clitoris. When her lover sucks on a nipple, crossing signals in the brain do her a loving kindness.

Imagine trying to urge a man to completion without touching his penis at all. Or perhaps, by just stroking the shaft and not once touching or even brushing against the tip. It would be an act of pure sadism.

Yet without direct bump-and-grind to the small clitoral area that is her most precious asset, a woman must fall back on far duller sensations and expectations, even altruism or a tiny engraved participation trophy on the shelf. Brutes who failed sex-ed and read centuries of smutty literature are told things like this:

"I had longed for her for so long and I was long but as a proper gentleman I took her gently and slowly. As I parted her soft opening with you-know-what, she gasped with delight. And as I glided slowly within her, I felt a sublime sensation that transported me to great heights, and she matched my pleasure. As I finished, she gallivanted about with joy and happiness."

Bullshit. That poor woman. She was probably faking it, the saddest thing ever and the most shameful outcome for any man. Brutes the world over just assume that the vagina itself must be as chock-full-O-nerves as he, that the mere slidey presence of him will make the Earth move for her the same way. I buy the gasp, for she was desperate and his entry tickled her near the opening, where most of her nerves actually are, giving her a warm flash of hope. He was on top of the world because the walls of her you-know-what were sensuously massaging the top of his glans. But she would have felt little during the exercise as described.

My hope is that while he was distracted, she went to town on herself with both hands. One spreading the labias with outstretched fingers that stroked them lightly, and with the other bringing the middle finger down upon her own glans, the clitoris and hood, stroking it vertically and smooshing it around. She could get in five lovely strokes to his one and build, with all the pleasure of sex-for-one when you are feeling randy. Good for her. Then as she felt his finish, pressed harder and ramped up the rate until she flew over the top, just as she did while he was out fox hunting. Then her tired arms collapsed as she surrendered and gallivanted about happily like the good society wife she was.

The labia minora is literally the shaft of the penis. And vice versa. It is a pleasant place and delivers good promises but it is a dull part of a woman. Nature takes short cuts. The vagina is one of those purpose-built female contraptions, a tubular muscle with benefits. But to her, it is no Xanadu where did Kubla Khan, a stately pleasure-dome decree. Her most scrumptious nerves just aren't there. But its walls are ribbed for his pleasure. And when he delivers, it becomes the place where Alph, the sacred river ran, through a cavern measureless to man, down to a sunless sea, babee! Or if you prefer, a Chinese finger trap for men.

There are some delicious and exciting parts near the opening, and she would be glad if you found them. But the rest of the tube is low-bidder stuff that allows her to perform her marital and motherly duties. It gives her a comfortable sensation of love, but women deserve so much more.

So bump and grind front and center is good for her, and mind your angle. That part of you is padded and designed for this contact. You can play with her, using lips, tongue, fingers and buzzing objects she likes, but mind your fingernails. She is delicate and precious, even when aggressive. She will usually maneuver herself against you and use your hairy pelvis to clean her carpet and rub out the tough stains. Sometimes they can be very creative and greedy about it.

Oh, and women lubricate themselves! If you're doing it right. What an amazing and clever thing that is! Songs should be sung about that also, with choirs and orchestras. And when they rear up on their hind legs and just walk around, like it's nothing to them. Astonishing! I see men doing it too but it just looks clumsy and imitative.

We live in a world of wonders.

———

INTERMISSION: MOM ON TOP

He is thinking, she is rubbing her beautiful scent all over me to claim me as her own, forever. And it pleases me.

It was a pleasant thought, but he also knew she had reached such a state she was desperately seeking release, and she was exploring his body for new points of contact, new sensations. He had offered his lips and fingers but she had just kissed his face and wrist softly while gazing at him, and gone off exploring.

His legs were drawn up and she had finally discovered his bony kneecap. She flooded it with warmth as she applied herself to experiment with it, then found a smooth, slow primal rhythm against the ridges of his skin and across the raised part. Her throat buzzed softly.

And after a time she froze stiffly and quietly and her body shuddered, for she had found what she had been seeking, and the sweet reward was so deep and strong she had no inclination to move or cry out. Then she collapsed on him with exhaustion and deep breaths and began to snuggle, and soon after her breaths grew slower with sleep.

She is so lovely in the moonlight.

He is still surrounded by the shrill, desperate sounds of lovers striving around him, and he feels a flush of pride that his own precious love has brought peace to him, and then to herself. That last was a quiet one, a good one. She is so very special. He stroked her hair gently.

It had been so long since he awoke from his nap.

He had opened his eyes to see her full presentation. It was intricate and lovely shadows danced on it in the dying firelight. The sight of it always filled him with gladness and excitement. It was no subtle affair like a debutante ball with a youthful orchestra, passable food and flowing gowns. It was literal and direct, her most prized possession spread wide as she knelt close to his face.

She had said, uuuh, for words failed her at times like this. Uhhh! And her need was intense, for she usually snuggled up to him and planted wet kisses on his mouth and face while stroking his chest, then descended out of sight as her hair brushed his cheeks, and she nibbled along his neck. And bit sometimes. And apologized with her eyes. Then bit again.

But this time hands drew around the back of his head, and lifted it. By a slight miscalculation on her part, she impacted his nose on the intended target. Then after a sharp intake of breath, she grasped his head more firmly and began to rock it slightly against her hips as they trembled, and the tip of his nose explored her latest innovation to love. Such a smart woman! Her scent was warm and lush and he inhaled her deeply, and her springy fur grazed his cheeks. He stifled a sneeze. Her hands became more spastic and he knew what was coming, and he feared injury, so it was time for him to take control.

He grasped her buttocks tightly and spread them apart for a moment, a sensation that always made her gasp in delight as it commanded her attention, and drew her down, which is a fine way to steer a woman. As his parted lips spanned her center with undulations of their own and working of his jaw, and his tongue swept across her making probing circles and tiny journeys. He knew he had her. He retracted his tongue and pressed his clenched teeth against her a bit more firmly and smoothly than any pelvis or finger, and her mind flared and she moaned with heat. Then the tongue again, and she reached a higher moaning echelon. She had so many. She leaned against him and her hands were making clumsy wringing motions to stroke his hair, which was praise of the highest order, because he knew that was all the attention she could spare them at the moment.

He was holding his own head up now but he could keep it up for as long as took to fill her with delicious fire and hold her there indefinitely, by easing off for a moment until her secret dread rose, then resuming with so much vigor her dread melted into the most exquisite joy. And despite that he had done this one thing hundreds of times, his tiniest idea of a new rhythm or pattern, even ones he had used before, seized her whole mind like an undiscovered country, because women crave new sensation and each subtle configuration of his mouth muscles arrived to her as an exciting new flavor of pleasure.

And she wanted to taste them all. Still no words, but her vocalizations and whole-body shudders changed with every flavor, and grew shrill. And even her powerful urge to move was stilled by her mind, for fear he would lose contact with her.

And at last his neck was tired and getting shaky, so it had been about as long as it took, and it was time to end her, so he eased off for a moment to fill her with dread that he would turn into powerful sweetness, and began shaking his head from side to side vigorously, his rough lips dragging across her pleasure center in a continuous blinding flare that no sliding man could ever achieve. Or she even could herself, for her own finger would be abandoned as its master was called elsewhere. And all the while, the edges of his lips flapping and brushing her center folds alternately to give her an elated, timeless thrill of opening. And flapping her buttocks as fast as he could. Because he could. It was more than this lady could endure, and she would rise almost soundlessly on a sea of magma and shoot into the sky as certainty claimed her, and she would pull away from him and collapse on his chest breathing heavily, and float down gently. And then start planting soft kisses upon his chest.

That had happened the first night they met. And many times since.

But tonight the volcano kept rising and never reached the top. Her arms and hips were trembling, but with effort, not release. She ascended with his vigorous ending much longer than she had ever been able to hold out before, and finally collapsed in more of a swoon of exhaustion than satisfaction. But pleasure was still with her and she was happy. And he could barely see now but her face was lit by a sliver of moonlight, and there were tears in her eyes. She embraced and kissed him. Then she felt him erect, shifted, raised her head and took the end of him into her mouth.

This was love by another, and instead of gliding his mind floated. And like the happy fool he was, he gazed at her stretched body and slowly moving hair in the moonlight and fell in love with her all over again, from moment to moment, with each sensation. And his love for her grew beyond measure, and he was clenching like a madman even though he didn't want to douse her. But it turned heat and bliss into fire. And she kept on for a long while, at least as long as he had tasted her. And now she was moaning, but the moans were more like sad whimpers. She dragged her hips against the bed and he knew she was feeling an incredible surge of desire and yearning, but she was fighting it all to please her man. And that made him angry, that she should suffer so.

So he sat up and reached for her hindquarters and rolled her over strongly onto her back toward him. And with one hand he lifted her bottom from underneath, and the other grasped an ankle and lifted it up over his head, so her taut leg swung her around to face him. She was now propped with hands behind her, and sat up on his belly, looking with open mouthed surprise. He lifted and tugged her ankle once more, centering her on him. Then his other hand pushed under her knee, bending it, and placed the foot on the surface beside him. It had just taken a few moments. She was facing him with knees apart and inner thighs open, stretched taut with the inner hollows men love so much.

Now with both hands perfectly mirrored he stroked along the tendons of both thighs and explored the hollows, then slid along the inner thigh and back, and her body shivered, a low growl issuing from her throat. She stirred as if to move but his thumbs were upon her, his fingers fluttering against her folds and hollows. This was no tease, he was applying pressure and lifting his thumbs and placing them again in slightly different positions in the center, and the very width of her sensation made each contact a new and exciting place. She did move then, she whimpered and stretched wider and his fingers found a place to rest on those beautiful tendons as his thumbs continued to impress her. And her eyes were shut for a moment then opened, she gazed at him while breathing heavily, and it was her turn to fall in love with him with every delicious push.

Then after awhile she blinked, and forced her feet to plant themselves on the ground, slid them along both sides of him and beside her, and nobly sacrificing a moment of pleasure for coordinated movement, rose shaking into a low squat with knees apart, her eyes begging him not to stop. As she rose his phallus popped up, for it had been laid down sideways under her bottom. She lowered herself onto it until it was almost between his hands and he swiveled them aside, and watching him with loving eyes she leaned hips forward and enveloped him in warmth.

It was her favorite position, and she had built incredibly muscled legs and buttocks from lovemaking alone. She would squat with knees apart and use taut arms and hands on his pelvis to spring herself up to the point legs could assist. She loved to bounce. She would draw him inside and begin to explore many more angles and pressures than he ever could. And she would linger him inside her opening until the angle was extreme and he was pressing more directly against the top or sides of her, and she would swivel her hips softly and moan. And even then he could command her attention and steer her experience by thrusting upward in rhythmic gentle motions. This would transfix her and she'd lean her head back and draw breath.

And after a long time of that, she had fixed him with that one-eyed half smile of mischief, as her hair was always all over the place, and she began to long-stroke him slowly with her pelvis tilted at an angle of incredible sweetness known only to her, that triggered every ancient circuit of elation and urge to deliver in him, and built steadily.

While being long-stroked he would busy his hands with the idea of something special he could do for her, and she would watch with grunting satisfaction as his eyes glazed and his hands grew spasmodic and still, as sensation overwhelmed him. She would hum a lullaby to him that they sung to the children as she did it, in slow rhythm with the strokes, as her head drooped and hair swayed slowly back and forth across his chest. He could only gaze at her while being the happiest man alive. Then she grinned at him again and hastened the pace.

The moment she felt his release she had suddenly tossed aside her limbs suddenly in the strange way she usually did, while cleverly keeping hips still and him inside her, and landed flat on him with a slap and impact that knocked the wind out of him. And she rubbed her hips against him as he spent and rose quickly herself with a throaty roar, and as her own ecstasy started to peak she propped herself up on her hands and shook her torso so vigorously breasts flew from side to side, and arched up into the air higher on her extended arms and leaned back until the tip of her nose was facing the sky.

And howled.

She has such a beautiful voice.

And when he arose again he rolled her over and loved deep inside from above, for a long time. She was a ravenous creature, and this time her own hands were centered on her hips. But his lips found a couple good places, and he teased her in a special new way.

——

INTERMISSION: HOW IT WORKS, IF MEN STOP WORKING

Men had better take note and remain useful. For Nature has a back up plan.

It is the tradition of some spiders that as soon as the final act of copulation is under way, a tiny notion begins to tip over in the female's brain, and the male's value as sustenance rises to equal his value as a provider of seed. While he is still busy enjoying himself, her coital see-saw tips a bit further still. Transported by waves of ravenous ecstasy, she takes the first bite. And his lower abdomen continues to deliver, heedless that he is now missing a head. Nature has taken him out of the loop. He is fully consumed in her afterglow.

A woman with the skill and intelligence to prepare a man and render him helpless to her own desires, who has undressed her man with eyes alone, processed animals to make food for him, and has had babies with him, such a woman also has the capability to separate the head, truss and skin, remove viscera and entrails, and carve the rest into steaks and set aside the bones to crack for good soup. And prepare a delicious meal that will long be remembered, to set before herself and the children. To serve man. This happens the moment he has outlived his usefulness, while he is still enjoying himself. For she knows he contains all the nutrition she and her family need. If our clumsy tampering removes Nature's love from the equation, this is a likely result.

Nature has endowed women with strength to surprise to subdue a man, render him disabled or unconscious with found objects or bare hands, but only if she makes the wise choice to develop muscle and skill, and play unpleasant and dangerous situations in her mind as practice.

Muscle and brain hardened women can surprise a man with delight, but they can also tightly grasp hold of the thing a rapist holds dearest and literally rip it from his body. And Nature has given her the pistol to finish him off with two shots to the head, so she will not have to endure his piteous lawyer-coached whimpers as she is dragged through the legal system, or live in perpetual fear that he will stalk and ambush her and her family some day. After she is exonerated the body should be released into her custody, so she can carve it up and prepare cauldrons of hot stew to drain and then discard in a lidded dumpster. To serve as a closed casket for the funeral. And there must be a funeral, it is the right thing to do, so relatives and parents can grieve over their mistakes. And Nature applauds.

Nature's gift of love is sacred.
Rapists must be removed from the gene pool.

Future generations will thank us.

———

GATHERER AND THE CHILDREN OF THE MOON: PART III

Under the irresistible cascade of moonlight, they drank it in greedily until what composure they had was shattered. Surrender was complete. Instinct flared and it was so delicious and exciting, minds snapped and bodies set to work.

The people in the village loved one another deeply, which is and is not a pun, and even witnessing a partner struck mad with bliss was enough to send them into it themselves. But Moon sent a barrage of energy. It all began suddenly and every little thing they felt and did, even sounds issuing from their own throats, drove them wild. It was the end of all modesty, and its sounds arrived from many directions at once. The whole village was on fire, and its flames were people!

And it sounded something like this.

Pure instant pandemonium. And the story audience did their very best to mimic wild lovemaking. Some did it with grunts and groans, many exclamations of words, and lots of sounds from personal experience. Any who had a distinctive sound in loving was sure to be trolled by their partner. A man imitated his woman's ascension and triumph, and she replied with his bellow of satisfaction and grunts suggesting his release.

And the children were completely over the top because they were the true stars of this part, and a common theme was for each to specialize and practice some shrill and urgent animal sound.

Wild boars, cawing birds and screaming monkeys, lots of monkeys of different species, bellowing bison, laughing hyenas, rutting cats, trumpeting elephants and grunting hippos. In counterpoint and varying rates, but all deliberately slow and rhythmic as a parody of the human act.

There was even call and response as groups alternated with other groups. And rehearsed compositions of these noises, with a conductor.

Any descent towards silence would be punctuated by someone starting up again, as a parody of the couple who cannot get enough.

At long last, shared laughter would slowly replace this symphony of the primeval.

After motioning for silence repeatedly, the storyteller continued.

And finally, a long procession of dark clouds began to cover the Moon. Those in the village felt a fading of that sublime energy and desperately redoubled their efforts to reach a final peak, which was attainable. They sensed its nearness and the whole village howled with delight! Then the energy of a thunderstorm flooded their senses and the night grew stiller as the lovers were rewarded for their efforts and carried away by ecstasy. They immediately fell into an exhausted slumber.

And the storyteller continued,

It was over. The jamboree on the hill erupted in laughing conversation and eventually grew quiet. Gatherer and Baree sat outside and spoke quietly long into the night, both grateful to be free of tension and compulsion.

Baree finally said, what a glorious mess! referring to the night itself. And he said, It's been good to hear so many young voices again, and they really are such fine people. Perfect guests. And I am sure there will be more little ones after this. We planned to have... and he stopped, for he was racked with sobs. Planned... and he had to stop. His young wife had already started one and had died with child. He wept. Tonight he had stoically resisted the memories for so long.

Baree embraced him, then took him by the hand and led him to his sleeping area, which was only infested with two children. Once they had arranged the sleeping forms on the floor with the others, she banked the fire and undressed the quietly sobbing man completely, then herself, and pulled over the covering. She cradled and rocked him gently, alternately stroking and snuggling with him.

And as the lurches of his grief subsided, she kept him awake by again pretending she was unable to get comfortable. Her gentle thrashing always seemed to result in some warm and beautiful part of her sliding across him slowly as she stretched her legs. And her arms would move across his chest and lightly brush parts of him that had been such a desperate focus before. It was all calculated, as was the rhythm of clenches and relaxes in every part of her in accidental contact with him. It had nothing at all to do with her restless and catty stretches. And as she rolled to face him, his hands began to move and touch her, and she knew at last he was hers.

His hand drifted to her inner thigh. This time without any pretense, she tensed the whole leg until muscle became hard as rock. He traced the muscles so lightly it was a new sensation for her and she shook. She drew every part he touched tight until it strained and trembled. Then the back edge of the calf up the back of the leg to the buttock. By the tremble of his hand, they did not disappoint either.

He whispered, You are an incredibly strong woman.

She answered, Tell me a story.

She took complete control, always reserving a small part of herself to plan what happened next and make it happen. And he still managed to surprise her with unexpected touches. Clearly her tight clenches excited him and he was aroused and excited by her muscles, to such a pitch she had soon compelled him to do the usual things men do and her legs encircled him.

And she felt herself reach the plateau where some desperate women push themselves over in greed and abandon, but she tarried there for awhile by remaining still, and her control lasted until her bottom was grasped tightly with two hands and pulled tightly to him. She felt his arms tighten with a shudder as he was pulled over the edge.

And with her last bit of resolve, all her own past sadness forgotten, and with complete certainty... she said in his ear, You are an incredibly strong man, and I am going to have your baby.

And with all her might, she clenched every muscle below the waist and thought of him. Under the glow of the plateau every screaming muscle became a sweet reward. His tiny sighs were victory for her and the sensation of it pushed her over the edge into elated certainty. Her legs trembled with her interior spasms and suddenly shot out from under the covers stretched wide, opening her completely. As the fire finally subsided she drifted in the heat, and her legs again encircled and trapped him inside her until they both surrendered to sleep. Aside from a few whispers and a bit of labored breathing, it had happened very quietly.

And she had made it happen herself, without any assistance from the Moon. Because she was a practical woman and always did what is right.

The children awoke at first light, roused the young ones and padded about quietly gathering their things. A little girl whispered, Look!

and pointed. Gatherer was sound asleep under the covers, and her head was next to his. But there was an uncovered pair of legs circled over the top of him. A boy whispered something in her ear and she nodded, six times. They left quietly and motioned the others outside for silence. Inside, no one stirred.

The next day was surreal. There were plenty of embarrassed looks and smiles and allusions and wordless responses that meant, me too.

But in the early morning an announcement had circulated at the jamboree, don't say a word about it! It'll be funny! The day passed for many in silent introspection, but under it all, a glow of satisfaction for a job well done. Men refrained from mentioning it to one other but women were as talkative as ever, and whispered and laughed between themselves often.

And as for the Children of the Moon, total hilarity. As you have heard during that last outburst, the hilarity continues to this day. And yes, there were a lot of babies born that year. Everyone was busy building places for new and growing families.

But that is not the end of the story.

Baree had returned to her own home in the morning. She told him as she left with a finger on his lips, I will see you later. He smiled and said, don't bring food. I will make dinner. Gather your strength. She laughed, and placed hands on hips as she lectured him.

Water is what I gather. Lots of water is carried from the river in baskets and skins every day. Men love to help us carry and show off one day, and the next they are scarce and off on other chores. A blushing young bride will struggle under the weight of a skin and she is good in bed. A fiveyear later she is carrying two skins at a time and is great in bed. And a fiveyear after that she is carrying four water skins at a time, and in bed, she can snap a man in half and make him glad for it. So treat us with care and affection, and we will put you back together again.

And with a slow I-love-you gesture she was off.

That evening people kept glancing up at Gatherer's house, the house that had been touched by tragedy and had remained silent for so many years. It was silent no more. The same trick of sound that had amused the children worked in reverse, and all were treated to an evening of gasps and moans by a woman who was learning life-changing things about herself, and had never been teased by a man with clever hands, and other things too from the sound of it. She had also taught herself some tricks it seemed. For when the moment arrived to accept Nature's final reward, she lapped up every delicious bit in a shrieking wail. When he finally mounted her it was even louder. And when she rolled him over and started to tease him, they heard man sounds also.

When Baree heard about it the next day she was beyond any embarrassment with happiness. A gatherer's hands are good hands, she said smiling. He has good everything. We are together now.

His reaction was more sedate. With her embrace and long kiss of approval, he made arrangements to move in with Baree to start a new life and lay his memories to rest. And maybe the acoustics were better. When asked how much better the neighbors would just say, they inspire us to greatness. The house on the hill became a place of fire-watch and kids were always welcome. And jamboree night became a regular event. Quiet time for everyone.

Months later many women were heavy with child, and Baree was also. The couple was happy and completed each other. They had twin girls and a boy before her body stopped making them, and she would always say, I'm going for six. As a joke for the children. Gatherer made shorter trips and acceded to the men's wishes, and he traveled with companions. They now also came back with bundles of whole plants with roots also, for his final gift to his first love was to be a cultivated garden on Jamboree Hill.

In mixed company Gatherer always referred to her as 'my water-woman', and if anyone asked him why he would just smile. Of course Baree's friend asked her right away, and she stood and described that morning and told the whole lecture to her friend in the same voice she had delivered it, with hands on hips.

And her friend stood facing her with hands on hips and replied in the same voice, and so right you are! Baree embraced her in shared laughter.

After a few years their children grew steady on their legs, and the whole family traveled with other adults and children on long away trips. He introduced all to his places, his craft and the uses for each item, and how to spot and prepare them. They became competent gatherers in their own right and were in high demand.

And finally, the storyteller said, the tale of the Gatherer is now your own tale, and when you live out your lives full of good love and good friends and care for each other, you are all adding new chapters to it.

And cheers rang out.

It was always the first and only story of the evening.

———

STAR RISE II

He was standing, transfixed. When he had first seen stars emerging from the mountain a little while ago, it had taken on new meaning, and he shivered with the immensity of it. He counted things with a few counting-words and vast things without them, and the whole sky was too much for his senses. Some part of him would always try to quantify, and surrender in discordant discomfort. That is why he had only glanced at the night sky before. But a little group of stars could be known. As the thrill abated, he froze himself in time. To see stars rise in proper fashion, he decided, one must become more still than they, more still than he ever had been.

He followed the star cluster that had crested the mountain until it was high overhead. At first they were connected by the tiniest and straightest of lines in his mind's eye, following the path of his attention until there were loping and looping paths crossing the cluster. Triangles shimmered here and there also, confused by his path and uncertain if he wanted them to be there. He had to continually tell it all to go away. He finally bounded it by hopping from star to star around it until it made a complicated shape. He left the shape there and just watched, and pondered.

He was not wondering what they were, just browsing his mind. He knew many stories. Some had said the lights were the campfires of people or hunters. Why would they move? Torches more likely, but they were smaller, and where ever there were torches there also must be campfires. Campfires would be just as bright and fixed in the sky, as torches moved past with the night. If it was people-fire, it just didn't add up. Children told stories, as eager for a scare as later theater-goers, that the dim ones were the eyes of predators looking down upon them. That brought waves of shudders through the group, as such a multitude suggested an inescapable nightmare. But predators never looked up. What would they do, jump across the sky to catch something? Prey and stampeding animals did not look up either, if that was their eye-shine. Was the prey on fire, cooking themselves for the feast? (He smiled). Traveling folk had planted the idea that they were ancestors looking down with pride or wrath. Peoples' eyes don't shine. Were the ancestors on fire? What strange thoughts. His tribe embraced the idea of a great herd being driven and did not delve into detail of what was actually seen.

The explanations were like a slow moving circle in his mind. If you asked he could explain each theory to you, but nothing reached out to anchor the circle to anything he knew for certain, and stop it from spinning. It was doubt, but he did not associate doubt with untruth. That would be expecting others to have done all the hard work. He must do the work, and solve the mystery.

He needed to map the great herd, as he had mapped so many other things.

What to do next.

There was a large climbing-stone at the edge of camp, four times the height of a man. It was a giant smooth boulder that had been rolled away from the mountains during some ancient upheaval, and its edges were rounded. It would have been impossible to scale but for previous generations patiently chipping hand and foot holds up the side. The stone was a popular playground for children. The unusual sight of it once greeted a weary migration from the South, and they liked the cooler weather, and it felt like a sign, so they settled their permanent camp around it. Slightly oblong with a small mesa on top that could accommodate a dozen people standing. It was a good place to view the camp, the slope to the river, mountains, and the night sky.

There were things on top that had been hauled up with no small effort. A large log for sitting and several smaller for anchoring a tent, and a circle of stones for a fire. Upon it a sentinel could keep watch in the open, or a sky-watcher could doze without fear of eyes creeping in the night.

He cared about the people he visited during the day, and to their continued amusement, he had never ceased making formal appointments for their next encounter, even if it was the next day at the same sun-time. From long ago when they had invited him to come, to him it just seemed like a necessary step to navigate the world.

His day was a polygon whose points were people or places, with lines that represented time spent until the next. Sky time was slow time and sleep had to happen some time, so he reassigned the identity for sleep as star-sleep. But of course it was not long enough. He moved the points until the line was twice the length. He anchored it to span darkest night, but he knew that the whole thing was more than a day!

As the other lines shrunk until the whole thing became a day, he started to feel like a madman and each encounter was a hello!-yadda-yadda-goodbye! Or actually, just one yadda? Maybe it already seemed that way to some. It was silly even if he ran between places. He tried deleting people-points but every deletion was an arrow through his heart, and they reappeared. Then Thing One or Two offered a suggestion. He watched as his day-circle was pulled into two circles! And each had half the people, and star-sleep was still anchored to night.

So... he'd be telling people he would return the day after next, but also he'd be spending a bit more time with them. He was taking something away but giving also. If he did that for all, no one would feel slighted. He noted with satisfaction that parents-evening-time was on both. And fire-watch was not on either, since he was off rotation for now. And each was exactly a day.

So these were his next two days. And they could repeat until they changed. This contemplation took several seconds and was firmly decided, to give you a yardstick into the efficiency of his symbolic manipulation.

What to do next. Star-sleep was the next unsolved problem. The sky was slow and daytime was louder in time-distance than darkest night. He had measured both and he knew that with certainty. The ratio was expressed in his mind without numbers.

His ratios were pairs of lines and it was fairly obvious by looking at them. For disproportionate ratios the smaller line always wanted to tumble head over heels up the larger one, like how a stick would walk across the ground without rising up. And every tumble was a pace. It had started as a joke while he was practicing strides of several steps. His left foot would take a stride and his right would pivot, trying to catch up while measuring paces to check his prowess. Heel over toe and hop! Toe over heel and hop!

And what if a pace was also a stride? There would be another tiny foot on a short leg, and it kept turning while hopping on the ground counting tiny-paces. And another, and another. Very very many small toes and paces. He laughed at this and would have fallen over if it was happening in real life. He was a strange looking animal now with legs and feet of different sizes! He made the creature run and its stride side stretched out into the distance. Then half of it couldn't keep up and was swaying in circles. Circles were all around and he knew them, but was fascinated when thoughts traced that shape. It felt mystical because circles never just popped into his mind. He should try that some day.

Lines could also duplicate and flop over on themselves. He would start with night and flop it over for day, then put people and things on them as new points. Day and night would arch into something resembling a circle but actually was a shape with corners and his appointments were along it. It was serviceable, but the lines vibrated with uncertainty which was annoyance to him. Sometimes his day was as big as a country, other times as small as a bacterium, depending on the 'arbitrary' measure he had used to draw the first line. He stubbornly refused to pretend inaccurate things were accurate. What if he lost track of which is which? If you can imagine arbitrary as a dirty word, you will understand why he set out to measure the day for certain as soon as an opportunity presented itself.

With sundials, drips of water and sand through the hourglass... verge, foliot and mainspring... cut crystal oscillators and clock divider circuits... people have wanted to carve the day to bits. They have wanted to keep time, and have time keep itself while they are doing something else. You can keep time with a clock, but if you punch a hole in the clock does time run out? From the earliest noisy Rube Goldberg devices time has interrupted daydreams and sleep with its petty demands.

He had tried to measure the day once with a tall stick in the ground and stones following its shadow, but it seemed a pointless endeavor when looking at the result. If only I had a sun and rocks in my head!

But he knew he could stay awake from first light to first light again, if he was rested. And if he placed a lump of animal gristle in an ear he could hear his own heartbeat clearly. He had left it in one day and learned that his heart rested or raced based on what he was doing. Just as he had paced the ground, he must pace in time. If heartbeats were paces with every beat becoming louder, he could measure the day as a whole and every piece in it.

An opportunity had presented itself. He had sprained an ankle jumping off a handhold on the climbing stone. Bedridden for five days, his mother doted on him and she expected he'd sleep most of the time. And he appeared to. He could stay active in thought without moving a muscle, and chase sleep away until he was very, very tired.

He could also summon sleep at will. He would float a certain sleep-identity which lived in an empty place. Hold it in his mind without pushing, and pretend it had pushed into him suddenly against his will. He would imagine a seeping liquid warmth that was not welcome. The warmth drew thought into itself and doomed his struggles, yet he must try. A hurricane of ferocious defiance dissolving to whimpers as the sleep-identity became larger than vision, ever drifting closer. Helpless certainty that it would swallow him (soon) was the last thing on his mind.

He was a fast thinker and it actually took about twenty seconds to sleep himself, time enough for fail-safe ancient circuits to fire and chemical hormones to invade and quench the mind. Many things in the brain share cause and effect. Some ancient circuits are connected with thoughts, even if not driven by them. He had recalled his struggles in the womb with sleep on some level and invented it as a game.

He always lost the game. But when he woke, the sleep-game-identity floated in front of him. He remembered he had decided to play it. And that brought a warm sense of accomplishment. Sometimes when you lose, you win.

His sleep cycles were the same as yours and mine more or less. If something needed to be done he would always come to full awareness, with plenty of time to tell his dream-friends farewell. As a fetus his existence was a series of thought-games ending with the inexorable onset of deep sleep. But as a human no direct THAT identities had yet entered his dreams. They were there but cloaked as vague symbols or portals or people.

His REM states in sleep cycles through the night could be chained together into one continuous dream if he so desired. This was a symbol he knew well. He'd spot it as the dark entrance to a cave or hut, or a blacker-than-black rock in a stream, or the night sky, or even the pupil of another's eye. It would beckon to him. And if he felt weary he would submit. With the dream world around him slowing, even falling water perched in the air, he would draw the warmth and darkness towards him. It would swallow him whole, which took forever. Without a hint of fear or resistance this time, for that interfered with the remembering.

And his awakening would be a receding from darkness infinitely more quickly than it had approached. He felt more rested. In the dream world no time had passed and his friends were calling to him as if he had just stopped for a moment. He had passed through another deep stage of sleep back into REM.

So starting in the evening with water and covered food near at hand, he slept himself through the night and most of the day, pausing long enough to nibble or drink. As he became rested REM sleep lengthened, and he went on an expedition with the Things. They climbed the mountain together. He finally awoke in late afternoon smiling.

After a hearty meal with the family, he set some aside for later and asked his mother to open a small flap at the top of the doorway so he could see the sky. When dark night arrived he stopped an ear and started at First. Resting heartbeats were paces and he was rested. When the others went to bed in the dark, the steady sound in his mind of passing identities kept him entertained, and did not distract him at all from the soft heartbeat in his real ear. He remained awake for more than a day and pretended to be asleep when others were near. It was easy. In this way, he paced out darkest night and the rest of the day, and knew their measures, and their ratio. He committed them to memory. And by good fortune he was only slightly North of the equator, so the ratio stayed constant throughout the year.

Until the ankle healed, he slept himself on trips down the river and great beyond with the Things.

So now when he had anchored his appointment day-circle to darkest night and assigned it to star-sleep, it was proportional and accurate. He knew their measure in heartbeats.

Over the next few days he stitched together a pack with loops for his shoulders. He collected dried food and small things that might be handy. He had a sleeping fur bigger than himself, which could be worn if a leather belt lifted it off the ground and gathered it at the waist. A thick bare animal skin with a bit of legs to tie it shut, and atop it a smaller grass mat he had woven in two layers. The whole thing rolled up length ways and lashed to the pack. If wrapped and tied around the fur with the opening sideways, so maybe he could stay dry if rain poured. He wore the whole kit to test it and many remarked on it and noted the design, and asked if he could make more. His mother quavered with trepidation... are you going on a journey? He replied with usual seriousness, no. I am going to sleep on the climbing rock for awhile. She was much relieved, for he never told untruths, and she need not worry about eyes in the dark. She replied, don't roll off.

And he slept. He slept himself savagely, fighting and dragged under while crying and loving the only sleeping place he had ever known. His house had usually been somewhere he had already left in dream-time, but this time there was a tap on his shoulder and the Things were there, pulling him out of bed and to his feet, dragging him outside as his dream mother worked and his dream father smiled and handed him a piece of meat.

There was no camp outside, just a dried desert of mud that was baked yet completely smooth, and did not even reveal footprints. The Things had been busy. Small stones and leaves were scattered about, and with a sharp stick they had drawn a large circle around them. A squiggly line in one side of the circle was the mountains, and they had drawn in its tallest sharpest peak. Beyond them the circle was studded with features, even small holes poked in the mud for tiny members of the great herd.

A Thing stood astride a stone in the circle. His brother knelt on the mountain peak near him, and gave the ground a push. And with dream-magic, every object in the circle but the area of mountains started moving! With arms outstretched to the side and eyes closed, the standing Thing rode Sky World to its middle zenith, then approaching the other edge he became shorter until only his head was showing, as everybody knows happens to sun and moon. Then with a glance backwards and a smile, he disappeared.

Stargazer could easily imagine such a silly thing, but this was elaborate theater performed just for him, and his surprise and delight were unrehearsed. The ground was continuing to reveal previously unseen mud-divots and bits of stone and leaves from the mountain top edges, as happened in the real sky. Thing Two on the peak stepped off into the moving sky and dropped to a crouch, arms circled, grasping an end of the stick in each hand making a larger circle. With a stern comic pout. His eyes were fixed at Stargazer in mock disdain.

...Hello, Mr. Sun, who does not like to be looked-at! Please forgive me for following your regal course. I will try to look just behind you. Mr. Sun nodded assent and turned forward. After he lowered and disappeared, it was night again and Thing One came out standing from under-over the mountains and continued to ride. Stargazer dimmed the light for night and brightened it for day as the Things rode the sky and disappeared on their separate missions, in hilarious dream-time. Then after a while the Things jumped onto the mountains just after they emerged from them, and they all watched the world go round. Now it was just blue-night with no bright ones and the herd flying by.

All the objects were flying straight across the circle, which fit with his notion of things as they were. He assumed the sky does not stop in the night, and surely it was the same sky every night? Was it really a circle? Was there only one sun? One Moon racing by with garments of shadow? Which was faster? Slower? Had he ever looked at the stars near the bright ones, let alone beyond one night? So many questions. The Things nodded. Thing Two dug in his stick and stopped the world.

There were no clear word-thoughts in this dream from them, though they heard him. He didn't mind, and Stargazer watched them for awhile as they pointed, argued and crouched, Two poking a new star and his brother stomping it away, to be whacked with the stick. They huddled in animated conversation, but only jumbled and babbling thoughts reached him. It sounded as if they had decided what to do next. He did not understand them because he wasn't sure himself. He watched them taking turns with the stick to draw lines connecting the objects into polygons. Always shapes and shape-children. Then one moved a stone and they rubbed out the lines and drew them again. It all happened in dim blue night, for that is where he had left the world when it stopped.

Then the real sun crept over the horizon unseen, day slowly flooding the world. And he was still in the dream world, but alone, on a bright smooth featureless plain of brown desert. Not a single object or mark or memory or certainty was upon it. The stick was in his hand. Nothing. That is how it must begin.

He woke gradually, as if the desert was trying to hold him. So many questions. When he knew more, he would seek out Walker.

———

WALKER

Walker was old in years and like Stargazer in some ways. Spry but slow, and walking in almost-strides that were more than paces, but these days he preferred gestures for many things and spoke only when they failed him. Yet he could tell a tale with both word and gesture as well as any storyteller, and had himself been a famous traveling storyteller once, but most his stories had been about things he had done and seen and carried useful information.

Origins unclear, Walker had roamed the wide world and would appear several times in a year, bringing tales of other camps and real people, and always sightings of any herds in the far distance and how they were moving. Even the doings of small animals, such as spotting a rabbit nearby that was upwind of him, standing tall on its hind legs as if scenting a predator.

Sometimes he could even outpace the night when herds were still and arrive in time to help organize a hunt. He would describe clever things he had seen, ways to tie things and build things, ways to catch slippery fish and sharpen stone blades. Even strange weaves with angles and folds. It was impolite to mention that any of these were already being done, and no one did anyway, because his manner in telling was like a child's wonder of discovering for the first time, and they felt it too.

Even as a young man traveling he had astounded people with his Silent Companion. It would be stowed in a secret place if he approached a camp whose language and ways were unknown, but in the realm of the mountains and lakes people were distant kin and he knew the language well, and was confident to explain when necessary. After the first telling he preferred others to tell it among themselves.

It was an ibex skull with horns mounted tightly to a thick leather headdress. It was worn facing backwards and the horns curved over his head. A flap that was also a sunshade for the neck descended from behind the snout with a cord passing through slits at the bottom, so he could bring the cord under armpits to tie it off in front. It would stay on securely even if he leaned or stooped. But suspended in a nest of smaller stag antlers between the horns, was a grinning human skull. It gazed backwards also.

He would place the headdress grinning at his feet. This is not my father. And pause, it was always a good sign if someone laughed. He is a traveling Companion and friend I met while hunting ibex in the mountains long ago. He had hunted the ibex also. He had fallen with his prey from a high place and broke his head. He lifted and turned it so they could see the back of the skull was missing. There were only the skulls and horns and no other bones. The rain may have carried them from somewhere else, but they were together. Hunter and prey walk with me over the land he once knew. When we approach his home I am sure he will guide me to it. He is a head taller than I and his eyes gaze where mine cannot, so any eyes that follow me will see a tall strange creature looking back. Murmurs in the crowd to the effect, that is a good idea. And if I wander my whole life and he does not find his home, my final resting place will be his also.

Topics also ranged from animal reports to broad philosophical rambles to the task of pushing down hard on the capstone when fire-twirling, even as it made twirling difficult and a firmer grasp was needed. It makes the fire come faster he said, excited. And then all can rest their tired arms in front of the fire. This had been a wonder, for obviously the magic was in the twirling and the capstone was to hold the stick steady with firm pressure. And it worked. How much more magic could there be? Someone brought a kit and they prepared a lighting, handed Walker the capstone. He examined it closely and fitted it on the stick. They let him hold it while twirlers descended. They perceived greater difficulty and his strain in pushing the stone was evident. But lo! Wisps of smoke appeared earlier than usual. Twirling continued, for they were waiting for a sign from him. And the tinder popped into flame in the light breeze and needed no breath to wake it.

One should hold the stone and never rest, he said. The stone bearer
never takes a turn. Twirlers may rest. The bearer must hold it steady
and push hard in complete stillness and attention, that it doesn't
wander on the stone, and the stick does not bend. He pointed to the
top of the stick. This should be sharper. He held up the stone to
show the chipped divot in the middle. This should be deeper.
Because the stick is a spear in flight, and it will SLAY THE MAN-
BEAST! The last was shouted and everyone jumped. But they could
see he had grabbed the stick and clamped it between stiff fingers as if
it had impaled him, and he writhed in agony to bring the point
home. They had seen this almost happen. And they had been
prideful of the handoff between tasks and practiced it like a dance.
But it was clear, that the easiest task should become the hardest.

I love fire, he had said then simply, as a man would declare love for a
sweetheart. And so they thought about it and realized they loved fire
too. He then added, it pains me to leave it behind. This was true
also, for he traveled alone with a small kit and carried shorter spears
for small game that were also fire sticks. But unless wrapped in kit in
a dwelling near a fire, sticks, tinder and fire boards tended to be
damp from the world, and a concerted effort was needed to make
fire. And he could not even employ the technique he had just
shown. In the deepest wilds he would wrap small kills away from
flies and dangle them from his shoulders until conditions were right
or hunger gnawed at him, and patiently make fire. And portion the
meat for several days.

Walker would have danced for joy if he had ever seen a fire-bow in
action. A tough sinew held in tension by a bending stick. Even
glimpsing the moment where the stick and sinew are held together at
the top, and the bow circles around it to place a loop around the
stick and slide the loop down to the middle, would have made him
cry out, for he would have glimpsed its purpose already. And then

with one hand holding the capstone, the favored hand moving the bow forward and backward. The stone pushed down in concentration. Fire thus can be made by one standing, for hands never travel down the stick, and yet the stick twirls faster than hands could. Physics just is, but applied physics is magic. It is the gift of fire to lone wanderers in the wild.

A mixed blessing, for if he always had fire he might have desired people less. As it was he needed them and they needed him. Far to the South there were geniuses using fire-bows at that very moment, and in the distant future North his descendants would use them also, and later, as backup for flint and stone. He had been content with wandering life and in several camps there were ladies eager for a tryst. He had many children, though he knew them not.

And in his later years, the man who loved fire had finally arrived from afar once more and settled down in age with one of his past flames. And her children became his children. The Silent Companion watched over his new family, and was content.

Walker was often at the hunters' place of training, giving advice on technique and method. He had hunted with many peoples, even those far away whose gestures and prey were very different. With many others driving herds into makeshift corrals or over cliffs, engaging and finishing with spears. Fishing with baskets of woven vines. He had stalked ibexes alone and with others in the mountains, where stealth and quiet breath is as crucial as the first cast and keeping oneself balanced away from the precipice.

The children were always fascinated with far casts and distant targets, but sometimes he would gather them to a place where there was a rounded stone and a melon dangling at chest height close by. They mounted the stone and were given several short double-pointed spears set in a cup like basket dangling from the shoulder, opposite the casting arm.   He described the game. Stand still for many slow breaths, move quickly and cast through the melon, and remain balanced on the stone turning all the way around while reaching for another and cast again, and you can hunt the ibex. If you miss the ibex, that is life. If feet touch the ground, that is death.

Terse announcements always moved them to great seriousness, for the less said the more it means. And there were other challenges. Instead of turning they might grasp and cast backhanded with force and accuracy, so the second spear is already in directed flight leaving the cup. Or a forward cast with twisted arm. He had demonstrated both. Which was why the double pointed spears.

After a tense round of this Walker might spot any who was new to the game and say to them, now you must practice dragging your kill down the mountain keeping him from falling. Tie yourself to him. It was a parody of the too-studious acolyte doing nonsense things the teacher had asked. Despite rising giggles from behind, if the child's gaze remained fixed in seriousness, Walker would suddenly shout, No! Just push him over! And ride him down the side all the way into camp! Walker never laughed at his own jokes, not even with his eyes. It was strange.

Laughter would break out, and yet they would glance at the newcomer to spot the onset of genuine mirth. Such was the protectiveness children felt toward one another. If the child thought the laughter was directed at him and not the joke, there was a possibility he may not have realized it was a joke, or was held absurdly transfixed by the pronouncements of adults, such as an abusive parent. Or he was in social terror from the laughter and had not even heard the words. The ancient notion of 'sharing a joke' is based in part on this watchfulness and if there was no mirth, he might be taken aside by the group who would frame the joke by pleading, yes push him over, but please don't tie yourself to him or ride him down! as if they were asking a favor. The earnest asking for small favors is an effective remedy for social terror. It is transactional, and small transactions bring healing.

And when they could balance on the stone while going deep into the melon but not always through, when their opposite side technique, forward or backhanded, was true enough to hit every time, and they could hit rolling melons on the ground, he would say you are ready. Ready to hunt small game. Hunters grow weary of it because they are so big and noisy. But when you are small and know where your balance is, you can walk and stand quietly, your spears will fly true and you will cast twice without thinking when it changes direction.

Start with rabbits and ground birds, they are good eating and fun to bring home. You can even spear fish while standing on a slippery rock. They are not always where they seem to be. Shoot low and you will hit them. You must figure it out. Even a crude straw basket underwater can bring home dinner, if you pile stones in the shallows and make walls that gather prey to you. And of all the great hunters I have known, the one I respect the most was the woman with the frogs. Dozens of them she had caught in the night with her hands, and she prepared them for us. We were all weak from hunger and it was the most incredible meal of my life, and it sustained us in the wild until the hunt was successful. Become that friend in time of need. I will leave you now. And he left them confused, but some were resuming the contest. There would be no more talk of ibexes from him that day, but they were thinking of them.

Walker was in quiet awe of Stargazer's precision. He knew the boy was different in a way beyond being older than his years, how others explained him. He seemed to master without practice. He would take any length spear, find its balance point quickly, then shake it both horizontally and vertically. then left foot lifted and forward he leaned back sighting the target, letting the spear fall in his loose twisting grip as the hand slid back from the balance point while pushing the back down a little faster than its free fall, then a grasp and hurl as the left foot swung behind, releasing with a twist and palm under its departing tail. Seemingly brushing it to aim or spin it, or just say farewell? He had watched it a dozen times. The boy hit the target ten of those times. Of the ten, the smaller spears he had been given hit but swung to the side, lacking the mass and sharpness to penetrate. It was early morning and they were alone.

He knew the boy's weaknesses too. When targets were swinging slowly or being pulled along the ground, when he was told to jog or run all the time, or make casts quickly in two directions, each cast went wilder that the last. Which was expected of a beginner. But he didn't improve gradually like the other beginners. He was grappling with some invisible thing that threw him off completely, forced him to start over, do what ever he had to do. Sometimes he would freeze in place and the others had to dodge him for a moment.

The most rigorous test was a game where everyone was given blunt spears and there were targets all around. Some were the hunters, the others animals wearing dyed scarves. Everyone was in motion. The animals would run in herd like patterns and when an animal passed by and dramatically tagged a target, the hunters cast for it. If an animal ran past and did not tag it, it was a losing target, and the animal would call out after he had passed it, so anyone who had already cast knew it was a losing target. If anyone got hit or even grazed by a spear, the day's game would be ended as a 'successful hunt' which was a joke of shame. It was the best compromise for what could be a deadly game, but it did offer real world conditions. And it forced young hunters to be constantly aware of the positions and paths of their peers, above all else. Hunters kept their own scores for casts, and hits to winning and losing targets. Sometimes one would only go after losing targets for fun, to be given the title, hunter of peoples.

Stargazer-as-animal played with verve and abandon. His long strides took him all over and he tagged almost every target he passed, and dodged wayward spears well. Stargazer-as-hunter never cast once, though he often pretended to get ready. When hunters called out their casts and winning and losing targets acquired, they would glance at Stargazer and he would remain silent, without embarrassment. Walker concluded, he trusts others but does not trust himself or his skill, even in this game. They know this, and they respect him.

With other children he was always relinquishing the spear to another after he hit a target, when the tradition was to take victory casts until one missed. One time an annoyed friend handed it back to him and pointed at the target. He took and examined it closely, tossed and caught it, smiled and handed it back, as if indicating his approval of it. The friend just shrugged and took a turn.

He Who Casts the First Spear is not here to become the greatest hunter, Walker thought. He is here to be with the others.

When Stargazer had been placed on the stone for the ibex game, Walker wasn't watching the cast at all. He was watching the feet, because everyone was unpracticed at first and each turned in a different way, with halting steps or swinging toes planted, or spun on their heels because it seemed easy and that was good for spinning quickly but not keeping balance. It was a challenge to spot the first hint of their loss of balance, and suggest something that might help. He needed to draw their attention to maneuvering and keeping balance on one spot while doing other things. The real objective.

Walker almost missed it. He heard a Thunk! and was starting to look up when after a slight pause, the left foot lifted and kicked sideways and the torso spun round, legs twisting until the right foot almost started to spin, then with the left still in the air swinging around, the right foot hopped into the air and spun quickly. It landed facing precisely the opposite direction with its leg now twisted the other way, clearly under strain. The boy swung past the opposite side and the next spear was vertical in his hand. The left foot swung in towards his center and with the spear held against his chest, the right foot hopped and spun again. He landed with both feet almost in a crouch and was already casting. Thunk! Then the spear cup rustled and Thunk! Three spears in the melon, one a little to the left. Almost through.

After a gasp and stunned silence, the others cheered and one shouted, Now you are the one who casts the first THREE spears! Most had not been watching the feet, a blur to them. But some had seen. They pulled him off the stone into the crowd with a babble of questions. His answers were brief. I don't know. I have practiced spinning before. Yes on one foot, then the other. For balance try standing on each foot with your eyes closed. Then with arms out. Then swinging them. No I cannot go all the way around. Something might break. I guess, but going the other way you couldn't cast as part of the spin. I must think about it. And so on, and in excitement with no hint of deliberate rudeness, the crowd drifted away. Stargazer glanced at Walker, then turned back to answer another question.

Walker stood alone in thought. I must think about it, the boy says. What lands have you journeyed in, young friend? I will ask you some day.

———

STAR QUEST

The brown desert would not leave him alone.

He had changed into his every-other-day schedule and there had been no complaints. In fact, he had triggered a wave of concern and whispered conversation. Some suggested he must be pressed by some demand from elsewhere, though no one knew what. They felt uncomfortable to see it. He was an older boy now, so dedicated yet uncommitted. So on the second cycle they had suggested the briefest of visits. They would save the most intricate and demanding work for him, and he could even take it elsewhere to do as he found time. And besides, there were plenty other young hands that needed to learn and his adult-friends promised to keep them busy.

So many saying that at once, it was obvious they had discussed him. He saw through the excuses and understood they had witnessed his abbreviated childhood, and wished him to reclaim a bit more of it if he could. He loved them all, these outside-parents. That was all right, he would accept their gift of time for now, and try to use it well.

Instinct had failed him. At home wrapped in his sleeping fur late at night he was restless. When ever he had decided to do something in the past, asking himself 'what to do next' had always yielded some reasonable answer, even if it was a roundabout course of action that eventually led to the result. But when he had declared he would map the great herd, no easy next thing had presented itself. Perhaps it was just make-busy work that had led to him outfitting a traveling kit, such as one you would wear around the mountains and through distant forests... just to climb a rock outside and watch the stars! He thought of the pieces around him, and they seemed silly and small. The shoulder pack and grass mat were some fine work, it was true.

But those things did not tell him what to do next. He slept himself.

And the desert did not tell him either. It was as it was, as it had been on the first day. He was always alone with a stick in his hand. Alone, and the Things were just a presence. They were waiting too and hung

silently on his every thought. Light was all around yet only blue
empty sky and no sun. Not even a wasteland as stories told that
deserts were, with shrubs clinging to life, insects burying themselves
from the heat and bales of dry weed rolled by the wind. There was
no wind, no low hills in the background. No sound.

Then he was in the dream world desert. Again. He remembered the
wild dream with the Things riding the sky and how it had ended.
That had been two whole empty deserts ago. How did he know
that? Are all his dreams connected now? But it was desert. Nothing
connected to nothing. That was funny! He had spoken that aloud
to himself in waking life when he last woke, he remembered. He also
remembered making fun of his travel kit before sleep. He even
remembered remembering the wild dream vividly in waking life.
Something had changed, something big.

The dream world and the real had always been echoes of one
another. Now each seemed a continuation of the other. Was this a
new way of getting ready for something? Was there only one sky?
Was there only one sun? He remembered those questions, the whole
stream of questions. They were strange to ask, and he had mused on
them in the desert, and in waking life.

What if there are suns-plural? Two? Three? One for every day of
the year? Or a new one every day from an endless succession of
suns? Ask the mountain how many ants are upon it. And the
mountain says, none that I know of. Ask the ant how many
mountains there are, and it says, one that I know of. That seemed to
lead somewhere but was unclear. The transition from none, to one?
From a mountain that cannot be bothered to know such things, to
an ant that measures the mountain with its legs?

His people measured the year with predictable weather and the
swinging sun. Its rising place swung back and forth over the

mountains in a year, between Buffalo Tail and the chin of Resting Face. These had been named by his people as features on the peaks, and Buffalo was a hunter's joke because the beast was laying on its side and its giant stomach was its tall rounded peak. Not as one would see a buffalo in life. It was a hunters-eye view of a fresh kill.

At the mid-point of the sun's point of ascension was Left Bosom, named by a man who spotted bosoms everywhere. As the story went, soon after they set up camp he had a bosom name for every rounded peak in the range from highest to lowest, and a special bosom name for the sharp peak near the center. He told raunchy stories about them. This led to a calmer discussion of naming and someone asked him, how many bosoms in all? And his wife answered, just two, glaring at him. So it was decided he could only choose two bosoms to name, and he picked Left Bosom and Right Bosom nearest the sharp peak. And the sharp peak is your nose! he shouted back to her, and everyone rocked with laughter. The story tells she joined in the laughter after a mock-struggle. And so it is still The Nose.

So when the sun's rising passes Left Bosom on its journey from the Face, the heavy rains are near. When it passes Left Bosom on its way from the Tail, one can expect gentler rains. It is common knowledge in the village whether the sun is currently traveling from the Face or Tail.

Parents and friends gather on the morning after a birth to witness the rising of the sun and note position and direction on that day. And they note its anniversaries. The posts framing doorways have marks that count the years of each child. These traditions were old, as the swing of the sun and the year had long been known. As his people used the mountains to measure this, far camps and those without mountains needed to find other marks on the landscape. And some used the setting of the sun to measure the year. It swung too.

He consciously decided there was only one sun and only one bigger sky. And something happening that revealed one or the other over the course of a day. And the sun was doing something over the year that made him wobble with precision and certainty. All the other ideas seemed like clouds. Stargazer was only one small person after all, and he had no time for the most fanciful and complicated of theories he could think up. Some people were like that, he knew. They were the storytellers, the ones who spun mundane life into the most incredible tales with twists, revelations and superhuman feats. He was not one of them. He would operate on the simplest of assumptions, unless any were proven wrong.

And so it was that almost a million years in our past before the birth of William of Ockham, the Razor was used. And probably not for the first time.

But he was tired of this thinking, and a black bird no bigger than a speck circled high in a clear sky. And with a clarity he had never felt before, he knew he was in the dream world. It drifted closer and he watched it for awhile, and then he knew it was sleep coming for him. He brushed it away and it did not go. Sleep was spent time, and it was darkest night in the real world, and he did not want to interrupt this chain of thought.

I desire to awaken... now! Nothing happened. A warm breeze stirred in the desert and he knew sleep had him. He had waited too long. He had been fooled by the illusion of the sky. The speck had not ever been distant, it had been a tiny thing floating in front of his eye. It was so close now, drifting slowly, and the most powerful mind would be fragmented and swept away by this littlest of things at the first touch. He dared not fight. Remembering had become so important. It was closer. Any time now. It took a very long time.

I desire to awaken...now! His eyes opened in the dark. When sleep had finally released him he knew there had been no dream world again, just a desire to awaken floating in the void. Remembering had become so important. He retained that memory to the last but the remembered thought was drawn out near the end, as if it spanned the sky. Remembering was sooooo iim-poor-taant. What a strange creature he was! Do other people experience this too?

He rose and dressed quietly with care as to not awaken his parents, and put a hand directly on his stick in the dark without feeling for it. He crouched and lifted the door flap near the bottom where it made the least sound. And crept into the clear night. A small part of him was procrastinating and urging him to gather his kit before he ascended the stone. You must be ready, it said. Or just watch from here, if anything. Don't go far. And come back to bed soon.

And he made sport of the little voice with brutal eloquence. Right! And I shall toss logs into the hearth and stoke it to a popping flame, so I will have light to gather my things. And rummage with a great clatter until dear Mother and Father are startled from sleep, and as their alarm fades I shall say to them: you must prepare yourself for the climbing stone leave-taking ceremony. They will nod and don the appropriate garments and beads, and place sacred objects in a circle. I will step into the circle in my adventure gear, and chant as I gather spirit energy and become as ready as ever. Then Mom will stoop and remove objects from the circle so I can pass from it unhindered by fear. And Dad will hand me a whole dressed animal carcass to sling across my shoulders. After I have passed through the doorway of course. And Dad will throw rocks at nearby huts to awaken them also, and as I trudge into the darkness all will sing the climbing stone leave-taking song. Does that sound right?

And the little voice had no answer. Sarcasm is as ancient as thinking a lot, and he certainly did. And it was not some enunciated paragraph of pretend-speech, it was a series of notions that were flashes of past events and imagined events and stories told, with a bit of extra effort to place him at center stage, which contributed notions of the twins absurdity and hilarity. It was a twist in the what-is, and that beckoned them. Notions were overlaid into a weave that progressed in time, but the pieces already had shape, and were just dwelt-upon and drawn out.

His people had spirits that give little pushes to the world and people to set things on their proper course. He accepted this, but he was sure spirits also had a sense of humor and could share a joke. For otherwise the world would be a lonely place. And it wasn't. And he never asked the spirits for help thinking things through or anything else really, except rain, which everyone did. He would no more do so than ask Walker to cast his spear for him. All this musing had taken time, to build a good sarcasm and make the spirits laugh. Time enough to walk across camp.

So he was at the climbing stone already. He thrust the stick in his belt and started up.

He sat on the log. He looked at the sky. And as he looked, the sky went by.

He spotted a group and let its outline and shape-children rise without connecting others. That was easier now. He saw many stars rise from the peaks but did not follow them upward. He was noting how often they appeared, and just thinking.

It was all begging to be mapped and he was rested. But if he could even do such a thing, by the time he was part way through more sky would have emerged and he must map that too. Would it never end? And what was that stone the Thing had moved, so they had to redraw the lines?

And surprisingly, an answer came! It is the bright one who wants to marry the sun, and she is seen in day and night, and is seen to have moved towards and away from him. So she moves with the day and night but also with much-slower speed of her own. It too must be measured over time. Like a man walking on a river. If he goes forward he is always moving faster than the river. If he turns around and walks he is moving slower than the river.

Thank you. It felt polite. And if he runs backwards on the river he is standing still, though he and the river are running hard. So the bright one is connected to the river and she moves, and the shape changes? A flick of assent.

And the bright orange hunter is known to appear in different places of the herd. There are tales of him being much brighter than people remember from childhood, and tales where he has faded. Maybe both are true. Maybe they are tales from different ages. And when he lingers in the night he stays for many Moons. His movement within the herd must be very slow and steady.

So the sky is a river, and I must jump onto it and stand still very still to see bright ones move. Their changing shapes to the others will tell me. Yet the herd has a measure I have not seen. I know there are lands beyond the mountains to the East with people, and those people must see the sky being swallowed by our mountains as surely as my stars emerge from them. If I stood on The Nose I would behold the entire sky. I cannot. It is cold beyond imagine and makes men shake even far from the top, tales tell.

I have seen animal herds mingle and reshape, as individuals move. If that is happening, they must be reshaping in slowslow time, for I heard there are shapes in the sky and people have spotted them and followed them for generations. They are heard in our stories seldom, but have been told by a visitor. It seems to me that aside from the bright ones I know, the night sky is one thing and it moves as one, the sun with it. What is the measure of the whole night herd? And what if I am the one standing on the river, watching still things on the bank go by with speed?

Or... what if the whole world and all of us are spinning or tumbling, and the sun and great herd were still? And even the bright ones were closer than the herd, and yet far away?

He thought about this for awhile, his mind literally spinning, while holding on to the log.

It may seem uncannily prescient for him to pose that, but it is simple child's play. Adults seldom spin in place and they have forgotten. Bipedal humans and great apes seem to be alone in this regard. Everyone turns around looking for trouble or to plan a new direction, dogs chase tails with eyes on the tail, but the human child will do it, eyes fixed on nothing, with verve and dedication. They do it as long as motor control and balance will permit. And beyond, when they fall down. To rise and do it again. With the modern invention of the swivel-chair children continue to explore this realm. The merry-go-round existed in Stargazer's time as a young tree trunk grasped in one hand, and the child swung around it and spun the world with no fear of falling.

And it is a different realm. It is the only motion where nearby and distant objects, even to the horizon and into deep space, remain fixed in place relative to one another. And the mind perceives this as everything moving by quickly at once, ridiculously without end.

The human mind has no predilection for snap-shotting things from a whirling tapestry and doing comparative analysis. That must be learned with difficulty, for it has never been necessary in evolution. Or at least in situations where survival is to be expected. It is the realm of people picked up by tornadoes, falling off cliffs, or being

dragged by the feet along the ground by a predator. Perhaps children
are imagining all these things.

But Stargazer knew motion parallax very well. One of his earliest joys
was walking and feeling the shape-children between things and him
change shape as he passed near objects quickly and distant ones slowly.
And when the mountain peaks and other features made a shape, not at
all.

And he did spin like other children, but very slowly and with
fascination as his shape friends were nailed into place despite the
movement, and made a continuous jagged band of tessellation
completely around his head until his mind joined the ends and fit it all
together perfectly. He could even close his eyes and see it, bold shapes
all the way around with a few blurry remembered images of some
objects at the points. Connected with straighter-than-straight lines.
He loved spinning in place. It was the dog finally catching its tail.

But he also valued precision and certainty. The sun seemed anchored
to the great herd, but was it? He would need to prove it somehow. If
the sun was not anchored after all, the night sky could even be bigger
than day and night. By seeing stars fade in the morning and reappear
in the evening already high in the sky, and knowing of the bright one's
courtship with the sun, he strongly felt that the night sky was always
there but cloaked by the sun.

The Moon was troublesome. He seemed to wander much faster than
the night, or at least in the sense of slow-time. How else could he be
seen in an arc near and far from the sun, through day and night, all in
recent memory? And Moon got so much attention in tales because of
this. Stargazer did not dislike the Moon, but he felt Moon was an
outlier, a different mystery. He would turn to it later after he had
solved others. And try to ignore it in the meantime. He would ignore
the bright one near the sun as well, since he knew she wandered.

The Moon had kept him company and was high in the sky when he arrived. It was lightly cloaked on this day and the landscape glowed. The mountains were big enough to drive their tales but when one ascended the climbing stone, it was easy to see the mountains had ends. As you gazed at Left Bosom, or even lining up your nose with The Nose, turning to the left where your ear had been the mountains fell quickly and there was a great forest, a Northward continuation of their own. At the right ear to the South one could see mountains' end again, a more gradual slope and thinning forest. Far South of the camp he knew was a lake and grassy plains where North-traveling herds made the crucial decision which way to veer to pass by the mountains.

Low treacherous marshland extended past the lake so better or worse, a herd might find the decision made for them with an impossible crossing of rivulets and waist deep mud. So they would continue along the valley, our side of the valley. Its grass was rich, there was plenty between the trees, and they never liked to venture too far away from a source of drinking water when they found it... so fate would deliver them down the river into our hands.

Many a successful hunt began with sighting a huge bonfire or smoke on a foothill to the mountains South of camp where shifts of spotters surveyed the land. It meant, they are coming. Hunters would take positions along the river and they knew their own number, so all would wait until the leading animals of the main group passed the last. Then they lay in to them with shouts and first casts were usually kills. And among trees herds were confused in motion, so there were many casts and kills.

So the mountains bracketed his view but gave his effort a point of focus. And in all other directions the sky was almost unobstructed from the stone, an occasionally taller tree in a carpet of trees extending to the Western horizon opposite The Nose, where there were low hills in the distance.

He fixed on the madness that was the great herd.

He needed a measure of brightness that would pick few of many, so that his sky shapes could take general outlines at first but accurate ones. He practiced making shapes of only those in a group. It was a variation on preventing objects in his vision from making connections unless he wanted them to, and this was hard because it was all tiny lights in the sky and he could see the suggestion of blurs that could be several together. He became annoyed with the dimmest ones, and perhaps annoyance was his greatest gift, for when he looked at them they went out as if a brush had painted them over, and the lines connecting the brightest were still stable and strong lines.

His eyes grew tired at first. He tried to tessellate a group with brighter ones without moving his eyes at all. That didn't work so well. In fact, he had touched on the limit of his analytics that spoiled his aim with motion. He could only make inferences about things and merge them with memory if he had looked at them directly, even briefly. Not a tiny focal point, but the broader portion in the middle of the eye where Nature provides us with a dense mass of vision receptors. So he didn't have to look directly at every star, but he had to plant his vision on a group and keep it there. Only then would it connect with others he knew.

By contrast, when he had spotted the first emerging star in the corner of the eye, that had been a native human trait we all share. The eye is optimized for no-color sensitive detection and tracking around the edges. And the most important event of motion vectors is to sense something not there before.

By starting annoyed he could now stare at a large patch of stars and lines would connect only the brightest and the lines and shapes were bright and memorable. By relaxing the annoyance very slightly, another line network would overlay the first with dimmer lines making 'islands', connecting to the bright lines only occasionally if they were near by. Eventually if vision was not confined with conscious thought his annoyance ramped up again sharply to a wall of frustration, because he was actually trying to prepare hundreds of objects for visualization and recall. He did not know how he did this but felt discomfort when it was happening.

And now he was really tired. He wiped it all from memory by pretending he had been very annoyed by this first effort, to start fresh. His mind was a jumble of disconnected star groups.

So after slow tides of thought and intense practice, the first hint of predawn light was in the East and he finally descended his post and crept back to bed. The first night of sky-watch had been interesting, but not fruitful in the quest. But he had the beginnings of a plan.

He would climb the stone in late afternoon when the sun on the ground was shadowed by the trees, and rest with some weaving or leather work. When the last bit of fireball dipped below the distant hills, he would note where it disappeared and start at First, listen to heartbeats and their ascending identities. In a while the light would fade and he would scan along the entire pathway of horizon across from his left ear, on forward up the steep slope and tracing the mountain peaks, down the slope to his right ear. He was looking for the first star to emerge along this outline, not any already risen.

When he spotted the first-risen he would note its time measure from sunset. This was an important measure and an important star, and it would mark the end to listening to the heart. What ever the star, when connected with others it would still carry the heartbeats-from-sunset measure.

Then in slow-time he would connect first-risen and every emerging star to the best of his ability, but confine himself along the horizon to a narrow band of many stars, so over slow-time he would have the risen sky mapped and tessellated into distinctive shapes. The shape-band would consist of a narrow progression of shapes from left ear, to and up the mountains in a raised shape, then down to right ear. The rising crest.

He would sweep it repeatedly until it was a band of shapes rising in the night, and he'd give it its own identity. And would watch for new ones, adding them as they emerged and re-tracing the others in the band. He would ignore the rest of the sky and Moon.

Then he would sleep himself and when he woke, he'd spot and identify the earlier band now more directly overhead. He would stripe it East to middle peak, remembering that path and its measure along the shapes. And another from the band overhead to the horizon behind each ear. Then mute the lines' visibility and begin again to draw a new shape band along the outline of horizon and mountains. He hoped to populate two or three crests a night until morning.

He knew it would take concentration, but it was little different from what he had done while walking in the woods. Even easier, since he was looking directly at them and not also judging angle from the ground. While walking his mind could see shapes connecting objects all the way back to his house. With vivid learning as a series of actions, he hoped to memorize an expanding grid of stars that began to represent the whole.

And then he could spot past bands in the sky and their measure along perpendicular paths to new bands. He was particularly interested to see if the whole herd mingled aimlessly in slow-time during the night in ways resembling a real herd, or the wandering bright ones.

He hoped not. If it did, he'd just have to give up. He could not remember a swarming hive of bees, no matter how slowly they were flying. That was even boring, a pointless exercise. The biggest puzzle of all would be a herd that marched with the night in absolutely perfect formation. Night after night. That is what they appeared to be. Fun stories aside, it was not animals or people. What was it?

He made time for a rare luxury, a nap during the day. He slept himself into the desert again. Still empty. But this time he desired to escape. And looking straight over his head was the sun as bright as ever, and it was there above him only because he had looked for it. Another strange dream-thing, a sun that doesn't hurt when you look at it, and doesn't mind being looked-at. And with his thought he pushed the dream-sun and woke up, just like that. This is good to know. And drifted back to into sleep.

STAR MAP

He had no idea what a spectacle he was. In late afternoon there was foot traffic near the stone, and they had never seen him keep vigil there. Always visits and questions. I will be watching the night sky. It moves. There was a couple who had made a habit of watching sunsets from the stone and noting its point of departure against the low hills, with knowledge of its year-cycle. They just weren't morning people. Since the sun was not an allowed topic of conversation, the talk rambled through everything else.

He had practice measuring heartbeats while interacting with others, but now he wished for quiet. He blocked an ear to get ready and one asked if he was having trouble with it. Just itches, he said. The sun set. His first measure of time to star-rise was serenaded by talk of plugged ears and sinuses and remedies. He could never mention heartbeats to them, there would be no end to it. He imagined them asking why, do you think yours will stop soon? He closed his eyes and remained silent, and at last the voices drifted down and away.

He spotted the first stars in the sky and finally one emerging, and took its heartbeat measure. He imagined his heart skipped a beat afterwards for spite, but that was a joke.

He claimed first-risen for his own. That one was his. It was not bright but there it was, and he hoped it would guide him to the end of his days. He traced it out with its neighbors above and those risen after and shapes formed as still others rose, until a band of shapes appeared in his vision along the horizon boundary, from his left ear to face to right ear. He retraced them countless times, sweeping his vision back and forth and sometimes in his mind with head still and eyes closed. They were important to him and the mental lines shimmered brightly. He had not brought any work to keep him occupied and he realized that would have been silly, for he knew now he'd be spending a lot of time on this project. He had played with shapes but now it was important to remember. It was urgent to remember!

He became weary though he had been rested in the afternoon. The urgency of remembering was weighing heavily on him. He finally closed his eyes and put up the vision of the shape-bands he had connected, from one ear to the other. It floated in mind-darkness, and he opened his eyes to spot the points of light that had inspired them. There was sometimes a tiny shift as the actually-seen points drifted towards the corners. But the shift was slight, and they locked in quickly because he really did know how to turn his head and look precisely.

He decided to pay more attention to this re-alignment shift, so it would alert him if things were not aligned closely or his attention was wandering. He did not consider it a game anymore, and that changed the flavor of everything. Finally satisfied he could remember, at least in the short term, he closed his eyes for a long while and his chin hit his chest suddenly, startling him awake again. He lay on the fur and slept himself.

Desert again, daylight. The weariness had left him. But something was different. He could see things on the brown ground. Not stones or leaves but an indistinct hatching, as of something drawn when it is viewed almost from the edge. He walked forward and realized he was floating, and scale in this world was what ever he thought it was. That in itself was nothing new for the dream-world, but the direct control was sublime. And as ever the pointed stick was always in his hand. He looked down and knew its purpose.

There were shapes on the ground! It looked as if they had been scratched with the stick and some furrows were deep, others shallower. Holes poked in the dirt at the corners depicted each star. It was all there, and it was the band of shapes he had just toiled over. Where the last part of the band had cleared the horizon-edge, there were faint figures that looked like they had been drawn hastily, showing the horizon curving over the mountains and down to the other side. It made a huge half-circle open to the left. This was a representation of his forward and side field of vision. The ones who had drawn it even added an embellishment for The Nose and Bosoms. He thought of the first star he had claimed and it was there at the leading edge of the mass, as a deep hole and heavy furrows of lines leading to others.

As he panned his attention across the figures, he could see the furrows deepening. There was no distraction like dirt clods being kicked up by a digging stick, the deeper furrows had always been more pronounced it seemed, but hadn't been a moment before as he swept the shapes with recognition and familiarity.

So he spent an ageless time in the desert with stick in hand, deepening the existing furrows of memory. He could have been on hands and knees scraping the stick along each, he knew. Or as he was doing, floating above it and everywhere he looked while tracing them in his mind, they deepened. The stick was a metaphor too. He was looking down on the shapes he had just traced from the sky and there would be more. And he knew the outline of horizon was moving right now, and a growing gap stretched in the record because he was asleep. And when he awoke and set to work, a new connected band of shapes would appear in this place. And the dream-world was different now, he could perceive identities as directly as in waking life. It was an extension of waking life.

Somehow, he knew he was looking at deep memory. Incredible, even in one for whom the usual was unusual.

Thank You. He said again to no one in particular. And felt a tiny nudge of assent.

Incredible feats of memory do exist in the animal world also. And who's to say how a metaphor for this ancient memory mechanism might appear in the mind of an animal, such as a migrating bird? He found it breathlessly exciting. And he looked up and pushed the sun and awoke. It was night still, and there were new stars, and the old ones had moved.

Fall rains had subsided and the sky was clear but for an occasional cloud. As long as there was space between clouds to concentrate on, he could do his work and the drifting cloud in his real vision might have shapes and lines projected upon it. He was doing only these few things and gave his attention to them completely, because he knew answers would not just pop out at him. He had to toil in this slow-time.

Two or three sessions a night, every night. And time in the desert, surveying and tracing the whole. If in the desert there were bands that were distant from others without much interconnection, or there was uncertainty, upon awakening he would bring them both into view at once and retrace a new band of points to bridge them and make their connecting measures known.

Ten days passed, and he watched the stars. And grew bewildered and shocked. The figures in the desert were always there fresh from memory and he had a massive grid of connected shapes. His virtual sky spanned the night from sundown last light to almost sunrise. Such was his discipline that he thrust the bewilderment aside for later and focused on precision in the now, so he'd have certainties to puzzle over.

He was stymied by light pollution from the sun. To make star discrimination work well he needed blackest night or his perception of brightness suffered. So his first and last observations of the night had a shimmer of uncertainty. But for evening objects progressing West as the night darkened, they could be retraced in the mind, even poking new holes in the desert and new lines to connect faint stars that had not been visible at first reading.

Moon cast a silvery patina of light over the sky that could be seen even if a finger shielded it, and disrupted his perception of stars around it. The Moon was wandering quickly all right, and moved in relation to the herd even over the course of a night. So the stars are the river and Moon is standing on the river running upon it. But his parallax sense also told him that Moon was floating over them, and thus was a nearer object. It was definitely a bigger thing. He was sitting still, but what if his world was walking?

The stars were currently rising from the mountains in a band he had recorded several times before. He could even perceive imaginary shapes down their dark slopes, 'seeing' the ones that were soon to emerge. He had time to rest and just think for now.

The sky was stranger than he had ever imagined. No tale he had ever heard even touched on this strangeness.

In the wild dream everything had been flying straight across the circle. Even with East mountains to the right, above him in the sky things were going straight across. And the Things had chosen the middle path of the sun for their funny ride. The circle itself representing the sky carried a taste of metaphor also. He felt it was a 'guess' in some way. But you have a field of vision and as you slowly turn there is always something to see to the ends of the world. So why not a circle? He was prepared to accept his world as some sort of polygon. To trace the boundaries of the world, that was an exciting idea! But to do that he'd have to find corners. And to his amazement, he had not found any. The night sky had no corners!

The problem was his ears, or more precisely, what was happening in the sky in the places where his ears looked when his nose was aligned with The Nose. He had expected to see stars flying straight across close to the horizon. He had even imagined that if he made a great journey in that direction, he would come upon a sky watcher such as himself and they had the same straight path of sky overhead, and when that sky watcher looked far in his direction on the horizon, the other could see his own sky marching straight too.

His whole idea of the sky had been seeded by what was clearly happening along the path of the sun. But what was happening at the ear-ends of the world kept bringing him to and from the desert in confusion. Along the path of the sun shapes were predictably straight in their travel. It was so obvious he had never bothered to even note direction over time.

But what was strange, stars rose near his ears also. But they moved in slow-slow time and when he had traced their course through most of the night, they had risen above the horizon only a short measure and had arched over. Some were actually descending in an arch, as if they would set close to his ears! There were so many it could not be an error. He called them 'star-arches' at first in confusion, after the familiar arch of color beside rain. Nothing in the world but a rain arch made that precise smooth curved shape. He had long pondered it, and now he is thinking it may have helped him prepare for the stars' bizarre behavior. But only at the ears of the world.

Everything happening in slow time between sleeps, and the weird stars making a star-arch in the distance in slow-slow time, as if they are traveling a circle. A small one. It challenged the projection he was constructing in the desert, and he was forced to imagine a continuous correction. Because over here was something happening in a straight line. And over there was something drawing a circle. He decided to call the straight E-W path 'eye stars' and the curving paths around N-S 'ear stars'.

And the relative shapes along long paths between eye and ear stars never changed. They were the same angles relative to one another to make the same shape. But the shape itself rotated in an arch at the ears. This made it easy to see that the curves of the paths extended outward, even to the path of the sun. Small circles at the ears, to a large circle along the sun's path so large that its edge appeared almost straight, to small circles again at the other ear.

In the desert with great difficulty he tried to make a representation at his feet. He traced a tiny circle, then above it an increasing radius of arcs until the last was so large it was almost straight. Then a straight line. Then smaller upside down arcs to a tiny circle again.

So this is how the great herd moves in the sky. As one.

So precise. Yet not straight in most places. No idle milling about about could confuse his shape perception. Some shapes would change and not change back if things were drifting in different directions. These are not animals or people. What are they? He left the figure etched into the desert, and he would return to it often in thought or sleep to ponder.

But he had another problem, something just as perplexing. His measure which was sundown-to-first-star-rising was of great concern. He had half expected it to always be the star he had claimed, the one he had noted first that was etched so deeply in his memory. But that one was already in the sky above.

And the heartbeat measures he had taken over ten days were pretty close to one another, considering how far they had ascended from First. And for almost all that time he had not been able to make that measure as his own star, since it had already risen. In fact, it was now so high in the sky that he would have waited a long time to see it ascend to that position. Had the sun revealed the sky sooner. Later. He tried to think it backward and forward, and it suggested a conclusion.

The great herd was moving faster than the sun. Every night. Not by a lot, but it was moving faster.

That was a big idea. For it meant Sun was not standing still on the river of the great herd, swept along. Or if anything, he was walking slowly upriver. And the sun was also walking back and forth a little bit, such that his journey would take him back to the same place again every year. Who knows how far he actually walked, but to Stargazer it was the measure of the sun's rising from Resting Face to the Tail and back again. It was mesmerizing!

But it also planted the confusing suggestion that the great herd was closer than the sun. Because faster moving things relative to oneself are closer things. That seemed strange.

He had three general classes of objects now. The great herd. The bright ones that wandered across the herd and moved faster, Moon much faster. And the sun, who moved a bit slower. A pretty puzzle.

If the herd was drifting faster than the sun, it also meant that the herd was drifting a little faster than the night! The lead star firmly fixed in his memory was his own star. Its first appearance in the sky when the sun disappears and uncloaks them all, would be higher in the sky every night. Then that place would creep across the sky over time and even approach the far place where the sun sets. And then there would come an evening when it would never uncloak his star because it was following the sun and outrunning him. Then where ever the sun goes at night, his star would follow it and slowly outpace it.

And his star would rise with the sun in the morning, unseen, and remain cloaked by it. For a long span of days his star would creep through the day. At least as long as its slow creeping procession had been through the night. Until one day, if there was only one sun and one great herd... he might once again see his star rising in the evening when the sun uncloaked the sky, as he had seen it on the first day.

Was that in a year? He only picked that because it was the only long celestial phenomenon he knew. And for the life of him he could not connect the yearly wobble of the sun to the great herd at all, without some amazing proof. He dismissed it but kept it tucked away in his mind.

He decided that he would track the sky for another ten days, until the bands merged into mostly continuous memory. And just as important, he wanted to see where his star would emerge from sunlight at the end. He wanted to have a more accurate measure of how much faster the herd was than the sun. He knew that when he ceased his vigil the gap of previously-unseen stars would start to grow. But he was just one little person in the wide world after all.

The ears of the world were crucial to the mystery. Little star-arches. He had something in mind to ask Walker when ten more days had passed.

———

THE IBEX HUNT

But it is a forbidden hunt, he had said.

You mean, forbidden for little children to climb mountains instead of searching the meadows for rabbits? his brother Grale replied. If you'd rather do that. His brother was almost a man. Grale had already joined the hunters and could outrun many of them, even while casting. His casts were true and deep.

He said, someone told this place to me long ago. It is a place where you leave the mountain stream and walk straight uphill into the woods for many paces. And there is a cliff split in two, and a large crack big enough for a man to enter rises up, going left and right. There are plenty of places inside to climb easily, and even rest. And when you reach the top, you can see the world below. And there are paths leading from there few have walked. Will you come? Three must go, but I am two men! And I choose you third, little brother. Come with me. We shall bring home a feast!

I will go he said, trying to sound older than his years.

They were given leave to camp in the woods for a few days and set out heavily laden with skins, cutting stones, some food, a fire kit and dry sticks to burn. And nestled with the sticks on his brother's shoulders, many short spears. There will be no rain, he said, and I must find the right stream before it dries up. In fact the stream was fed by snow melt

182

year round, but the one who told him the place in the stream had been told that by someone else, and he had not known the land very well.

Even though Grale had hiked directly towards a particular cleft in the hills it took the whole morning to reach it and find the small stream. He had once been waiting at the bottom of the stream with others when some returned down the stream. That hunt had not been successful, but one of the tired men had described the place to him and the manner they had ascended. Even as a child his brother had found the secret place in the stream and ascended alone. And stood on top of the world.

Grale was tireless and he was already weary. He sat for awhile. Come now. It is not too far up the stream and we can walk beside it most of the way. Come. And he had pretended he was on an urgent errand, and found new strength. Grale splashed up the stream in and out of it, but when ever he even put in his foot it was cold. He shuddered. Come, Grale said. Keep moving and your feet will stay warm. And tie your skins at the waist so they stay dry. You will feel a chill but dry things are better than wet things! And after a trudging miserable journey for his young legs, including one place where he had to walk a pool in the icy stream almost to his waist, Grale said, this is the place.

Grale had said to himself, two boulders together and a third apart. This is the place. He said the last aloud and the smaller boy was distracted by his own concerns, and was in no mood to ask questions. They filled bladders in the stream, literal stretched bladders of wild boar with ureter tied off and urethra as a spout encased in soft leather and hung on a loop from the shoulder. He paid little attention to surroundings and followed Grale into the woods.

Many paces indeed. But it was steep enough that uphill was always evident, and the trees' grasp on the mountain was so tenuous that their roots would have been a hazard to one running. They were young mountains as mountains go. But no one was running, and they provided a foot ladder up the hill. It was afternoon when they approached a sheer rock wall. He rested and Grale ventured back and forth along the base. Finally he heard Grale beckon and he headed off in that direction. And spotted the crack. It was wide enough even one with things on the back could climb. It looked like a meandering river going up the cliff.

We rest here for a little while and start up. It is not so far and an easy climb. You can rest often without worry. Then you will emerge like a rat from a hole and have the sight of your life!

It was. The sun was still three fingers above the horizon and the world was golden. The mountain blocked the view to the North, but the lake shimmered at the mountains' foot to South. And a wide world spread out before him. And they twirled together expertly and had a fire as the sun dipped below the horizon. There was a place next to the higher cliff where erosion had gathered, and generations of plants had clung there. Green leaves poked out of low bushes so grazers were few, but it had been attacked before. The cropped plants had left a tangle of dry stalks. These cut easily and burned well, there was enough for many fires. The view was from a wide horizontal shelf between cliffs, and the crack ran through it and up another. On the horizontal it was narrow enough to jump over in places.

He warmed in the fire and listened to his brother. Grale was a great story teller and put himself into every story. When the hero demonstrated some superhuman feat of strength he would pause and show off his own muscles with a big smile. Behold! I am two men! And his little brother asked, what do you show the girls when you tell a ribald tale? And they both laughed, slapping each others' backs. It had been a good day.

They slept under a bowl of stars.

Wakey wakey, Grale whispered. There was a bitter gentle wind and a cold light of dawn. I have heard the clatter of small stones. It echoes in the hills and it is not just stones falling, it is the click of hooves as they jump from rock to rock. They climb where men dare not. The beasts do not feel the cold and they begin feeding at first light. There must be plenty plants up there or they would have stripped these already. Thorns do not stop them. When they are picking at leaves among thorns is the best time to get them. They close their eyes so thorns do not poke, and you only have to mind the ears, which are keen. You must move silent and still your breath. And the first cast is all you get, and your spear is lost if you miss. I have hunted these in another place, and my first cast was true. Our party brought one home. I think this is a good place. Bring some food, the cutting stone and a spear. We travel light.

The way up was a steep tortuous path on stony ground, more vertical than horizontal. It had tall boulders that could not possibly be just standing there, for they were perched on steep ground. It was not a path made by people. Many animals had walked it and hoof prints were visible. Perhaps the land had been pushed aside somehow and the boulders were the tips of ancient cliffs buried by it, still attached. They finally topped off and walked along the spine of the hill to its end overlooking the valley, and the final bit of the hill was crowned with giant stones and bits of cliff, with a glimpse of vegetation here and there between them.

They crept between them. There were several places with carpets of thorny plants, some cropped of green. It was a maze and sometimes they would enter a vault of shadow from the other side to seek new paths. And always Grale would tilt his head around the corner and scan the area first. Finally he tilted back and covered his mouth for silence.

He spoke in gesture, he is above us, and eats with head down. We must creep closer quietly. After five steps I will cast. Grale held his spear at the ready and prepared to step out. But a tiny sound escaped the younger one's feet as he reached for his spear. There was a clatter of hooves unseen. Grale peeked again and the beast was gone. He looked down at his brother's feet and made a silent gesture like slapping his head. He smiled and pointed down, and knelt to unwind his brother's leather foot guards. Soon the young hunter was barefoot as Grale was. We must move silently, Grale gestured. Now is the time to find a closer place and wait. He did not see us, and the sound was not a voice, so he will be back. These spook easily and forget.

They crept forward and Grale found rounded stones with a gap between they could retreat into. It was three strides from where the beast had been, but they were out of sight and around the corner. The breeze was at their faces, so it would carry their scent between the stones and down the mountain. They waited. Grale dared not even look.

At last they heard a light sound of hoof and later, snapping of twigs. Grale smiled and made crude eating gestures with his mouth. He closed his eyes for ten breaths, Then at the next snapping of twigs he peeked and stepped out. The younger dared not move and watched his brother plant his feet, and cast out of sight. There was an animal scream and thundering of hooves. Grale jumped for joy and beckoned the younger. And dared to speak. It was a good cast, the spear is firmly planted at the base of his neck. We must pursue him now.

They bound between the rocks and scaled along cliff ledges at the sound. There was an occasional bleating in the distance and spots of blood. And finally they came upon the animal in a narrow dangerous place, open air on both sides and a floor of uneven stone. A narrow space between two boulders led to the place, and the spear had done even more damage as it was brushed sideways by the entrance. Blood was pulsing out from the neck and matting its fur and staining the rocks. The animal was flicking its eyes and swaying back and forth.

Grale said, We must bring him down quickly or he will fall off the wrong side of the mountain. He is showing me his heart. I will go for it and end his suffering. Give me your spear. He accepted it and stepped out onto a smooth stone and cast. It was true.

But the animal snorted blood, shook its head and lurched. It dimly realized that the only way out was the way in, and charged the opening blindly. The younger found himself staring down the animal and did not flinch, but grabbed with his right hand one of its horns. He pulled it forward. But the beast had brushed past Grale and upset his balance on the stone, and one of his feet slipped out into space. He grabbed a handful of short fur and having nothing else to grab, wrapped his hand around the other horn.

Now the younger was pulling on the horn he grasped to bring the beast and his brother out of that awful place. But it died suddenly from the spear to the heart. Its haunches collapsed and the ibex went limp and slid on its own blood towards the edge. Now Grale was dangling with both feet, hanging from the horn. And the boy held on too but it was pulling him.

The haunch drooped over the edge and the weight became terrible. All he saw of his brother now was two hands, grasping. He kept his grip but his feet were dragging.

And the last thing his beloved brother shouted was, Let go! It will take you! And they were gone.

His own long wail was all he heard. Then silence and a whistle of
wind, and he was alone.

———

THE WORLD AS IT IS

Walker had thought of him often. But the boy's life had taken a
strange and sudden turn, and it had been almost a Moon since he
showed up on the practice field. Or most other places, it seemed. One
who had been watching him long said, he had taken on such a burden
as a small child, he has already reached the point when adults
reconsider their lives. And the child would emerge from it headed in a
new direction, and he would do well as he had always done. To say all
this for a boy of so few years, Walker had thought. These are amazing
times.

Stargazer came to his hearth after sunset. Without a word he had
waited for the man to rise, held out his arms and stepped forward to a
full embrace. It was the custom of friends who had not seen one
another for ages, yet seemed appropriate. Or wait. Is it not also the
custom between shamans and healers at every meeting? Which will it
be? Neither cared for small talk and just held one another at arms'
length. The boy was clearly waiting for the elder to speak first. Ever so
polite, he thought. So he spoke. What far places have you been, young
friend, even as you walk among us by day?

I have been living in slow time, watching the paths of the great herd.
There are many paths! I have discovered some things, and others
remain mysteries. I am confused. I have questions.

Walker said, To me the great herd is a place where stories are born, but
those grow in the minds of people. Surely you have not come to ask an
old hermit about people? You are Star-Gazer to me now, and you may
call me Stumbler, for I am feeling my age more these days. Do you
know people are telling tales of you now? You are the one who

watches the stars, and they expect you to make a speech from the stone one day to announce your findings. Others are comforted by the sight of a sentry on the stone every night, just like old days, even though he is looking in the wrong direction! And you are always so lost in thought it is a wonder you don't step off the stone or tumble to the ground in your sleep.

Don't roll off, she said. Mother I mean. I must obey her. And rather than gazing all night I do sleep. The first part of it is sleep, but later I walk in an endless desert of sunlight. There are marks upon the ground that are star observations I have made, and no weather to disturb them. It is a desert of memory. The great herd is not fixed with the sun. It travels faster than the sun by a small measure, such that the sky shifts its place a little every night and stars rise sooner. Have you ever seen this?

Stargazer brushed the sand smooth and found a short stick. He drew the curves carefully in the firelight. A small semicircle at the bottom, a series of expanding arcs until almost straight, a straight line, and the same figure upside down with a small semicircle at the top. And the ends of every line this time were now bounded precisely by an invisible circle. This sand was good for drawing, and where he drew it was darker with moisture. Walker was silent for a long time.

What amazing times. I have seen something like this before. It is a sacred symbol in the South. Far South. Years ago, in the farthest of my journeys. I never met one who spoke my language there, but I traveled with a friend who spoke theirs. And to see a boy of my own village draw it before me after all these years is like... like the wildest story come to life! How did you come by this?

It is the true path of the great herd in the sky. Our mountains are here, from my eyes. He indicated a point in the middle to the right, then the lines. Those stars rise and head straight across. These stars come towards the middle and away again. And these move in very slow time, and make little circles. But the whole circle is beyond the world I can see.

World! yes. The name of the figure is, 'the world as it is'. But even the one who drew it was recalling it from long memory. And that people he was with were obsessed by symbols. It would even be forbidden for us to draw it. And yet they adorned things with it, like the walls of caves and sacred places. To them it was another sun symbol for they worshiped the sun. But even just a circle to them was a sun symbol! Maybe Mr. Sun had fried their brains! But he had seen it elsewhere too. He said it came from another people even farther South, and its true name had been lost in time. And 'the world as it is' had been its true name. But he knew nothing about the world. He just liked symbols.

So what would that mean? How could both be true? That we are the ones living in the sky, and the ones who drew the figure were looking up at us?

I like the way you think, friend. That is a strange idea. I'll make a story from it. No one will like it I am sure, for around here it is Moon-fever and tales of the heart. But I know you did not come for a story. If the herd moves faster than the sun, that is news. But as to its name, even the wildest tale has little tales within it that are true, or false. I propose that the name might be true, but the one who said it long ago had completed an observation in the same world and same manner as you, and excitement carried away their words. Or maybe it was the great herd itself that had fried the brains of his people, and they worshiped it as if it was the whole world.

Walker smiled, for he knew he tended to be cynical and irreverent about things untouched or unseen that others worshiped, for he had seen hints and heard tales where such casual worship created arbitrary hierarchies of privilege and division in societies and over time, turned them against one another, even leading to people hunting people. He reflected on it for a moment. And realized that this boy was his equal, very likely greater, and was entitled as a friend to know his own thought process. So he told the boy all this, confident he would follow and understand well. And added a word of apology, and a warning that his views might not be appropriate to share with others.

Stargazer listened with interest and was silent for a moment. But that is of little matter, the boy finally said. I heed your warning but not your apology. Your comment about the name rings true, for it is a simple and likely explanation, far simpler than a symbol crossing between worlds and people in the sky. It is you I name the one who sees 'the world as it is', and I feel your wisdom was gained by listening and watching and not talking. I am glad I came to you with this.

Walker was stunned and felt unexpectedly warmed by the praise. It was so surprising and direct. He wished he had met Stargazer long ago, even absurdly longer than his young life had been.

How can I aid your quest? Walker asked, once more getting to the point.

I am seeking a place. A high place where I could better see the ears of the world. It would be a special place that looks in the directions... he stepped outside for a moment and examined the mountains in the gloom and stars as they were, and returned and raised his arms extended, pointing opposite. He noted with amusement that he must look very much like the Thing riding the world.

These directions. Towards the lake to the South and the wild lands to the North. Along the mountains, and yet also the lands below. Have you ever ventured to The Nose?

No one has ever stood there, as far as I know. Lone explorers have walked near there who ascended from the other side, where the climbing is easier and there are many more paths. And it was far above them still. But that is a bitter cold land of white water that moves not, and no plants are there, and no animals. It is a place you can only visit in dreams, or with such hardiness as men cannot spare, if they wish to return. I do not visit it, even in dreams. It makes me shudder to think of it, that there could be such cold and emptiness in the world.

Is there no other place? I need to see in these directions only, to learn more about the ears of the 'world as it is'. And it need not be a high or cold place, if eyes can see farther beyond the trees to the North.

After a time of silence, Stargazer realized that Walker was battling something in his mind. It would be the easiest thing in the world to say he knew not of such a place, or that he did. He could not recall a time Walker had ever refrained from speaking for so long, about anything!

He did not know why the man was not speaking, but he felt a growing personal shame in asking.

Finally Walker said, there is such a place. And I will take you there.

Stargazer relented a bit in confusion, but Walker was having none of it and even made light of his condition and unspoken battle. He said plainly, you are making me cross now, so I shall make a demand. Only we two will go, or I will go alone! For it is a journey without worrisome danger, and I am also cross with myself for not having made it in so long. Which is not your concern. You are on a quest for learning and wisdom and I must help if I may. And if I may say, it is a pleasure to help you, and I enjoy your company. We will leave when these clouds pass and clear skies return.

———

THE HIGH PLACE

And so they left one bright morning and set out for a tall mountain foothill that carried no name anyone could remember, for it had never resembled an ample female bosom. Walker traveled light and soon found his legs again, seeming to enjoy ambling along clear paths with a destination firmly in mind. Stargazer had been asked to bring straps to gather bundles of wood, light food to ration over three days and small skins of water to sip so that, Walker had said, you will have your full night of star-gazing, and another if you wish it, and the morning after we will be off again. The way back is much shorter, if you can believe it.

As they approached the hill Walker started cutting and gathering dry branches, and he suggested the same. While you are huddled in your furs in darkness watching stars, this old man would crave the heat and light of a fire. There is a chill up there. Stargazer was sturdy for his years and rearranged pieces into a tight bundle of the straightest wood, accepting more from Walker until he refused to give them. His heart is heavy somehow, Stargazer thought, so I must help him travel light.

And so it was that they reached the small stream in mid-afternoon and quickly ascended it, for Walker knew the way exactly and the boy had no trouble keeping up. And at the sign of three large stones they refilled their skins and veered into the steep forest and ever up, and Walker was climbing the hill bent forward but vigorously, like someone who had found a sudden lightness of heart. And finally the sheer cliff, and Walker bade him rest from his burden and sit while he scouted ahead. And just as had happened so far in the past, a voice called and he followed, and Stargazer saw the great crack in the cliff.

They climbed up inside the crack and stepped out, and at last stood on the large shelf on top of the world. Walker did not miss even the littlest thing, and when he spotted the boy looking anxiously at the cliff faces obscuring the North view he said, have no worry. This is not the place. It is far above and is just a long walk now. And they set off up the steep hill.

Stargazer found himself straddling the adjacent hill, walking along its rocky spine with an incredible vista to either side of him. It was the most exciting and incredible sight of his life. They drew towards the setting sun and there was the crown of boulders perched upon its West-most end.

If you try to spot it today you will be sorely disappointed, for the large crack was a portent of upheaval to come. Despite its firm dirt floor, the crack extended far below and above the small part they had climbed, and it separated a large part of the hill from the mountains beside it. Violent earthquakes over the last million years rent and widened it until it was narrow cliffs between taller hills, and then they shook until the Western foundations of stone toppled and smoothed out into the land below.

And yet... you are descended in life from Stargazer and Walker through a long line of evolutionary success and good breeding. Ponder that as you consider the strength and timelessness of stone, and the frailty of man. You are a winner! Congratulations!

They descended into the labyrinth and Walker led him through the shaded grottoes of hardy vegetation to its very end. And he finally stood in front of the two narrow stones leading to the high place of the whistling wind, with abyss on both sides, and he said, I will go no further. Take your measure of the place and see if it will suit your need. And do not roll off!

Stargazer stepped out onto the smooth boulders that floored the opening. There was a good one to sit upon and view either direction, and a high boulder that blocked the setting sun and the whole place was in shadow. But he turned again and again to see the foothills of the mountains curving off and down to both sides of the land. The ears of the world. And the breeze was gentle on his face, only whistling and moaning ominously through narrow spaces between the stones as it shifted. He smiled at Walker and said, this is a good place. Thank you kindly, friend.

And Walker smiled back with simple satisfaction and then pretended to be aggrieved once more. Help me find somewhere between boulders shielded from the wind and your eyes, and let us have a bite and lay out wood for a fire. And the boy collected many dry sticks and brambles from the dense thicket upon which an ibex had once browsed, and set them aside for the fire.

The night passed easily as he noted the slow spin of celestial clockwork. There were several stars at the ears he had never seen before, especially to the North between the familiar ones with wider arcs. The tiniest of circles anchored below the horizon described their motion, and a new one among them was so slow it had only slightly ascended and remained in place, and had shifted only slightly as dawn light cloaked the sky. And another under his watchful eye that did not ascend at all, just emerged and froze, and disappeared with the cloaking of dawn. The most tiny circle of them all.

It was very nearly a polestar of his time, far distant in the sky from the polestar of the Egyptians, and also the one of today.

Milutin Milankovitch eventually discovered why, for he was also a connoisseur of fine celestial clockwork in slow-time.

Such was Stargazer's excitement and wonder that first night, he only slept himself once, taking care to exit that perilous place and curl up on firm ground near the two narrow stones. And as he squatted in the bright desert retracing their new marks upon the smooth ground and completing their tiny circles, Walker crept up on him quietly in the starlight and saw him sleeping there, and was much relieved.

At first light Stargazer relocated to the still campfire by the sleeping man, and slept fitfully through to almost high noon. The previous day's trek and night vigil had taken more of a toll on his young body than he had realized, and he awakened finally to Walker lifting his head to give him a long drink of water. When he regained full awareness he noted that Walker had given him water from his own skin, and Stargazer's was empty.

Once again, camping humans had brought too much food for their immediate desire and yet placed themselves away from a reliable source of water, and carried with them not enough vessels to bear it. It is a scourge that remains to haunt us this day.

And yet Walker was not in the least fazed by this crisis and said calmly, did it go well? Do you need another night to complete your observations?

And the answer was yes. Then no, for a crisis loomed and he feared for his older friend. Then after a time of thought, yes again, for he was fully rested and strong again. And he had decided what to do next, and it was nothing really, just a concerted effort on his part that would yield the best outcome for both of them. He said,

Another night would be most welcome. And right now you should drink and drain the last of your water, and give me your skin. I see there is wood left so I will descend to the stream and drink hearty, and I will fill them both and return. And then we will talk about our lives and explore through the day.

And Stargazer raised his open palm in a very adult gesture that forestalled any objection, and pointed to Walker's skin. And the man finally drank, while thinking a phrase from one of his favorite stories. Confound this boy.

And when the sun had blazed not too much further along its arc he was back again and a dire crisis had turned back to leisure and adventure. Now they ate hearty and the boy reported his finding.

There is nothing to report on the great mystery itself, but from this new place I have sighted new stars with even smaller circles. I have not yet seen a circle complete, but I have a strong feeling that they are circles, for I feel the sky is always above the world and the thought of arched paths is uncomfortable. For the world I have seen is a place of smoothness and constant motion, and that would mean some sort of stopping and starting. Tonight I will confirm my observations and trace them again in memory, and give more attention to the South.

Walker was very impressed by this, because what he most secretly feared was that this wild little shaman would snap in some way and begin to deliver with complete certainty, some outlandish tale of reality. But the difference from his previous vantage point to this one surely must be subtle indeed, and he had reported a subtle result. It all still fit, and he followed the boy's working assumptions completely. It was a worthy endeavor, one in which he was proud to be taking part. He would have been glad enough for a fine adventure with a friend, and this seemed like much more.

And so as the elder he spoke first. He told the boy the tale of his life, and why he both hated and was drawn to this place time after time. He spoke of things he had even refrained from speaking to his love, for she loved him as she knew him, as he had long been. And finally he said, this is the last time he would ever come to this place, and yet he was glad to have come. And Stargazer held him for a long time in silence.

Then the boy told him of things he could see that others did not, and things he heard that others did not, and the Things and their playful games, and his own games. And the old man doubted them not, for it was finally clear that the boy was not merely 'older than his years' as others claimed. It was as if he had started life earlier in some other world.

And they explored the hilltop in late afternoon and took in the grand views, in thoughtful silence. And the South confirmed his finding over night and added to it a little, and this vigil was rested and meticulous. He slept himself twice through the night to ease the return journey.

Back in the village he embraced each of his parents the moment he sighted them, and they embraced him very tightly, for it had been his first long adventure away from them. And they both had secretly learned he and Walker had violated the hunter's rule, but it was less of an urgent concern these days, so they refrained from mentioning.

He resumed his daily schedule of appointments and volunteered for fire-watch, to the amazement of those who had posed that he had been suffering some sudden crisis and would soon veer off in a new direction. His study of the heavens had reached an impasse on four important points that he readily confided to Walker.

The first and foremost was the mystery of the arches in the sky and the little circles at the ears of the world. Walker had helped him confirm this and it was the greatest mystery of all.

The second and just as perplexing, was that the great herd actually moved faster than the sun, which still implied to him that it was closer somehow, though how could that even be possible, and he had fought the idea without success. His simplest notion had been that the herd was smallest individually, and therefore should be the most distant and the slowest to the point of not moving at all, anchored on the sky river. Then the sun and the bright ones moving along the herd as closer things, and finally Moon who raced through the sky, as closest.

And finally, the movement across day and night itself, which put the whole sky into motion. And with it the yearly wobble of Mr. Sun, which he dimly felt was related somehow, though no actual mechanism was apparent. He even remembered and mentioned his idea that the herd might be completely still and the whole world was spinning, to Walker's continued amazement. For in the end that was Stargazer's strangest idea of all, and yet it seemed slightly less strange than animals and people in the sky, or ancestors gazing down at them.

He had a broad and dense grid of sky memorized, and he found that vigils on the climbing stone every few days were sufficient to expand the grid and note a new band of fresh-seen stars after sunset. They were indeed all new. The crest he had cataloged before was still high in the sky and easily connected to it by the overhead path. The ears of the world remained as they had always been but every so often another would join the small circles in the slowslow nightly arc. He no longer felt he had to prove the herd moved faster than the sun with comparative measure. Its procession over time was very evident.

He felt that nothing about the sky was arbitrary, just smooth and ever moving in a way that he had yet to discover. He especially yearned for the full passage of a year, and he was always on the lookout for his own leading star, which was already appearing much further West after sunset. He knew now for certain it would disappear into day after a time, and if it emerged again after the passing of a year he would suddenly know that the great herd was one year wide. And only a small part of it was revealed in the night.

And such was his skill of observation as moons passed, that he could glance up in the evening as he went about his business, and note something new and file it away. The orange one had entered night after a long while and he was tracking it on its course and noting its shapes against the herd, day by day. The Moon's speedy flight and odd yet predictable shifting shadows were still a distraction he avoided, because he felt he possessed too few puzzle pieces.

———

A BETTER PANGOLIN

Not often does child's play change our perception of very nature of things, and bring something into play that challenges craft as it has been. And requires advanced problem solving. Stargazer had received such a challenge.

It was delivered by a boy of eight years. He called it a 'pangolin', from a game of that name. A hunting party in the South had encountered one of these docile creatures and witnessed its scaly defense from predators when it rolled itself tight into a ball. The men made sport with the creature for just a few moments, rolling it to each other until one caught it with the side of his foot and made it change direction.

When they returned to the village one of the men had the idea that if he could make a better pangolin, it could become a game that adults and children could play. He took a roundish river stone and applied grass weaves around it, trying to keep the stone in the middle until it was padded on all sides, in more or less the shape of a ball. He had applied narrow strips of weave with some success, but the challenge had been that in play the stone would shift within the weave, resulting in a ball that had started to unfurl or hopped along its path.

There were other games of throwing coordination that were played with ripe fruits and even dried gourds that had been carved into a more perfect shape and reinforced, yet they remained fragile. But pangolin was a rigorous kicking sport and was quickly coming into vogue.

And sometimes one would take this uneven balance strategy into account and deliver a kick to its heaviest side to get it to do some specific thing, and received a sore foot for their trouble. The one who presented it to him was limping from such an attempt. Can you make a better? He asked. Stargazer was enthralled by the challenge.

He decided the use of a stone in its center was the biggest problem, for a usable ball could be made much lighter and tighter if it was wound from something besides a stone. The village had a boneyard where members had collected cleaned animal bones they had hunted or found, and there were a few monkey skulls in the pile. A monkey skull was only approximately rounded, and he applied single strands of wet grass in weave with each end twisted onto another and held in place by the next go-round, until he had a constructed a spherical shape of grass around the skull.

He pressed wet mud into it and dried it by the fire, and at last had a compact spherical form he could roll back and forth. It was light and did not hop too much when it rolled, so now his challenge was to add at least a hand of radius to it, keeping what weight it had in the very center. He used the green tubular reeds that grew by the river and wove circles that anchored to the adjacent ones, rotated around the form and it grew it from the center in equal measure.

Now he had something big and light and suitable for play, but an outer layer of skin was called for to seal in the weave completely and spring back slightly when it was kicked. With light skin sections of several necks of deer and thorns poking holes at the boundaries, pushing sinew through them and pulling tight and squeezed flat, he at last had a spherical ball with very slight protrusions.

His first attempt was not quite spherical enough with only four skin sections. But then he standardized on a skin shape that was pointed at the top and bottom and wide in the middle, such that eight stitched pieces would cover its surface with no gaps. It was a lot of stitching but the result was perfect. Another technique was to cut flat pieces into interlocking rounded shapes that minimized deformation along their edges. Or his favorite extreme design where fewer larger pieces of skin could be given patches of horizontal and vertical slits that stretched over the spherical surface easily and it left some of the weave underneath exposed, but it still rolled well and was secure.

This elevated the level of skill as players developed new strategies for capturing and moving the ball in play with feet alone, and delivering the final kick to the goal for the team, which was a between a couple of stones on either side of the field. By spacing out more goals along a large circle several teams could play at once. Dyed scarves identified the players.

It was light enough that even a sideways or angled kick could easily outrun other players and score a goal. And the ease of this and their prowess with the ball brought into play a strategy of players on the team whose duty it was to linger near opposing teams' goals.

Such was the novelty of pangolin, its evolved rules and simplicity of play, interest by children and adults who could often engage with comparable skill... visitors placed orders for skull-balls on the spot to bring back to their villages. A new industry was formed in the communities of the river and lands beyond.

In place of an off-balance monkey skull, the skull of any small animal could be chipped to remove pointed edges, brushed with hot glue made from tree sap and ground bones, and fitted with other skull fragments until a rough but more uniform spherical shape was achieved, to be wrapped and mud-treated into a smooth core that was tested for its ability to roll smoothly and straight. Then outer wrapped to the desired size, the weave painted thinly with glue to repel moisture, fitted with slotted stretchable skins and the sinew stitches sealed with glue. But some still called them monkey-skull pangolins in honor of the prototypes.

Over just a few moons people had begun to travel between villages for a new purpose, teams heading to and from pangolin tournaments.

There were still contests of personal skill, but a new niche was opened where game play was extended and watchers could easily track the ball among players. Individuals were not stressed with tense moments where they must perform and best others. It was a very social event of no hushes and a constant stream of boisterous noise and banter between players and audience.

———

AS THE PANGOLIN TURNS

Stargazer was lauded as a skilled technician by the players and participants in the new industry, and peers were well aware of his quirks. Even a lack of personal interest in a popular sport he alone had transformed. But at times he could still surprise them with bouts of oddness.

They encountered him one morning on the playing field with a couple pangolins, and one of them was spinning wildly from a well placed kick as he had seen others do, or had been put into motion with his hands. It spun quickly and wandered around the ground slowly on the unequal footing provided around its axis.

It was all eerie in a way that had made him shudder. The rotational axis of the spinning pangolin had ears! Regions at the poles where the texture could be seen to describe slow small circles, a spinning equator that was a blur of more or less straight movement, and evenly spaced zones between that were a smooth mixture of the phenomena to varying degree.

It was trivial to see that any rotation would introduce simple cycles, such as the nearby pangolin standing still, if viewed from the equator of the spinning one, would only 'seem' to be rotating around it. But something gripped him about this and gripped hard. In trying to design a better spherical ball he had wrestled with the materials challenges and had spent a long time with thorn and sinew, just as ancient Greek philosophers later cherished their model 'perfect solids' and placed them on desk and papyrus, tracing their shapes or rolled paths and wondering about the universe.

Motion along curves had always been a sublime mystery to him, used as he was to polygons connecting his parallax views of points and solids in space. But he had adapted with a new form of model in his mind that was based on slow steps. It had been easy to perceive that the tip of the thorn resting on the ball's surface could only 'see' a tiny circular area around it. Its vision was straight but the surface dropped away below its tiny horizon. And when it was raised up it could 'see' a much larger circular region of the ball and what was beyond in the ball's sky.

He had an empirical proof in his mind that by raising himself up to the high place, he had seen stars at the ears move a bit further along their paths. And he had even glimpsed new ones in smaller paths.

He knew that people had migrated great distances in the world but where ever they went, aside from local obstructions they were always presented with a circular field of vision and a circular sky, as he was. And something flipped over in his mind on that day. That the world was a spinning ball if such is possible, was much more likely than some grand celestial ballet of objects that happened to be spinning around it. That is, IF he could fit all his observations into practice.

The universe had done Stargazer a kindness. Not just by positioning him near the equator which offered a viewpoint that showcased modes of spherical motion. It was also the fact that Stargazer had not investigated and become obsessed with the physics of centripetal motion, as later natural philosophers had become. It exists on all scales. The very same force that would fling kids off a merry-go-round would surely fling people and animals off a rotating planet, they felt they knew with complete certainty, and it trapped their thinking.

Therefore the Earth must be absurdly and completely still, and the universe itself must be in complicated motion that strained belief and defied all practical attempts at modeling, with any in that universe hanging on for dear life or anchored in place by that same force on the side that faced us. This became the orthodoxy.

So ignorance of gravitational attraction between the centers of masses and the very specific case of the mass of a person versus the mass of a planet. Or even a subtle difference in static charge between a dust mote and a spinning tennis ball, anchoring the mote to it in the ball's flight. These remained unknown until people became very clever and observed well.

So after a short lifetime of mental tool-building, one eventful day of thought was all it took to fit almost everything into place. Day and night were cyclical, so there must be some fast circular motion governing it. The year was cyclical also, but its period was so different there must be a separate motion describing it, yet he knew it must be a circular 'something-or-other'.

Ironically, it was the wandering motion of the spinning ball on the ground that resolved his greatest paradox of all, that the great herd seemed to be moving a little faster than the sun. For he was operating on mental snapshots of imagination where everything would be frozen in time while he literally 'ray-traced' from the surface of the ball to some feature around the playing field, features that collectively represented the herd.

If the spinning ball was itself also rotating around the other, perhaps in a grand movement so slow as to represent a year's travel... a tiny new slice of the herd would be revealed with every new day-rotation as it circled around the other. This would mean that the herd was not actually moving faster than the sun, but the world was. And the great herd was perfectly still and very distant. And the sun may be still also, yet much nearer.

And the ears of the world were revealed to him, as a distant great herd object could be a bird hovering in the sky looking down upon the axis of the spinning ball. From the observer at the ball's equator looking sideways across the land at the bird, the bird would always appear to be making perfect circles that were small and slow, moving with the ball's spinning day.

And finally, after a long period of ignoring it altogether, Stargazer attacked the Moon suddenly and solved him. For all his speedy wandering Moon was always seen as about the same size as the sun, and yet he was cyclical in a much briefer cycle, ever beginning his cycle again after a month. So his circle could only be around the world itself, and he was much closer.

And now only Moon's shifting crescent and straight shadows remained as a mystery. But. If all his light was gathered from the sun and reflected to us and he was a ball too, his crescent shadows could be the angles between the observer, himself and Mr. Sun. When you saw his shadow traced vertically down his middle, it meant he was beside us and we were seeing directly across the curve of his surface and the parts of him light can and cannot reach. A round stone on the ground placed next to his spinning world revealed this clearly when he saw its own light and shadow in the direct morning light.

Stargazer was silently floored by all this. He forced himself to meticulously re-think everything through that day because the rolling epiphanies made it seem like something awful was happening to him, rather than some unfolding realization he was having.

So for awhile the anxious feeling even got worse when he unexpectedly decoded the yearly wobble of Mr. Sun also. To suddenly have a firm idea about something that had troubled him for so long, seemed like an ominous artifact of the mind.

But he had struggled to find the perfect axis of rotation for the ball on the ground that would place its rotating top still and immobile on the surface. And found that he could not in any practical sense. It was always tilted a bit and wandering around, and the blur of a straight equator was always shifting, and the hypothetical observer on its surface was always rising up one end and falling on the other with each spin.

But he was perverse also, so when he mentally lifted the ball from the ground to remove the annoying effect of friction against its surface, he kept it spinning on a slightly tilted axis as it rotated his hypothetical sun. It was a simple exercise of imagining some new annoying perversity to feed sarcasm. The spirits will like this, he thought. And the very stability of its course over his mental year hit him suddenly. Because of the tilt, the observer was often seeing Mr. Sun appear and disappear from different angles. And they were slight. And only when the tilted world was beside the sun would it appear to rise and set in the exact middle. In other parts of the year its rise and set points would continue to trace out a wandering course between two nearby places.

As actually happens!

With the herd-moving-faster paradox resolved, he felt he was once more on a solid ground of reasoning. The great herd was still because they were very tiny and very distant. Sun was much closer and whether he too was still was impossible to determine with the cloaking effect of his light. But he was likely still to a great degree, for the passing of a year was very stable.

Moon was very big and close and circled the world. And the other bright ones that wandered in the sky were much more distant, yet still moved against the herd so they could not be very distant after all. And maybe their light came from the sun also.

And the world was spinning quickly, and it was tilted a bit on its axis, and revolved around Mr. Sun. And that had been stable over years uncounted.

And finally he wondered aloud what they were, and the Things who had been with him all through this day of great thrills, spoke aloud as one in his mind. They were shrill with excitement, for they had discussed that very thing among themselves.

The Great Herd are all other, distant suns. Mr. Sun is a big deal to us, but he is also their child and descendant. And this greater world of sky is larger than any story has ever imagined!

———

BRAVE HELIOS, WAKE UP YOUR STEEDS

Walker was blown away when Stargazer approached him that evening and after a polite greeting and a bit of small talk, proceeded to describe and diagram the known part of the heliocentric solar system.

So the world spun, in two ways at once! It seemed a bit disorienting but he grasped the reasoning behind it and accepted it, including the bizarre transformation of a pangolin ball into a very model of the world. And why should it not be that simple? Must everything always be cloaked in mysticism and story? He was reminded of one of Stargazer's early pronouncements that was confusing him then. The sky has no corners! And a shapeless timeless world had taken shape and was placed in time, and a valuable clue was the sky's path as viewed from the world. Walker finally said with admiration, So the sky as it is, tells us about the world as it is. And Stargazer nodded and embraced his friend.

Walker reveled that Moon's shifting garments could have such a simple explanation that was clear and concise at first hearing, after decades of subtle and spicy drama that had him shucking and donning his clothing as he spotted loose mortal women in oestrus and they bore him children after a night of celebration. He was that Moon also, and so Mr. Sun it was who managed his wardrobe and illuminated his raiment for all to see.

Stargazer was in a better mood than Walker had ever seen him, so heavy had the quest been on his shoulders. And he reported that lately the bright orange one was as bright as it had ever been, and everyone was telling stories about him. And the boy's confusion was evident when he said its motion relative to the herd was slowing, and soon might even stop still! This troubled him because he now firmly believed nothing in the sky ever slowed or actually stopped. Either ever still or always in motion he said.

Walker suggested, perhaps if you place yourself in front of the goal and start intercepting pangolins, you will gather enough to riddle out this latest mystery! And I am sure all the teams will eagerly await your results!

And Stargazer smiled and said to him, it seems even your jokes have good ideas in them. If you could father children with jokes, half the children in the village would be laughing with you and the other half would just think you were saying outlandish things!

THE PANGOLIN AS MATCHMAKER

Stargazer attended the evening tales around the fire with a light heart. He had concluded the major part of his investigation without standing on the climbing stone and announcing his findings, which was just as well, for it would have made a poor story anyway. But he had ended the solitary and thoughtful interlude that had him sleep-walking through the day, and had rejoined the social order around him. And his peers were happy to see his old self and happy that he had resolved what ever crisis he had faced, because they loved him.

He was now awaiting the completion of a whole year since its beginning, which was near by, and was hoping beyond hope that he would see his own star re-emerge from the mountain to confirm the passing of the year and bring certainty to his measure of the herd. He reluctantly held on to a bit of doubt in case all was proven wrong, but the Things were in complete agreement that it must be so, and their certainty brought warmth to his mind and helped calm his anxiety. So he just waited patiently.

And there was even speculation among several girls of the village that he might turn out to be a grand prize indeed, if one could manage to stir him. His voice had changed but there was still no hint of restlessness in him, so they concluded he was a still a bit young and they turned their attention to other targets in the meantime.

And there was no shortage of targets. For the sport of pangolin had changed the social order of the time in a way that was welcomed by all. People had been settled in communities up and down the river for generations now but aside from regular trade and the visiting of relatives, at any one time there had been few individuals or groups on the move.

But the groups engaged with the sport had not just fostered community pride and the desire to show their prowess and best other communities. Girls and boys had formed separate young touring teams, not at all from any perception of difference or skill, but by mutual agreement because they had all convinced one another with a smile and a wink that there was much more to the game than fun play.

Village children tended to feel like close cousins, and in fact they often had been in the past, as the opportunities to encounter others from neighboring villages had been few and far between. There had always been an undercurrent of intrigue and tension if older boys or girls were traveling in the company of elders and stayed in the village for several nights. They might find themselves subject to a bit of planned conspiracy and no small amount of matchmaking, and these encounters sometimes blossomed into young love.

There was an established tradition where young lovers in courtship between villages would decide by themselves who would bear the burden of separating from their own parents, and the other would put out quiet word in the other village to find one who secretly desired adventure and new opportunities for love. This was a known possible outcome for parents everywhere, and it was a bittersweet parting with less sadness if the village was nearby. And the exchange-child would meet with the young lover in strict confidence to discuss this, so that all would announce their intentions at the same time.

So to the great puzzlement of adults, it often turned out to be a mutual exchange of children between villages. The heartbreak of parents was shared by both and to replace one's own lost child there was an opportunity to adopt another who needed to learn the customs of the village and build a good life of their own. The population of both villages remained the same. And the exchange would end with a child from the other village arriving at the doorway of grieving parents in the evening saying, may I? And the ritual asking could be answered as yes, for always and ever.

And the village children would take in the new one with unbridled enthusiasm, knowing that they had taken part in a secret equation that had brought joy and happiness to one of their own. And between villages lovers always maintained the direct bond of brotherhood and sisterhood with their partners in exchange, for life.

But the pangolin had brought an exciting new pageantry and a measure of pomp to the duller circumstance of their lives. The tables had turned and now there were many older children traveling between villages in the company of fewer adults. And it just so happened that pangolin tournaments extended to several days each, so players could rest up between matches and put forth their best performance. But of course. And visiting teams gathered at night in the places of fire-watches, and there were many comings and goings, not all of them to borrow and bestow fire. While adults kept score and coached their members to athletic greatness, tallied between team and village, there were unexpected new currents of teenage excitement flowing up and downriver.

Home and visiting teams arrived for each game clothed in matching outfits with a team symbol and specific colors of natural dye. And adults who preached the sameness of girls and boys in contest were tolerated by the younger with understanding and affection, for their only true fault was that they were a bit dull-witted. For each game was actually a pageant to see potential mates in action, and not some iteration of age-old gender conflict for the boorish to declare winners and losers.

This related to the ancient declaration that the menses and the hunt must never be placed within any hierarchy where one was over the other. Which also meant that either would never be denied to the other as women proved their hunting skill to men, or men proved their menses or child-raising expertise to women. It may seem women got the better deal, but men applauded this also.

But also, the speed and agility of players at peak performance often resulted in violent contact and injury between them, which always resulted in a ritual apology and embrace between games. And the players of each team and audience simply never wished to witness that between girls and boys. It would be unfair to both of them in the circumstance of that tragic meeting, and none would be well-represented. And it would just feed the opinions of the dull and boorish, and not properly guarantee the safety of players from undeserved personal shame and anguish, among other things.

So in every audience there were ones who were admiring prowess and fitness in the sport and gathering strategy they could use. And there were others admiring prowess and deciding potential fitness for the greatest sport of all. And they might choose to approach a player and seek a private match of their own in earnest, for it was a noble sport where both may become winners.

Such was the power of the pangolin in their lives that none had foreseen.

And the young Stargazer had touched it all off and maintained a small interest in it, and yet he would one day benefit in a way he could never have foreseen.

———

THE WANDERER AND THE WALKER

It was like any other night for everyone else, but over the course of two moons he had seen the likely become the certain, and the improbable become the impossibly true.

It had begun with the jubilant sighting of his own leading star recently risen, and he now saw it among its companions in the precise and perfect remembered configuration as they had risen together a year ago. He ascended the climbing stone and admired them as they rose.

Then in the desert he was at last able to connect his figures end to end. He connected the ending of the figure with his own star to its deeply remembered beginning with a long crude stroke, and it annoyed him, for his flat representation of everything had caused nothing but trouble and such difficult markings at the ears of the world. But this was even worse! So untidy! He would soon remedy that.

So he tried to lift the whole floor of the desert and curve it into its true spherical shape so he could plant the sun and his own small world inside it, but what lifted off the ground was a large dark shape that carried away all the markings and was the deep black of sleep.

And he felt a sudden warmth but it was not sleep chasing him after all, for both Things carrying sticks sprung from both sides of him suddenly and started beating him on the head with them.

You must not do that! Stop now! They cried. He put away the dark shape with some effort and the desert brightened and markings reappeared. We tried to do something like that once but we were smarter about it, or so it seems, for we stopped trying sooner than you! You will fry your brain or your brain will become a happy little boiled vegetable, just to please you! It just wants to do your bidding and it will destroy itself trying.

Or so we think!

Good thing we were here. Shall we hit you some more?

And he smiled at them, crossed his stick with theirs and they danced around each other and fenced for awhile. It was like old times. Then

214

the Things bowed in unison, each holding a stick sideways with both hands, and disappeared. He smiled.

But he would have erupted into tears and wailing sorrow had he known it was the last time he would ever see their beautiful faces. Which were now each distinct, and no longer his.

So rather than doing any dangerous transformation that would tax a supercomputer, he awoke and revisited the last crest of star-shapes before the year-connection completed it, and when he saw it was firmly attached to the beginning, he slept himself again. And traced it in the desert with a flourish, and walked his crude mark back and forth just as he had first explored distance so long ago. So this is a good measure of a year by world and star, he thought. He would keep the ugly mark, for now he loved it after realizing what it really was. And he would keep his brain too and cherish the marked desert for as long as it lasted, like the happy little vegetable he was.

Walker was glad for him again once more, and when Stargazer reported his other news, Walker once again proved himself a most worthy fellow observer, even as he had only ever observed by proxy. And he summed it all up after he sat in a long silence. His eyes were closed most of the time as if he could sleep sitting down.

So, Walker finally said. You now know that the sky moves forever only because the world moves forever and the same distant sky appears after a year. And the sun moves forever also, but only to our eyes from our spinning and circling world. And you have posed to me that the bright one near the sun who courts him and ever lingers near might be another world like ours, spinning or no, who yet circles him and is bathed in his light. And her circle is much smaller than ours which is why to us, she stays near to him.

And now you feel shocked and spooked that everything is somehow called into question, because you have seen the orange one slow down and stop moving against the great herd? You know, the same great herd that is actually always moving but you have stilled it completely in your mind, by power of thought alone?

Consult your pangolins, friend. I have done so in the muddy river that is my own mind. If all worlds circle with a speed around the sun, which seems to have captured them somehow, then the orange one whose movement seems strange to us might be traveling a larger circle than our world. Think of how long it takes to pace around a circle. The circle he is pacing has many more steps than ours. It may be possible that all these worlds were started in the same motion by the same hand, or nearly so. And what will happen as our world with its shorter path begins to overtake him? How would that appear? And how would it appear after? This is a puzzle of eyes spinning on inner pangolins and circles within circles.

And Walker fell silent once more, because he knew the younger could make fantastic shapes in his mind and make things run slow or fast with equal skill. He felt privileged and honored to know such a person, and was especially happy to know that this beautiful young one was also humble and kind. What amazing times!

And Stargazer finally opened his eyes and said in wonder, he will slow to our eyes. Then appear to stop. Then reverse his course. Then stop and resume his original path. Because all the time we are moving and he is moving. That is the world and the sky, and it is certain!

Stargazer embraced his oldest youngest friend in tears and laughter both, and they held each other a long time. For the last time.

It was a year of bitter partings and new beginnings.

THE WALKER AND THE WANDERER

Stargazer glimpsed the orange wanderer and was sure he began to see the shapes begin to shift once again. He ascended the stone to see it away from bothersome lights, and smiled. There was a tiny star near to it and that tiniest difference of distance revealed its new motion quite clearly. He descended and rejoined the community fire.

It was a lull between stories, and a runner approached the gathering and passed to the middle in front of the fire, and held up her hand. She spoke loudly with difficulty and was crying.

Our own dearest Walker has passed to the realm of the spirits, quietly in his sleep. Please, let only two come with me to keep the family company through the long night. He will sleep in his own bed this night, and we will all approach the house to lay him to rest at sunrise. Then with a racking sob she said, remember him. In story.

Waves of wails and sorrow passed through the crowd, young and old, and people embraced. Stargazer was overcome with grief and cried with them, but a growing whisper in his mind stilled him by asking, what to do next. And it offered a suggestion, and it was a good suggestion, and time was short and he must begin. And it would take a great deal of effort, especially now.

He gathered himself quickly and walked in front of the fire, and with tears streaming from his eyes, he faced the crowd and raised his head to them, and held his hands behind him towards the fire.

And they paused in wonder and curiosity because he had not once ever done this, and they recognized him quickly for his face was adamant and he was the first to ask. And the boy projected his voice loudly as he spoke.

I will tell now tell a long tale of Groll, for that is also the Walker we know, and some among you or at his house may know it, but may I speak on his behalf and beg forgiveness if any did not know it, for it was the name he left behind in despair and sadness, and he took the name Walker as he was a young man and he wandered, for since we have known him and even before, he has had no family or close kin remaining in this land.

They were all paying attention now and fixed on him. Some had indeed heard that name. Stargazer had dreaded so many eyes on him at first but they were kind and sad eyes, and as time went on he found it easier to speak to them.

He told the tale of the two young hunters who had once fancied to bring home an ibex, which lured them onto the mountain and a high place of great terror and peril, which ended as the older brother and their prey fell. This ever so briefly touched on what Walker had once said, that some wondered if it was the same tale. But it was not exactly. Walker had mentioned the tragedy only in passing and it involved someone long ago. This tale had far more detail and riveted them, for it was well told nonetheless. They loved Stargazer and respected him, so they did not even consider that he might be re-telling Walker's tale and adding his own fiction to it in some simple conceit, surely not at a time like this.

And as the younger was left in that high place alone and he wailed in despair, Stargazer identified the younger by name as Groll for the first time. And but a few finally knew for certain that this was a tale of Walker's own past that he had told to the boy, for they knew of the close friendship between them.

But of what Stargazer knew, that was just the beginning. He continued.

Groll wandered alone on the mountain for the better part of two days in complete denial and moments of delirious fancy, that Grale would suddenly return and offer his hand and say, come with me brother and we shall claim our prize! It was almost a whole day before he could bring himself to step part way into that terrible bloody place and look down, and all he saw below was a tilted cliff face with another spot of blood on it. They were below that somewhere, fallen perhaps even into the valley beneath.

He spent that night and the next whimpering and nibbling through the food and briefest sips of water to its end and he was of course unable to start a fire at their camp spot, which had become dear to him as he re-lived their night together and even faithfully slapped the air that once held his brother's back and he re-told their jokes, hoping against hope that his supreme effort would roll back time to that moment and he could give his brother fair warning. He fell asleep in his and his brother's furs, and they brought him to tears also.

For he blamed himself now for everything that had happened, from his assent to the hunt to the giving of his spear instead of throwing it off the mountain to the final moment of release of his hand on the horn. It was a perfect storm of blame and it broke his heart savagely.

And on the final afternoon he hiked again to the terrible place and looked once more for his brother, and this time he was brought to helpless despair by the sight of their foot coverings. And there was still strength in him, for he gathered them and put his on, returned to the campsite and he decided to leave his brother's furs and foot coverings there for when he returned. For even with that deceit a small part of him wished to survive, and he finally left then only because the last words he remembered were, Let go! Or it will take you! And now that meant the mountain itself.

He hated that mountain and would not let it have him also.

He scrambled down the crack somehow and after an endless downhill torment his face hit the cold stream and he drank greedily. And again without noting his surroundings he stumbled down and out and across the land and took a wrong turn at the river, but his senses returned after sleep and a drink in the dead of night, and the morning's glimpse of the mountains revealed his error.

He turned around and backtracked until he spotted familiar terrain. On the fifth day after they had left he wandered into camp scratched and bloody and reunited with his family, and he babbled the tale. No one presently there knew of the high place or could draw clues from his words. It was obvious that something terrible and final had happened and they knew Grale would surely die before leaving his brother in the wild, and so they mourned for Grale.

His parents consoled him and rocked him past nightmares, and they ignored his pleas to help him find his brother, for they knew that Grale's bones would never console him either. He grew to become a young man racked with guilt and his parents did their best, even as he became moody and misbehaved, and was prone to sudden fits of anger. And almost ten years passed and the drought and the famine we all remember from tales set in.

Our own community was more populous than theirs and yet we scarcely had enough people to forage and stretch food to the end of it. And they were a proud people and few and they were hunters, so it is not surprising that those among them with greatest foresight made a firm decision to migrate North while they could, almost a year before some of us resolved to do so. Both of Groll's parents died suddenly with two others from bad food or some poisonous plant, and he was taken in by an uncle, for his own empty house was full of sorrow he could not bear.

When the briefest mention was made of an ibex hunt to sustain them, Groll seized on the idea with demented resolve, for it was a chance to redeem himself and wear the shoes of his brother and return with the prize at last, and the part of his mind that was still a terrified child whispered to him that he would return with his brother also and all would be forgotten. But none would hunt with him, and the idea was abandoned anyway as too risky and not at all assured, for no ibex had been sighted recently. It was far better for them to strike out and hope for more sustaining lands along the way, or fish from the river. So they resolved to leave.

And on the day of their leaving, Groll came to blows with his uncle who had been imploring him to come, but he irrationally felt he was abandoning Grale and refused, and he left his uncle unconscious and stalked off into the wild to find his brother. And as he did he felt a lightness to his steps, for as a man he had resolved to make this journey but the child in him had delayed it. But the years had clouded his memory. He knew ways to catch fish in the river for that had been his parents' specialty and they had taught him, and he was a doughty and capable woodsman and he was obsessed, so he searched for two full tendays without finding the place or his brother, before he returned to camp.

And of course everyone was long gone and his tiny village was empty. He later supposed that his stern uncle had probably insisted they all wait for several days, and before long almost came to blows himself with others. But perhaps his wife finally convinced him to leave with them, for Groll knew he loved her and was afraid because she was frail, and survival for them all had become so dear.

Once again little Groll had been left alone in the world. And that proved to be too much for him. So he died on that day, and Walker was born.

Walker maintained his quest and at last found the crack and the high place by sheer perseverance and a few recalled clues, and by following every cliff up the hills until he encountered the crack directly and not via the stream. He ascended and stood in the terrible place again, and the blood had long been washed away by rain and yet he was able to gaze down at the valley with a more mature eye, spotting landmarks and hints to the way below. But he never spotted an ibex and was reminded of his people's wise decision that he had flatly rejected. And he felt sad for them putting up with him, and at last he wished them well.

Then with a woodsman's resolve to survive he descended again to the stream and noted for the first time the three stones Grale had been watching for, and he faced them as he apologized to Grale for the act of turning his life into such a hopeless mess and failure. His guilt knew no bounds and he now blamed himself for not fishing for his parents when they had grown weak with hunger, and hitting his uncle. Such a worthless self-centered idiot he had become! Then he headed for the river to replenish his own cursed strength.

And resumed his quest and at last noted the landmarks he had seen from above and found his brother, and their prey. They were just disconnected bones cleaned by carrion birds and insects, and they were laid out almost as they had been in life, with no sign that any four-legged predator had ever found them. His brother's head was broken in back, probably in the fall. He carried his brother's remains down from the low cliff and he dug a grave in the soil with a sharp stick and scooping it out with his hands, and finally laid his brother to rest.

But the child within him screamed in agony every time he even thought of tossing the first handful of dirt into the grave. His brother's vacant eyes were looking at him, but not in any accusing manner, for that was not the way of his dear brother. But he stared imploringly, as if he did not want them to part after waiting so many years for the younger to return.

So Walker of no-people did something that some would find distasteful and abominable. He took his brother's imploring stare into his hands and cradled it like a baby, and kissed it. And tucked it into his pack. And because his sweet brother had no need for them any more, he buried the rest. And ascended the cliff to fetch the skull and horns of their prey.

And he made up a little story for curious people he met to hide his own shame from himself. And for the rest of his life he was never separated again from his Grale. And from atop his own head Grale watched over him and stared down any predators stalking him from behind, just as he would have gladly done in life. He was the Walker you knew. Always fighting spirits he had created in his own head, but a very capable and good man to the very end. And he wanted to keep the promise he had made to his brother, that they would be buried together. No, he once said in jest, this is not my father.

The only reason I have spoken tonight and the only reason I have told his secret, it is important that the brothers must be laid to rest together as one, and I implore you to help me send both Groll and Grale to the spirit world as brothers and under their true names.

And as you all know, I have been watching the stars and the bright ones in their midst. And lately I have been following the bright orange hunter in his very slow journey across the sky night by night. And for days he has been paused in his journey, and today he looks to be starting to move slowly backwards along his path. That is because... he sobbed.

Stargazer felt Walker whisper in his ear. Or was it a Thing?

He choked again with emotion. It is because a great hunter who once boasted that he was two men is finally about to leave the world after waiting so many years. And his little brother, a great hunter who was two men in real life, was fading yesterday. Two brothers wish to rise together in the sky. So as both men are two, it is a true hunter's complement and the orange one is moving backwards on his path to gather them. And they will all hunt the great herd together.

Let us lay them to rest in our world tomorrow morning and wish them good journeys, brothers Grale and Groll. And Walker, my friend.

He stepped forward and sat down, and as he cried viciously with his eyes shut someone sat on his lap and embraced him. Her voice and hands were soft and she murmured as she stroked him gently. He opened his eyes slightly and saw a blurry dark blue shape with a crescent Moon in front of him. And his grief resumed in spasms and she stayed with him until it was quiet again. And he dared not move or open his eyes for a long while, for he would start again. She left him with a final caress. And later he was off with the men and helped them dig a grave by starlight.

THE PANGOLIN AS SAVIOR

As the first beam of sun illuminated the world, the headdress that had been watching over the family was disassembled, and the Silent Companion was gently taken out and wrapped. And the deer bones and ibex skull and horns were wrapped separately. And Walker was wrapped and borne out of the house he had settled in and loved, and a slow procession followed him to the place of final keeping.

All in silence and without a word, for all the words had been spoken, he was laid to rest, and his brother's head was laid next to his, and their prey and the other bones were laid at his feet, and flowers were set on him with a tearful kiss by the ones who loved him still, and all of the weary hunters departed this world as its fertile soil covered them.

And somewhere unseen by day, the bright orange hunter gathered them.

He walked alone in thought for awhile.

Someone had approached quietly barefoot and was walking beside him.

You are Stargazer the weaver?

He recognized the voice. You have soft beautiful hands and a lovely voice, he said. I am sorry I was so overcome last night.

I have never heard such a story before, and such a great tribute to a departed friend. Every bit of it sounded true, as stories so seldom are. I know he loves you still and more than ever, and his brother loves you too. You did them well.

Stargazer had refrained from turning because a part of him was terrified that no one would be beside him. But he did turn, and she was there.

Taller than he, ever so female and amply curved. Kind eyes and a round face and short dark hair, and a loose shirt of soft leather with a brilliant dark blue square in the middle, pigment in solution applied to it with small brushes of straight animal hair. And on that a different pigment, an opaque bone-white crescent Moon and a few white stars. She had sturdy long legs that moved almost two paces with each slow step, and delicate feet.

This. Do you recognize it? And she reached around her back and brought out a faded woven grass pad of the same design.

He took it for a moment, and it was still warm from her. He turned it over to see the other side and remembered.

Yes I made that, it seems like ages ago. So it has become the sign of your team?

He offered it back to her. She took it slowly, while raking his open palms lightly with her fingertips.

We are the Lost Girls of the Moon and I started the team. The other is on the back. See? And she turned with a pivot and a flourish, and on the back was the same design in white and a blue crescent, and the blue stars were perfectly positioned.

He clapped his hands in delight. That is amazing!

She whirled again and faced him. So it is true that the orange hunter has reversed his course?

Yes. I do not know how often it happens, for I have just seen it for the first time. But I do know that he will keep that course for a while, then pause again and resume his journey.

And how do you know that, if you are seeing it for the first time?

She was fixing him with a little smile and an amused, very intelligent stare. He felt flustered for no reason. He took a breath and calmed his voice.

It is a long story. But I have discovered the shape of the world and that it turns, and the movements of the world around the one who brings daylight, and the journeys of the bright wandering ones. And the Moon and its shadows, and the many dim and still ones behind and far away. I am not certain what everything is, but I have ideas and know their movements.

And the movements of the little fishes in the river?

No not those. But it is a long story, and you will follow I am sure, if I have time enough to explain.

So then, tell me a long story. But now I have to start practice and the last game of the tournament in the afternoon. If you approach me when it is done and we are celebrating our win, will you feed me?

Yes. I will start catching little fishes in the river, for I remember their movements now.

She laughed and it was a musical sound. No fish if you please! We get too many where I am from. I heard someone brought in two large boars last night. That is what I crave, and some greens and tubers. And if you feed me I will follow you anywhere. Even onto the climbing rock and into the sky!

He looked at her keenly.

Yes I know your movements, or what the little ones have told me. I have been trying to find you, weaver of this Moon pad, and I had to form a pangolin team just to get the job done and scour the land! And it is a fine team. And they are the finest by the way, your pangolins. And the little ones are very sly here. They led me to the council fire and sat with me because I had been asking about you. When the awful news arrived they pointed you out as you stood up, and told the saddest truest story ever. And you were taken with emotion and went to sit, and they made room for you. And then the little foxes made silly excuses and peeled away out of sight. And I am thinking, he is in great need, and here I am sitting next to him! Where have I heard about that game before? But no worry. I would have stepped on their little heads to get to you anyway. I am Breeta. Breeta of the lake people with the soft beautiful hands. See you tonight!

And she was off like a fox herself leaping in bounds, almost five paces a stride. And he was left with her memory, and it was wild and strange and alluring, and he would see her that night.

His regular rounds took him past the fire pit and he saw the boars. There was even a third. Runners had been sent back to gather more people to carry them all, and it was so satisfying that all burst into song as they carried them into camp, the boars hanging by the legs on a stick borne on several shoulders. They had been well fed and were tremendous in size. They were being roasted in a giant hollow on strong sharp sticks that had been run through them, and baskets of water and spice were being dipped with grass brooms and applied to the flesh. Everyone would eat well tonight.

And when they spotted Stargazer he was hailed as a celebrity, for Walker was a main topic of the day's conversation and eyes had not dried yet. So when he asked that a good cut of meat be set aside for him and his family that he would gather later, there were nods and smiles all around. But like the plain spoken boy he was, he also added casually that there was this girl he wanted to impress, and she had asked him to feed her. This caused quite a row with raised eyebrows, and several men and women gathered in conference and finally announced, shoulders you shall have! They will be cooked but you can apply a bit of flame and spice them to your liking.

There was also a savory soup of tubers, beans, peas in a meat broth that was being prepared for the feast in bulk, at another place. And he gathered some loose crunchy greens and soft edible leaves, some that had been destined for the soup. And finally some delicate sweet fruits as appetizers.

Stargazer was fascinated by the precision, choreography and regimentation of organized sport. But mostly he had been watching her. She was dance in motion, going at a run and then bounding, bouncing, stopping and twirling. Leaning into other players to keep them away as she was controlling the ball and changing its direction.

The final round of the tournament was two well matched visiting teams, and they had equal scores when a runner arrived from the climbing stone to signal that the sun had disappeared behind the hills. The next goal would declare the winner. But attempted goals were intercepted well and play continued into twilight.

But then someone kicked the ball to Breeta, who stopped it with her foot. Their goal was blocked by one standing in the middle and two others were running to help, and Breeta took several steps back for what looked like a dramatic lineup for a straight kick, and he could see that the line from her to the ball to the goal was aimed on its right side. The other saw this also and drifted a little to the right, but her connect sent it on a different course altogether, with incredible speed. It passed just within the left stone and she jumped in celebration with the others.

———

AFTERPARTY

The spectators and all the players flowed together and there were was congratulations and conversations and some embracing. He stopped close by, reluctant to approach because the exuberance was overwhelming, and after watching the game for so long it seemed like everything happening was part of some choreographed ritual. His eyes were ever on her and she stood apart from the rest and looked around. She was holding the ball and as she spotted him, she pointed to him and shouted,

I found him! I found him!

The meaning of this was apparently known to them, for the entire team of the Moon broke from the crowd running and surrounded him. Breeta stood in front of him and held up her Moon pad in one hand, and an animal-skull pangolin in the other. She declared, He is the one who wove this! But also, he is the one who designed this! Did I choose the right sign after all? Let us bathe him!

And Stargazer was grabbed all over and lifted over their shoulders, then suspended above them on the palms of their upraised hands, and the girls marched him from the playing field all the way to the bank of the river and set him down. Then they wiggled out of their shirts and skirts and short pants, and the stream of bodies began to enter the river.

You may bathe with me if you wish, Breeta said, standing by him smiling and beautifully nude. The custom is, winners bathe first and none may join us but the ones we carry. They have no choice. And it is very necessary to bathe. Shall I give proof?

And she raised an arm over his head gracefully with bent arms and extended fingers, and a sweaty hairy armpit was offered to his face. Stargazer dutifully leaned forward and inhaled deeply, and there were waves of laughter from the other bathers, for it was a fine joke to them.

But not to him. He said, I love your scent, and it excites me. If you let me sniff the other, I will follow you anywhere.

She beamed a smile and stretched legs and arms in an exaggerated athletic pose as she spun lightly and offered him the other armpit. He sampled it deeply also. This new development and the sight of him straightening up and nodding his approval of both of them, touched off another round of laughter and some whispers.

He disrobed and offered her his hand, and they stepped into the river together.

They squatted in the water facing and took turns bathing one other. He did not let his hands wander too far from the parts she had offered him, and she followed his lead and her hands touched him the same way. But there was still plenty to explore, and he cupped water and pressed it up under her arms, rinsing and tugging the hairs gently. He traced the curves of her neck and then between her breasts, giving them only the lightest of strokes, but his coverage was complete. She turned and he washed her back and he felt an involuntary shiver as his fingers traced her spine. But it was the wrong kind of excitement for the moment, and he raised his hands quickly to her shoulders and squeezed the muscles firmly as if to say, another time. And he ended with a soft slow stoke of his fingers across the width of her upper back. And he turned and she performed the same motions, and ended with the same stroke.

So this is what a promise feels like, he thought. His mind was reeling.

He straightened and stepped out of the cool water, grateful he was not presenting any added spectacle to the others. He dressed and stood with his back to the river as he waited. She joined him shortly, skin glistening in her bright uniform. She offered her hand as they waited for the others, and they squeezed hands in turn. Then the team followed them up the path in the twilight, in subdued but excited conversation.

On the journey he asked her, are you ready to eat? And she said of course, right away! She expected they would join the feast already in progress, or some cute and clumsy little picnic of his own, but she was surprised when they broke rank with the others heading to the fire-house. She waved goodbye to them with a smile and with raised eyebrows they waved back. He led her on a circuitous route through the village and through the doorway of his own house, where his parents were waiting.

He formally introduced them and Breeta received a warm embrace from his mother and a smiling wave from Father. Father had brought out the table surface and set it on its supports, a contraption of light straight young trees bound together tightly on cross members with rattan fibers, and he had rolled their hollow sitting-logs up to it. The table had been his own invention and could be stood up as a door if it should ever be necessary.

Mother had kept the food warm by holding it over the fire on pointed sticks and dropping cooking stones into the soup basket occasionally. There were rough hewn wooden bowls with drinking water in round gourds, bowls for soup meant to be raised to the lips, and flat and curved pieces of wood to set things on, some already with edible leaves and greens.

Stargazer bade them all sit, then began to load the table with glazed slabs of meat, poured soup, and there was a bowl of ground black peppercorns and most precious, a bowl of loose salt, the most trafficked item from the far South where it was mined from saline lakes. Breeta dipped into the salt when she spotted the bowl and consumed two pinches of it, for after the workout her body craved it.

She began to politely thank his mother for the meal, but his mother just pointed and said, Stargazer is the gatherer and cook of all this, and so many good things we have eaten, and you should have seen him fussing over this meal! Adding seasoning to soup and painting meat and touching it to flame. All I have provided is warm food and a warm welcome. You must be a very important person to him. You are his very first girlfriend I am sure, and I hope you will help him make up for lost time.

Breeta caught herself smiling as Stargazer complained, Oh mother! Must you be so plain spoken?

I learned it from you, dear.

Trying to change the subject, Stargazer asked, you lined up the kick to the right and sent it to the left. How often does that work?

She looked at him for a moment. Less and less. They call me The Twister now. I'll have to think up a dozen new things. There is a rule now that players can dive and let it bounce off any part of them but their hands. So you have to second guess them and drive it on the ground and fast.

Then his father took over and asked her things about boats and herd migration patterns in the South, and points of strategy in the game, and he admitted he had watched all the tournament games with interest. And not just the ones with the burly men! he said, looking at his wife.

I was sifting for new ideas, she replied. And then to Breeta, I like your outfit.

Breeta had an answer for this, but by now everyone had tasted everything and Stargazer sat himself down, and he alone ate silently while his parents lowered their eyebrows and gazed sternly at one another while murmuring and growling loudly through every bite, as cats do while eating to guard their own meal. Breeta found it hilarious and joined them. As her mouth was full and she chewed, she became the mighty lioness snarling at her own mate to keep him away from her choicest morsel. She snarled at his parents, they snarled back at her, and then they all turned and snarled at Stargazer through the food.

He smiled back at them and took it as a compliment.

Then they all took a drink of soup and fished pieces from it into the mouth with their fingers, and resumed conversation as if they had always been people. And Breeta grabbed another handful of greens and a pinch of salt. And showed his mother the pad he had made long ago, and told her how it had found its way to a far village by the lake, and held it up to her shirt.

At last Stargazer rose to clear away things, and his mother rose and pushed him down again. As she busied herself Breeta rose to help her and his father did also. Then when they were all done, the girl placed her hand on his mother's shoulder to get her attention and moved to stand in the open doorway.

With arms crossed in front and head slightly bowed, Breeta asked, may I?

And his mother turned to his father for a moment and held his hands, then turned back to her. And said, of course dear, you are very welcome. Always and ever.

And then they walked out into the night holding hands, laden because Breeta had said to him, bring plenty of water to drink. You are going to talk to me until you whimper like a frog. And I will croak to you also.

———

ON THE CLIMBING STONE

They sat facing in deep conversation, and now he was about to tell her the story of his life, for she had told him things about hers.

But first he must show her something. Anything!

As care free and wild and boisterous as she had seemed, she had told him a tale that frightened and moved him. As she recited it, the tale had captured her mood like a dark cloud and held it. In the end she said plainly that before she had found him, her whole life was poised on a cliff.

She had long watched the stars and other objects in the night sky and asked herself as a child, will I ever understand them some day? And she had so greatly desired to understand them, her dreams were captured by them, but as she grew with sameness around her she had to abandon that hope. She felt a growing despair replacing it, for she was in a place with people she loved dearly and they were comfortable and happy there, but she was not happy with the place. She hated the place and dreaded the life that was approaching her, even as she stood still.

She was not just a tomboy but a seasoned expert, could hunt and build boats and tame the wild like the best of them, was an excellent swimmer and could catch fish with her hands or baskets. And even navigate at night on land or water by the stars, and all considered her the perfect specimen of young womanhood, the model child, and some day the perfect mate. And she felt a burden of guilt, for they were all good people, and yet she felt empty inside.

And like a silly young child trapped in a dream, of all things, a little grass pad had spoken to her, and it had reminded her of whom she had once been. It had said simply, seek me, and find answers. And she had seized on the silly idea because a growing part of her felt like leaving everyone and walking into the wild aimlessly, and it was a gruesome and tragic idea, and that silliness was also the part of her that fought to survive.

She began to shape a new life around it, gathering every new thing that came to her into a plan of escape and survival. It was similar to Stargazer's own mantra of what to do next, but it was desperate and dangerous, for if anything to do next had failed completely she would have been in deepest peril.

The pad had come to her and became a sign. The pangolin had come to her and became a distant hope. A better pangolin had come to her and gave her a firm idea, and the sign became the team and then a regional sport, and at last she had a plan. And to put it into practice she had to become mother and manager and player and cheerleader to them all, and more of an athlete than she ever had been. And it came to fruition and every place she went she liked better than the one from which she had come, and that gave her hope.

And finally her very survival was assured because she knew she could settle anywhere else and find contentment, if not happiness.

And then I found you, she had said. It is a silly thing I know, but you are the weaver I had sought. If that weaver had been a woman I would have tried to love her completely, though I do not know how. I would have tried, and I might have failed and perished. But you are a man in wisdom and spirit, what ever clothes you wear today. You are smart and able and kind and you keep much hidden without trying to hide it, and even the young in the village watch you and know it, and they describe you with awe, and you are a worthy prize to me.

But not just. You brought me the sport itself and true escape, without even knowing me. How lucky am I?

But not just. Moments after we met, you said flatly you understood the movements of the sky, something even the wisest I have known dare not claim, which has been a dream of mine since childhood.

And tears had filled her eyes.

Please forgive me or rise up in anger that is rightfully yours! For you are too perfect, yet so much what I sought already, and I am prepared to love you as a man who is a perfect match and the greatest prize ever. I do not know why you mentioned the sky of all things. I am questioning my own sanity now! Because I am thinking, did I take leave of my senses in some doom of delirium long ago? Am I still sleeping by the lake? Will I awaken alone in the wild one final time, having done the deed and now laying still on the dreaming cusp of death? Have I been captured by an evil spirit that wishes to torment me? Am I even imagining the win today? See how deranged I am! This is my will to survive speaking! It is ugly and strong, I know. But it is all I have.

Please help me! If you do not know the movements of the sky after all, and made up an incredible story to impress a girl, well you have impressed her all right, maybe not in the way you intended. But if that is so, you must tell me now. And I will forgive you, and love you. It is your peril. It is mine also. Please!

And she was sobbing, and he took her into his arms, and yet she let herself be consoled by him only slightly. And he felt so deeply for her, it was the most awful and dangerous moment in his life.

It all hung on certainty. Was he really certain of anything, and not deranged himself in the same awful way that was her worst imagining? This was so bad, a moment of danger as big as the sky! For all he had to do was claim it was just a story he had made, a lie. And not a story that was not a lie like the orange hunter gathering Walker instead of circles within circles, for the orange hunter could be both, for all he knew.

And if she claimed she would love him if it was all just a story... could that not be... another story she needed to tell herself right now, to survive? Did her sanity doubt his sanity in a way that was secret to her? And then she would be gone, taking that horrible sadness with her?

He felt like he was falling from the high place.

Everything had gone so horribly wrong.

But you are certain, a voice said. Look at the sky. And he did.

What to do next.

Stargazer stoked her hair and said, You are beautiful and strong without measure and I love you. And I love your will to survive. That was so well spoken by you, by your intelligent and keen mind. It is you who are the greatest prize in all the world. You made the perfect kick today. It is all real. And I need you to enter slow-time with me, that is just to say, be very patient and hold back your fear for a while. Okay?

And she sniffed and nodded, and after a little while opened her eyes.

He said, let me show you something.

The year had recently turned over and the sky was full of remembered shapes, those he had been watching and then tracing furiously in the desert. A crest was now rising, one that he knew well and it was actually several crests together, from that early time he had intended to remember the whole sky. Shapes and lines extended below the mountains to dark spots beneath the tops, blacker than black, that were to him stars soon to emerge.

Stargazer was about to take the biggest gamble of his life. He was about to recite the sky before it happened. He maneuvered her gently with his hands and guided her legs to sit crossed on the stone in front of him, so he might lean over her back and embrace the top of her chest with an arm as he sat behind, and position his head over hers and point with the other arm, as her eyes aligned with his.

He pointed to a place on the dark mountain. The first one will emerge from here, from now in the time it took... for you to say, you are Stargazer the weaver? and when you ran off for practice.

And she still shuddered, but she was very patient, and waited, and it did. Its glow appeared first and soon became a glimmering star.

He said, the next two will come together, way over here.`After about the same time. The left will emerge first, and then after... as long as you were growling and snarling with food... there will be another glow and the right one will follow. And they did.

The next one will be brighter than all so far, it will be there, in as much time as... it took for all to bathe in the river. And after a time, a glow appeared. See how the mountain crest shimmers? It is bright.

She asked, how are you doing this?

I am remembering. A year ago I was at this same place watching them rise for the first time. But it is important for you to know that I cannot judge the passing of a year, or the time between to great accuracy, and it is not like I am re-playing in my mind what happened then. The ones risen so far make shapes with others already risen in my mind, and by drawing the shapes completely, they extend to below the mountain top from our eyes to those not yet risen. I can see them now but it is my memory seeing them, not my eyes. They would be visible already to one standing on top of the mountains.

She drew breath sharply and grew completely still.

Four are soon to emerge. They are wide apart. They will emerge in the order... here,here,here,here. It will be a little while before you see the first. The third and fourth will appear near the same time. And he moved his finger to where the first would be, and waited.

And it did. And he pointed again, and it did. And they all did. In wonder she said, I am becoming convinced of something. So you tell me, what am I becoming convinced of?

Only that I am a fool when I speak, and blurt out all I have learned with no regard for the natural suspicion of others. They need it in smaller pieces, with proofs or logical deductions for each step. Especially someone so dear to me, for whom truth is necessary to her sanity and survival. Another is coming, a glow over here. That one does not count, for I could have spotted the glow already. The next will be over here.

He kept calling them out, and there was time enough for him to explain he could see shapes invisible to others connecting things, and remember shapes. And many things that had happened to him, both in the real and the dream worlds. And he added finally, all this in itself does not prove I know the movements of the sky, but it is a long first step of explaining in slow-time. I want you to understand and follow completely and ask me to explain if you do not, for that is the best favor you could ever grant me.

She said finally, I love to hear you speak. It excites me. And if you keep speaking, I will follow you anywhere.

He was smiling in the dim light. The next one will be about here, it will begin to glow after the time... it takes for you to kiss me.

She turned, and he leaned forward and she kissed him. She said, that kiss was for your strange talent, not you. It gives me hope. Yours will be longer and sweeter. And so there is that cute little star!

She let him call out five more stars and then she lifted her crossed legs and spun to face him. Okay, I am convinced of something important now. Tell me about yourself. And I need no proofs, but also tell me what you observed in the sky and the deductions you made.

And she was calm and her fear had fled, and he had her complete attention. And her interest as a fellow sky-watcher. Her attention in that moment was the most precious and delicious thing he had ever experienced, the greatest gift he had ever received.

All he knew to do was tell it like a story. And he started by telling her things about his life and the ways he discovered he was different, but also how his people had treated him like a child and also a man, and let his own actions decide which, and for that he loved them all so. And his walks with polygons, and his own games with sound, shape and distance, and his concept of identities and measure and the place of memory, so strange he admitted to her he was unable to communicate what they actually were, from one mind to another.

I do not have to know them, she said. You have shown me what they can do. For I draw lines between stars too and make shapes to help remember them, and they are fragile things and trick me often, but yours most be solid indeed! You discovered your talent first on the land and played many games walking as a child. You were a master of something unique then, and did not know it. So when you put your attention to the sky and yet knew it would be difficult, you were ready and equipped for a deep quest.

He was transfixed that another could follow him so closely and plainly describe his life given such small hints. She was not just following him, she was circling him! And he thought to himself, you are my very own bright one, and I will cherish you always.

She was especially intrigued about the bright desert and asked endless questions how it looked, how it felt. She told him, there are such places in the world, but yours seems like it had been built for purpose, from ideas you had heard from others. By those Things you describe, perhaps. They are odd, and they are funny! And they could only be the two boys from your childhood dreams, and they grew with you.

Do you not think it strange that you never gave names to them? she asked. My mind is spinning from all of this. It seems that of all the tales come to life and the ones you told yourself, that it turns out you are in fact three men! That would explain a lot. But we all have spirits living in us. When I talk to myself, am I one person or two? When I try to convince myself of something, am I really two debating while a third listens? Could there be people with no voices at all in their heads, and they just do things and only speak and listen to others all their lives? I shudder to think of it. It seems so lonely.

He gave her foot a tight squeeze and then leaning forward, he lightly stroked and rubbed both her feet and ankles, and they swiveled like little animals presenting their favorite places to be rubbed. And now she stood and grasped and maneuvered him into a sitting position on the stone leaning against the log, and she sat sideways to him and set both muscular calves and feet on his lap, and she leaned forward to grasp his hands and placed each of them on a foot.

You were saying? She asked. Yes, just like that. It helps me think sharper and follow you better. Oh, a little harder. Now between the toes. They like to be spread apart. I am sooo following you right now!

He told her of the Things, how their faces had diverged over time from his own and even one another. He told her of his method of measuring the day with heartbeats, and how it led to his measure of star rising, and how he had no need for counting words. And how he had originally assumed the sky raced straight across and the sky would repeat the following night, and the incredible discovery that the herd moved slightly faster than the sun, and it had a much larger measure. And how he meticulously noted its small procession night after night. And how it planted the idea that everything in the sky was always moving or completely still, somehow.

That is good, she said. Very good. I was so confused to look up after a Moon to see different stars in the sky, and familiar ones also in different places. But you were not watching stars as I was. You were watching connected shapes as one! And yes, I follow about how the great herd appeared closer than the sun because it was moving faster than the sun. You were inferring distance from speed, as eyes do when you move. We do that on the water also.

So that is what I was doing, he said. I wish you had been here to describe all these things. I would have felt so much smarter! I might have even kissed myself!

And she took his hint by sitting on his lap and giving him a full and tight embrace, and a much longer kiss. Then resumed her previous position and placed his hands on her feet again, because it was all so fascinating she did not wish to distract him any further. That felt right, but devious somehow.

And he told her of the year, how he had maintained the sun's wobble as the sky measure for it, but also as a likely hypothesis for the extent of the great herd, such that it would repeat after as that exact thing again. And how the herd had indeed repeated precisely as the wobble returned to its starting place. What she said surprised him.

242

That is known in the far South, where they watch for a repeat of remembered shapes after a year. It was told to me later by a visitor and should have rekindled my interest, but I was already lost in sorrow. And it was done by collecting the tales and observations of many people. Your observation was slow and meticulous and kept in memory. And you were right to consider that tiny stars might mingle slowly in all directions like animals, and how any movement between them might change the possible nature of the whole. And she urged him on with a hand stroking his cheek.

His life had been one astonishment after another, and she was his greatest.

And he described the true path of the herd and how he had discovered it. And he did his very best to describe the ears of the world, the small slow star arches, the obvious straight path across the middle, and the smooth progression of shape between each path. And how it matched a symbol Walker knew, and his bizarre tale of 'the world as it is' and the conversation they had about it. And she followed!

She said, this is also known in the South, though people argue about it all the time and those who disagree accuse them of making things up. Perhaps You Were Mistaken, she said in the voice of an annoying person. The smooth progression of shape you will have to draw for me when there is light, but I understand. The sky has no corners. You said that, and it sounds mysterious. And of course, none of them can explain any of it at all! So from here you saw no circles, but assumed they were making little circles?

Which led to his account of the observation from the high place with Walker. There is much to tell about that, he said, and even more Walker told me in secret about his life then, as you can figure. But from there I spotted new stars within those I had seen from this stone, in even smaller circles. And familiar stars reached further on a circular path. And though I never saw a circle complete the suggestion supported the idea, and so I decided it.

As would I, she said. And to take that extra step. You are a good observer. Perhaps there is one in the middle of all the circles. At each ear. I know, she said as he started to speak. You didn't see a circle so your assumption is all you have. For not stating it for certain, you have earned another kiss. Don't worry, my kisses will never grow old, yet if this goes on I will have to think of other things to give you. Would you like to be kicked?

He said, line me up and send me straight across the goal.

You are a sweet boy, she said. Do you know how many men have said things like that to me? But it excites me to hear it from you, because you knew I had lined up straight and kicked different, from your far position sideways in the crowd, and that was a difficult sighting. Do you know how surprised I was by your question? But now I am smart enough to know there was a line on the field, straighter than straight, that only you could see. You will have to teach me this thing.

And then she pulled close to him, and he felt her warmth as she cried, I am so excited! Where do we go now? The stars I mean.

And then he had to continue the story and finally admit that his assumptions were all he had at that point, with few certainties. And time had gone by with the greatest mysteries unresolved. But then finally he had discovered a model in the real world and his mind, for the world and the sun and the Moon with its shadows and the great herd and a couple of bright ones, a model that was so great that it fit all the observations he had made. And stepping through this model it became obvious to him that only those particular shapes, that configuration and those movements could account for the sky as it is, and the world as it is. And so, that is how it must be.

It was starting to get light, night had ended. She was silent with his
sudden pronouncement, for there was no joke or comment to be
made that fit the situation. He felt a tiny seed of discontent in her
and he knew it would grow, so what to do next. He sent her on a
bizarre errand that she would have outright refused, had it been given
by anyone else in the world, and any time other than now. She had
agreed because he had asked the ridiculous thing straight out and
then said,

I want to show you something.

And they climbed down from the large stone and she was off at a run
to stretch her legs, and she was the very sight of gladness and
happiness and future itself as he watched her go. Is this what life
wants to be like? He wondered. Every moment an exciting
adventure?

He gathered sticks from near by and busied himself smoothing the
sand and loose dirt around the climbing stone. The morning was
hushed and still for it was to be a day of rest after the tournament
and feast. All had agreed beforehand that aside from the perpetual
duty of fire-watch, they would sleep late and remain in their homes
as they wished. Visiting teams would slumber late also, then gather
things to start journeys on the following morning.

She finally returned with a skin draped over her shoulders. She had
filled it by venturing into two fire-houses and tiptoeing around
sleeping team members sprawled everywhere. And she had begged
favors of those who were awake, and made necessary promises. She
tilted it and spread its muzzle and just what he had asked for dropped
out onto the ground.

Four pangolins.

He had put a dot in the center, and drawn two large circles around it.
He placed a ball in the center and one on each path, and set aside the

last for the moment. This is Mr. Sun he said outright, for he had not yet risen, and this path is the one our world travels, and he placed the world. And this is the path the orange one travels. He placed the orange one. Everything here is very distant but this is its shape.

And then he led her away from the circles. The circular 'world as it is' sky diagram was drawn there. He said, this is not part of that all over there, but it is the path of the great herd in the sky I have seen, and drew from my observation. The one Walker and I puzzled over and he remembered, the one you asked to see. Those are the ears of the world and the small circles. Our place is in the middle of the straight path and as we look directly above, everything also makes a straight path. The sun makes a straight path but as you and your people know, his path goes a tiny bit back and forth over a year, like this. He held a stick across the path and rotated it sideways a little back and forth.

And he stepped her through it all from the diagram to the world on its circle. He spun it with his hands and as it wandered on the ground he pointed out the equator and he said, this is where we are, and this is the straight path where the sun is. See him over there. It looks like he is spinning around us, but actually our eyes are spinning with the world and he is still in the middle.

At every stage he looked at her until she nodded or asked more questions. When he spun the ball and pointed out the ear of the world that was presently on top, and pointed to the hidden one on the ground, she gasped with astonishment and became very excited. But he said, it is important to know that there are no stars on this ball. Only our eyes, which are here, and he touched the equator. We look across the land as the world is spinning and we see the ears as little circling stars, but those stars are in real life very still and far away. It is the straight path between them and our eyes that is spinning in small circles. Imagine a bird hovering in the sky looking down at the ball...

and he drove this point until she understood well, and she tried hard, and finally did.

Every time she indicated she understood something, he smiled and hugged her. She wanted to be more affectionate but her mind was highly engaged.

His next demonstration was for her to imagine the world spinning between his two pointed fingers on the poles of the ball as he held it. He kept it in an exaggerated tilt at the same orientation always despite its place along the circle. He said, A year is one full circle. He walked the circle and stopped at every quarter. Only because of the tilt, the sun is on one side of his path when we see him from here. From here he seems to be passing through the middle of the land. From here he is rising and setting on the other far path. And here he is in the middle again.

At this point she had to take the ball from him and walk it herself several times. There were too many things in motion and pretend motion for her to see directly, but she finally made the connection in her mind. She said, this is very important and it fits.

He said, I have another demonstration. He rested the world on the ground on its circle, and he held a stick against the side of the world, and the stick was pointed at the sun. She leaned over and examined it.

He said, this stick is the light of the sun coming from him. It is late afternoon and he is about to dip below the hill. We see him directly and the edge of his circle shape, for we are on the world here, and he pointed directly under the stick.

He rotated the ball a little bit. Now it is night and the sun has disappeared to our eyes, but his light is still shining on the world above us. His light is still bright enough to cloak the stars from our view. The sky is bright blue-purple.

He rotated the ball again. Now to us it is darkest night. We are here. See how far the stick is from us now? This is the dark night side of the world. His light is far up in the sky and can no longer reach us or what surrounds us. His light does not crawl along the edge of the world to reach us or it would be day always. His light is now invisible from our place in the world and we now see stars in the sky. Turn all the way around you and look. Every leaf on every tree is a star. Every bird in the sky is a star. The climbing stone is full of stars. But any one of those things you could see from here, and he pointed to the place on the ball again, is a star we will see because it is night. The sun is no longer cloaking our sky with his light.

And here is my demonstration of why the star herd looks to move a little faster than the sun, to us. IF the world was just spinning in place and NOT also circling the sun, this would be our day and night forever. And he spun the ball in place. Day, night, day, night. And every night we would see the same sky, forever. And everything would be in the same place every night. A child would grow to be an old man seeing the same sky night after night.

But that is not what happens. The night sky changes slowly every night as the newest bit is revealed at night's beginning, and the oldest bit disappears into the light of the morning sun. The same sky over us only returns after a year, exactly as before.

He picked the ball up and put it down again further along the circle, while rotating the ball one full turn.

This is the next day, he said. The world has moved a day-step along the circle, but has also spun to give us the rest of the night, the following morning and day, then night again. From our new place on the circle, a few new stars are visible. And a few on the opposite side of the sky have been swallowed by the daylight-bringer as morning arrives. This happens every day. And when a year of days have passed, and he indicated the whole rest of the circle's path, we return to this part and see the same sky again. I will return to this.

He had noticed that the rays of the morning sun had entered the area, so he was ready for a demonstration that would definitely pique her interest.

He stood. I will now explain to you the Moon, and his shadows you see during his time that repeat. It is easy and simple to see. He bent and took the fourth ball into his hand.

She blinked in open mouth astonishment, for that was the greatest mystery that people wondered and debated. And she thought, such a mystery it was, that it was no mystery that people had given up explaining her and retreated to colorful and whimsical story.

You are standing there, he said, and pretend you are the world and our eyes that look out from it. You are the world, to me. This is Moon and he is a ball like all the rest. Moon is a world too, perhaps smaller than ours, but very close, and he circles around our world. He does not circle the daylight-bringer over there by himself like our world does. He rides with us where we go, and he only travels in a tiny circle around our world. I will now walk that small circle.

But Moon has no light of his own. Remember when I said at night the light of day cannot reach us because it is invisible, and high in the sky above us, and like the stick, pointed in another direction? She nodded.

Well Moon can see the day-bringer all the time from his path, and he always has a circle of light upon his surface, and another circle of dark shadow. But from our eyes we cannot always see the full circle of his light. Where I am standing now you can see the light shining full on him. That is a full moon, and you can see his full circle. If you keep looking as I move to your side on his path... now you can see a shadow growing upon him. That is where the daylight-bringer's light cannot reach.

From the side you see him half in light, and half in shadow. And from here, you now mostly see shadow, and only a crescent of him is with light. That is what you wear, your sign. And here, only his shadow is seen. This is the dark moon as seen in the morning, day and early night. He still has a full circle of light upon him, but it is on the other side and not visible to us.

And after I pass between you and the daylight-bringer, the shadows are on the other side of him and they diminish, and he returns to full. That is the Moon, to us.

At last Breeta said in wonder and amazement, but that is easy, just as you said! She is a ball, and has no light of her own. I follow!

Then she swayed, and caught herself. He dropped the Moon and reached for her and said in her ear, you do not need to follow right now. You are tired and we can explore this model together and you can point out any error I have made. For I am one little person in the world after all. But you are the most amazing thing in my life.

This time she embraced him, and he could feel her exhaustion. She was literally leaning against him. He said, there is more, and I am certain of it, but you must sleep. There are exciting things but we must start again and your understanding will move quickly through them, and go further. This was a whole year for me! And you have just run around the world on the pangolin field and kept your mind sharp over a long night. I will tell a great tale about you some day, and make you believe it. You are my hero! We go now.

She smiled with shut eyes and murmured agreement and muzzled against him, and he promised to return what she had borrowed before he slept, and received an exhausted kiss. He gathered the balls and shouldered the bag, and led her to his house, lay her down in his sleeping furs and covered her, and she was soon asleep.

When he arrived at the fire house he had spotted a problem, and asked a girl team member to identify each and return it to its proper owner as a kind and special favor. She had slept well so she gave him a knowing smile and he was given solid assurance, and he squeezed her hand in thanks.

Then he crept back into bed in his clothes as she was also, and snuggled with her, and she awakened slightly and snuggled with him, and said some nonsense words. He fell asleep watching her quiet face, his mind racing again until it wasn't. He did not dream the desert. He dreamed of her, doing every wild little thing she had ever done. They slept long into late afternoon.

———

NEW BEGINNINGS

When they awoke the house was empty, and they breakfasted on what was left over from his feast. She returned to the camp at the fire watch to rejoin her teammates and promised to return. In the evening she was back and they once again ascended the climbing stone. Her face was beaming under a crescent Moon and it almost matched the one she wore.

The team of the Moon has been discussing us all day! she declared to him with a wide smile. They think you have teased me in love and driven me to the wildest state of ecstasy a woman could ever achieve, using four pangolins.

Is such a thing possible? And one would not suffice?

I would not know. But I posed in front of them and tossed my hair as a sighing woman glowing with satisfaction, and said to them, you should try it sometime.

That's funny!

I understand them. And I have given news that is very bad to them, but very good for me. I am passing stewardship of the team to another who much deserves it, and leaving that place and saying goodbye for now to my parents. Moon is a crescent now and her light is diminishing. But around the time she is a full circle of light again, because of course she is behind us and seen with the full light of the sun from our spinning world… and she smiled at him… by your leave, I will return and appear again in your doorway and ask, may I?

You may, always and ever. My parents had already said as much to you, and then again to me today before you returned. They are happy and excited for us and they look forward to hearing your growls and snarls again. But this is more than I ever imagined!

She asked, what is your answer?

And he embraced her for all he was worth. His arms tightened around her and then his arms separated, and one hand gathered the back of her neck and stroked and tugged her hair, and the other reached below her back to find another part of her he had never touched before and it was beautiful also, and pulled both places to him tightly. She did the very same and he was drawn against her and they both gasped for air. And kissed, and then their faces pressed sideways and she felt his need against her for the first time, and it grew strong. They clenched one another and remained completely still in tension and pressure, as slow-time passed.

So that's settled then! she said at last, smiling and breathing hard as they separated to arms' length. I am a den-mother still and must sleep a bit and help the team prepare to leave in early light, and we will all be off. But we will meet again soon by the light of the fullest Moon, my very own star-gazer!

She watched him in the moonlight, and she knew his mind was racing with the thrill of young love as was hers for the first time, for she had planned her escape well and it was now complete. She was happier than she had ever been.

Then they sat and he started plying her with odd questions. This must be one of those 'what to do next' things of his, she decided, and while we have been just standing here being happy, his mind has also raced forward and is now several moves ahead. But as his questions continued, she began to follow his mind before he made it clear.

He asked of her parents, what they were like, and how much of her sorrow had been known to them and whether she imagined they had ever figured the real reason. He asked of her mother, what age she was, and since he knew Breeta was an only child, whether her mother had ever desired another. And he asked of her father, who had taught his daughter so many useful and valuable things. What if he asked, a boy might come to their doorway from this village and ask, may I? Would they welcome the chance to turn back time and raise another, and share love with him, and new love with each other... for it might be an escape for them also, an escape from loneliness and the passage of time.

For I know of such a one, he said. He is young still but is close kin to lake-folk and swims well and revels in water craft, and he already expressed to his parents that he knows he must leave them some day. For he dislikes our shallow river with no boats or people who desire them, and he hates even the little fishes, though he likes fish. He would say, Yes! A very big fish roasted over the fire if you please! It is more of a deep yearning for him than a tragic sorrow as you felt, but then again I must also wonder how yours began. And I fear for him, because he speaks of such things to girls he meets and they know he will leave some day, but he is unlikely to meet any who would leave with him. Perhaps it is for the best that he finds his life there, and maybe his parents would feel the same. I will speak to him.

And she was crying quietly at this. At the thought of one who also felt trapped by a place, but they were also tears of gratitude that there was a great mind in Stargazer who could gather up hints about people he knew and help decide a possible course of life for them, a course that would be good to them. And he is mine, she thought. And Stargazer held her hand, and they became tears of affection also.

She finally said softly, I think Mother and Father would like that. Shall I give you some hints and pointers to tell him about them, to seal his success in asking? And he said she should, so she did. She felt sadness for leaving them but it eased the pain.

And when they descended the stone and embraced for the last time in a while that was so long for them, she was in wrenching sobs of greatest joy and deepest sorrow. He was crying with her and she could hardly trust her own voice, so she gathered herself to say,

But not just. You are so much more.

And she bounded off at her own blazing speed, for she knew it was the only way she could leave him.

WHAT TO DO NEXT

He crept into his house alone and snuck quietly into bed, but his shallow intakes of breath betrayed him, and his mother came to him silently in the darkness and raised him out of bed to her bosom and started rocking him gently and stroking his hair. Then as his mind slowly collected itself he realized she was consoling him, for she could only believe that something had gone very wrong, and she must now try to help him find the strength to face another day.

No mother, he said. She is coming back! he said between sniffs. I am crying because I am so happy!

She said, whaaat? And she called Father who had awakened her with a nudge and whisper and sent her over to him, and in the tiniest light they were both standing over him and talking excitedly, and then they locked arms and were dancing in circles before him, and he was laughing at them, then with them, and they started growling and snarling at each other as they danced.

His mother finally said, she is a real lioness, you know. She will chew you up and spit you out and make you beg for more! And you are a smart boy, I know you will feed her only the best and never approach while she is eating. And his father laughed and growled at her through a kiss.

There were so many things to do next they spun in his mind slowly and he had to line them up carefully. The first item was the most difficult for him, for it was to wait until he knew her party had left and had walked far South along the river, for he did not want any news of current happenings to reach them. For the one he loved was a great celebrity in her own right, and people will gossip given half a chance.

And to those he did tell in the following days, he would only identify her as a player on the Moon team. This seemed appropriate, and did not affect in any way the aggressive and eager promises he received, when he told his plans of action to several groups. They loved him and this was their time to shine. Each in their own way, the village would welcome her by helping him.

But first he met with his young friend who had dreamt of living by the lake. In this his information had been a little out of date, for the boy had already been making overtures to relocate, and an uncle in the lake village had agreed to put him up there, but the uncle's offer was given reluctantly because he was happy living alone and his own children were long grown. The boy had insisted and gotten agreement but there was also the matter of tradition, for a village generally did not want to be perceived as draining children from another, when all was done.

So Stargazer's inquiry fell on eager ears as a most fortunate circumstance to him, and the boy grilled him about what his potential foster parents might expect, even as Stargazer was telling him those very things. But I am all those things! the boy said proudly and a bit defensively. My folks are expecting this. So I will just say farewell and go, he finally said. Stargazer embraced his new exchange partner for life and swore him to secrecy for now, and made him promise that he would find a party of three to travel with... and if at all possible, try to relocate before the next full moon. My uncle will be pleased if they like me, the boy said. But he will still be a part of my life and I will show him what a wise choice it would have been, and he will regret it! And then Stargazer told the boy while smiling at him, that the village was also home to the Lost Girls of the Moon pangolin team. And the boy left, suddenly moonstruck.

Well that was easy, he thought. Then he went to find his father and mysteriously brought him to other places and gathered several men with more cryptic invitations, to a quiet place at the very edge of the village surrounded by grass and trees, close to the river. This is the place, he said. Though any of you might speak up if you know of a better. My father here does not know yet why we are here, and he will learn as you do. And then he told them of the thing that would happen there, and asked them to grant favors to him that he would repay gratefully and many fold. And then he told them how little time before everything had to be ready. And that he would be with them every step of the way and do the hardest work. And his father smiled and they all laughed and slapped him on the back and said it was nothing, and they all would see it done with his help.

Well that was easy, he thought. He then approached the gathering place of the hunters and asked their permission to borrow several things he would collect soon, and perhaps a bit of tasty meat he could gather later around the time of the full Moon. For there was a very special girl he wished to entertain, and he wanted to take her to a place where they could be alone and he could make her feel welcome. And they laughed at this and slapped him on the back, and said it was nothing, and they would see it done.

Well that was easy, he thought. Now for the big one. So this time he approached his mother who was still smiling at his good fortune, mysteriously brought her to other places and gathered other woman friends of his who were his craft mentors, the ambidextrous huntress, an old friend sitting by her house, a slightly older girl he knew whose lover was watching over their newborn just fed and sleeping and she could spare a while, and two others only because they looked worldly as all passed by and they knew some already in the gathering, and agreed to take part in a cryptic errand.

This errand was a glade of dirt ground surrounded by tall grass well away from other ears, and he stood in the middle and addressed then all.

I have gathered you here to ask a special favor, and I pledge that anything said here will remain forever secret by me, and such pledges as you each wish to make to the others. My own mother is here, and she has no idea what I am about to ask. However I will use the information you give me to make my life better and to make someone else's life better, and others who ask me about such things in the future.

He looked at each in turn as he spoke and they glanced at one another as he did. I need to know what really pleases a woman. What she likes best, how long you can love her with hands and other things, how often and how soon she is ready for more and how you can start it, where tickling or stroking may start it. And anything in your past that has transported you to great heights. Anything unexpected and surprising and wonderful that has given you joy in complete surrender by the very sensation of it.

Things you do not like in men, things you tolerate in men though you wish it had happened another way, and places you wish men would touch more often or in another way.

I want to please a girl so long and so completely and with such vigor and softness and delicate touch and delicious surprise, that her face from moment to moment alone will bring me the joy I seek. For I love her, and I will love every minute with her, and I love you all for listening to me so far. And maybe she would love you all too if she knew your names, so great would her happiness be. But there will be no names, for I just want to see this done and done right. Because she deserves it all and more, for just being the beautiful person she is.

If you want to indicate parts of yourself that is fine, and there are a couple sticks to draw things on the ground. If it pleased you, please spare me nothing that ever made you very happy. Who wishes to leave, and who will go first?

His mother said, this is my son. He is very direct. But he is trustworthy also. I love my boy. I will go first.

None wished to leave. And every one was heard from, and several who spoke often. Many told of things that had happened when they were young, or years ago, or yesterday. There were nervous smiles at first but all nervousness left them as they realized they had been brought together for a great purpose. The young girl who was nursing left after a time, but she came back, twice.

There was earnest discussion, laughter and hugs, at times debate and argument. There were stories told by one that riveted the others, sudden eruptions of questions and declarations of pride in oneself or one's lover. It was a giddy discussion at times, then they would all become serious as they heard about some wonderful thing that had happened, and freely admitted to their new friends they wished it for themselves. There were tales of women with women with varying degrees of personal experience. There were descriptions of things women had done for them they wished men would do. One floored a discussion of her on top, and what miracles could be achieved. And novel ways for her to get on top and stay there. They listened to that intently.

And two from that group later became lovers with great satisfaction.

They drew diagrams and laughed at the anatomy of men and women and animals, and laughed at the drawn faces and swinging legs and arms, clenched hands. They pointed to things and circled things, and if one brought up any regrettable thing about men, another might suggest a remedy that had worked for her. And eyebrows would raise and several would nod.

And they all became life long friends and shared secrets with each other, and occasionally referred to it as The Conversation in the Grass.

As the sun waned they carefully brushed out the markings they had made and gathered Stargazer into a group embrace, and left their separate ways. Their lovers would wonder what had come over them as they were presented with new suggestions and greater challenges. But in the end everyone was a winner.

Stargazer's mother was the last to leave. She looked at him for a long time smiling silently and then said, they are lionesses all. I hope this will help you make up for lost time. And then she left.

He would have to sift through some conflicting information, but the faces on the others as they heard it would guide him also.

And there had been no mention of pangolins.

Well that was difficult, he thought.

That had been the first day. And the following days he was busy also.

———

MOONRISE

She had stopped in the doorway framed in the moonlight. She had set aside her pack, and wore a plain leather jacket with frills that dangled at the breasts and at the waist, and sturdy pants that frilled above the knees. She stood for a moment and crossed arms in front, but Mother interrupted before she spoke.

Of course dear, always and ever. Must I repeat myself? I will, so long as you wear a new outfit every time. I like this one also. But where is your sign?

It belongs to the team now. But do not worry, for I still have the original! And all embraced her as she entered, and helped take in her things. They had eaten but Stargazer sat her down and started to gather a meal for her. But first, he brought a drink of water and the bowl of salt and offered her a pinch of it from his fingers. She licked it off greedily and flicked her tongue at him while eyeing him hungrily.

They sat with her as she ate, and she remarked, you know the strangest thing happened the night before I left. Father was silent and had put on his stony brave face and gone out to do something, but Mother was weeping openly and uncontrollably because she could not help herself

260

and life was changing so quickly. I was crying too, and I sat with her head on my shoulder and her eyes were closed tightly, and I was stroking her hair softly.

And suddenly there was a boy standing in the doorway and he was still for a moment and looked as if to say something. But I gestured him to silence and beckoned for him to sit next to her, and he did, and his eyes looked at me in confusion and there were tears in them also, whether he felt for her or felt uncomfortable himself I do not know. But he also started stroking her hair and opened his mouth again but I quickly moved in front and squatted down between them and embraced them both. Mother opened her eyes and noticed the other, and this time I placed a finger of silence on her lips, and lifted her hand and kissed it, then lifted the boy's hand and kissed it, and laid his hand in hers, and stood before them.

And the boy asked her, may I? And stared to cry himself.

And Mother slowly realized what was happening and said, of course dear. And the boy pretended to take it as permission to gather her and rest her head on his own shoulder, and he rocked her gently as he sniffed and stroked her hair and murmured kind words. And then she saw my smile and realized what was happening in a larger sense, for they had all heard stories of scheming children, and she nodded to me and squeezed my hand, then embraced him quietly.

While taking another bite and chewing, Breeta said, and what were the chances of that? What amazing times! She smiled at Stargazer.

Stargazer returned her smile and said, I am just glad he chose right. Or I might have a new girlfriend.

And his parents laughed, for they had heard those stories also, and his mother gave him a wink.

And then they rose and started laying traveling things out on the ground and Breeta noticed his fur was not in his sleeping area. He was actually wrapping it around him and gathering it at the waist. Then he took wrapped packets of food and stuffed pockets he had stitched into it. And handed her a belt of small water skins, most empty. And Father reached to the side and brought out an extra tuft of hair and stuffed it into the fire kit.

He pointed to his wife. That is her hair, he said. Hers works best. It is greasier.

His mother pulled out a few more strands of her own and handed them to him and plucked a few hairs from his head also, and he crumpled and packed them all.

Stargazer inspected Breeta's foot coverings and noted she had leather soles tied securely up the ankles, and he said, good work, and he put on his own. Her whole face was a question by now, and he said, if you are not too tired, we travel by moonlight. No need for a sleeping fur of your own, and bring for two days or less. I have the food. Father had packed and there were two equal bundles wrapped and ready.

So this is more than a night in the woods, yet not a far journey, she mused to him. A mystery in the moonlight!

And by starlight, he said. Not to worry, there is Moon but I can find my way in the dark anyway because there is a line that leads directly to where we are going. But I think it passes through a tree. You will have to help me with that.

And then he said, come! Let me show you something.

They chose good walking sticks and set out for the edge of the village, and he led them down the path to the river. They unclothed and bathed one another gently in reflecting waves of moonlight. He washed off her travels and left no hidden part of her untouched, and yet applied only the firm muscular strokes of cleaning, and so she did likewise to him.

So not colliding suddenly and losing our minds in passion is the game of the moment she thought, and she liked games. And her mind flared and body shuddered as he drew his fingers slowly and firmly up between her legs in front to continue a deep massage elsewhere, so she retaliated by washing the stiffest part of him and giving it and its accessories a bit of extra attention, as if its rise to power had asked her politely to do so. They rose out of the water with smiles of promise and after brushing and shaking off, dressed again.

They walked North until the river went around a bend, and crossed in the shallows. Then continued North away from the river for some time through woods until he spotted some shape in the dark mountains, and later still they stepped across a stream and started following to where it emerged from a break in the hills and they followed it up. And he offered her his hand and they took every step slowly and carefully.

Finally he pointed and spoke with moonlight now almost overhead. Two together and a third apart. You may recognize these from the story. But since the brothers Grale and Groll were laid to rest and departed the world, there is no echo of terror or sadness in this place or the one above, and no ghosts. It has become just an empty place in the world, a high place and a beautiful place. It is ours now, a good place to start lives together. I have been there since we last met. And there is no great danger there, but always keep your wits about you.

They drank and filled all the water skins. Stargazer took the belt around his neck and they ascended the dark steep forest with care, and at last stood beside the crack in the world.

The moonlight enters a bit, he said. We will enter and tell me if your eyes feel comfortable with climbing. He climbed the first level and after her eyes adjusted she followed. She saw the horizontal shelves of stone inside, and said it was easy. So they slowly ascended and at last stepped out on top of the world. The bright Moon illuminated near and distant lands, and she held him in quiet tears as she gazed long at the distant shimmering lake. She then turned and cuddled with him, as if she was scratching an itch with her chest.

How dare you brush against a woman without taking her to the very top!

Is that any way to treat a man who stands up for you? he smiled. Come, it is further still.

They trekked in light now up the tilted lands with the strange boulders and then finally up and along the spine of the hill. It was the highest off the ground she had ever been, and she felt better holding his steady hand. And at last they approached the place of rock in moonlight and shadow, and descended to it.

Through galleries of stone and patches of glowing vegetation he led her until at last they stood in the long gallery and to one side against giant stones where they had kindled Walker's fire, there was a wrapped bundle. And under a tarp nearby there was a pile of sticks and the smaller branches of young trees.

She asked, Now how did that get there? to hear his answer.

Some poor fool must have brought it all the way up here, he said. In three trips. Lucky for us! Amazing times!

He revealed the bundle as a large hunting tent for several people and he unrolled it, and started propping it with a series of sticks inside, stones to anchor the outside, and sticks hooked into others that were already wedged in cracks above their heads. In the bundle secure from rain was also three big sleeping furs. To which he added his own, unwrapping it to reveal the leather shirt beneath. And the furs spanned the interior space with a double layer in the middle, and it was a large triangle open on one end.

Now for a fire, he said. They twirled vigorously and finally a spark kindled the tiny pile of dried moss and crushed dry fronds, and the magic hairs of the two who loved him. He blew it gently to flame. They set alight a bed of dry needles from the kit under the wood, and moved the flame through many small sticks until it caught on the larger.

Finally they had a crackling fire that would grow. The fire cast light directly into the tent and also the stone above it, bathing the inside in soft light.

It is not too chilly and there is little wind, she said. Why such a big fire?

So I can see your beautiful face as we love, he said. She shivered in anticipation of it and stroked his face in the flickering light, for it was beautiful also.

They left the growing fire and ventured through the narrow pillars and sat together in the high place upon its center stone. A place to be careful and alert but he is right, she realized. There is no danger and sadness lingering here and the past has departed, to live on only in Stargazer's tale as it is re-told by others. This place is ours now, a new beginning.

It is beautiful, she said. And the sky fools so many people because it looks still even in the long march of night. And those must be the very ears of the world, but in fast-time it looks like any other part of the sky. Every star is still, waiting for something. She spotted and pointed. Is the orange hunter still moving back on his path?

He is, but after a few moons perhaps he will slow again and pause and resume his main course against the sky. That movement is something I did not have time to show you. So exhausted you were! And your mind needed sleep. You are an amazing creature.

I loved that night in slow-time with you, she said dreamily.

He pulled her tightly to him.

I want to love you in slow-time, he said. You must be very patient. I will show you the way, but you must try to let your fire build slowly and enjoy every bit of it. Taste it! Savor it! You will ascend from your own greed because you are a perfect creature and that is just what you are, and you deserve it to happen, and it will happen, and you will at last blaze suddenly like the sun in ecstasy and heat and happiness, and you will descend slowly in bliss that feels like the final conquest of love.

But I will catch you gently and touch you in other ways that you will feel as a smooth continuation of that love, and it will give you quiet fire also but you will be relaxed and happy, and after a time your most secret and beautiful places will have rested, and I will kindle them again in a way that brings you sudden joy and you will know you must rise up again. For I will make you ride it.

As you tire I will take your muscles firm in hand and revive them and love them, for they love you, and you will awaken from half-slumber fully with strength returned and your mind will suddenly blaze with the delicious heat of a new promise I have given you. And you will rise again. And this will happen many times, more than your busy mind could count.

Think of it as a game. Your every triumph is a point and a win. You are a natural champion. I will keep score for you with great pride, for I love you. And my greatest desire is to see you take the game as far as it will go.

You will want to take me and if you do, I will surrender of course, for I am no match for you. But for as long as I am able to surprise you, yield to what you feel and express your happiness with your face and body and voice. It is a gift to me. And your arms and legs are long and your feet are as nimble as hands. When you feel the fire, stretch them wide and tight and I will stroke places softly that make your body sing. Take me when you are overcome with boredom and I am yours. Stay with me if you find a better place and greater happiness, and we will both climb slowly together.

I am presenting you to the Moon, and you must surrender to her forever or how ever long it takes, so you can learn how beautiful you are, and convince yourself of it. You must be certain. At any time I know you could chew me up and spit me out like the lioness you are. But be patient, as I am. As days pass we will love in other ways. Your keen mind will decide what to do next, and you will take me by complete surprise.

But tonight, let me show you something. Are you ready?

She rose and offered him her hand, and her whole body was trembling with excitement, and she led him back to the fire. And they started to undress each other.

INTERMISSION: FROM THE CONVERSATION IN THE GRASS

I look to be the oldest here, and have loved men and women in my life and I have captured them and tamed them, and bent them to my will over many happy years, and some of us were completely devoted to each other, until others or this cursed world took them from me. To the young man with the curious eyes I will say there are secrets about you I know, but I would not tell them. For you must learn them from her and you will some day, if you are worthy and she is clever. Those secrets will amaze you and she will delight in the sight of your face as you discover them. I too delight in the face of the one who has surrendered to me. It is my best memory of them.

But as you take control and guide your lover, avoid locking your gaze on her face and keeping it there, as I know you will be tempted to do.

For her precious mind is also making memories as she tastes your fire, and she needs to see you in all of your expressions, looking in concentration at parts of her and intent on the task, even raising your face in a smile to the sky with closed eyes, for she will see that you too are transported in bliss, as you are with the mere sight and sound of her, and that will push her also, as you are pushed by her movement against you as she responds to your touch.

Lovers gazing at each other can be a quiet thing and should be the main thing, but sometimes it brings to others the desire to speak or kiss, to say or do the obvious. You want to hear no speaking from the one receiving good love that is timeless.

You want no long embraces, only a surge of greed as she swivels her body into you to claim greater pleasure for herself, her own exploration and discovery of what her beautiful muscles and limbs and breasts can do for her, and only noises of surprise and satisfaction. Her mind must be kept in amazement and wonder, and greedily clutching the sweetness that is happening to her, and desiring more.

If her hands explore you, that is love. But if you can steer her own hands to places of her that were nice when she explored them by herself, but while being loved completely by another they explode with beautiful heat, and her mind is held by this and she continues, you have done it right. For she will also be pleasing herself with such attention she can spare, and gazing at you in thanks for every moment, just for the showing. The purpose of your quest is for her to learn how beautiful she is, and see that she is wholly convinced of it.

All I will say to you as a man is, the thing you were given to please her must be used to finish love, not start it. You have my pity and your burden is great, for you must make and gather seed as love is happening to you, and you must give it all to her in the end, every time, every little bit. You must do this. If you do not, your mind will be destroyed as it wears away the joy and happiness that is rightfully yours.

But of the very thing you seek, I have some good news for you. You can do it. I was loved for the first time by a woman who knew my body as well as her own, and I gave complete surrender at her very first touch, and she kept me in a tight grip and ordered me with her voice to stretch things and do things as she loved me with her mouth and her fingers, and everything I did for her was delicious and beautiful. And then she said, now I will teach you to fly, and flooded me with sensation and such joy I cried out and floated above the world and pushed myself over greedily with the tiniest effort.

That was only the first, my beautiful lover said finally, as I lay glowing and her hands continued to move and I was held in happiness by them. She shared her wisdom and kept me in loving and flying surrender without stopping for the better part of a day. I was trembling happily from it and even the light from above caressed me! I remember what she said as she loved me, for her words tasted like warm honey in my mind, as did everything on that day. So here is my advice to you.

Women are sublime. They are different! The ability to receive endless love is a gift to them. Even long ascensions and many sweet endings might have been given to them to stay happy and contented while a man finishes. But they have taken it so much further.

A woman has many parts of her that like to be brushed or stirred, or even squeezed tight in a firm manly grip of affection. Strong muscles are important in this, hers and yours. And if the path of squeezing or gentle caresses approaches her sweetest and most delicate parts, her mind will seize on the promise of a journey and she will feel a tingle and yearning at its final destination, and you will kindle her desire. Only after her mind catches a tiny flame of promise do the best parts of her awaken. Any part of her will do at first.

But if she is friendly and you want to be direct, as your dear mother has suggested, only brush against the sweet center you will command later, as if by accident, for it is very sensitive and may be unpleasant until her desire is full and engaged.

Put your attention instead to the delicate folds around it and treat them gently and kindly. They want to be stroked and grasped and spread lightly and played with, if she has made them accessible to you, and they will whisper delicious promises to her and soon make her very ready, and kindle her desire to its fullest strength for you. It is why they exist, their purpose. And you must teach her about herself by treating them well, and give them even more attention than she has ever given them in her own pursuit of joy, and she will at last beg you for love.

And thighs inside the leg are very important, every bit as important as the delicate folds between them. For every touch to them and the folds as one, each stroke leading to and from the other and back again, will give her sudden joy in the act of knowing them, and spreading them wide and stretching tight. Too many spread or open as some dutiful act of receiving a man, and they do not discover this ancient magic. But thighs are magic! For my own lover commanded me to do this, and her gentle strokes against my tightness and the thrill of those delicate folds was her very first gift of surprise and wonder to me, and it was so hot and delicious with promise I happily became her prisoner.

Surprise and change from moment to moment in her kindled mind, especially from her most sacred and special places, is very important. If you lose surprise you lose her, and she will jump on you and finish you, and finish the job. You must be terrified of this or you would not be asking. Sweet boy.

Others will tell you how to excite a woman and push her over the top, and I encourage them to do so, but I will speak directly to your quest and tell you how to keep her your prisoner in love, and distract her in sweetness even from her inevitable desire to change course and please you, so you may see her rise with her mind bathed in fire she cannot resist, again and again.

You will command her as she rises, and after a time she will take charge of herself and peak with abandon, which you may bring also, and you must learn the signs as it is happening. It is not always easy, for some cry out and some thrash about and some freeze still and silent, some breathe in deep gasping moans and some hold their breath, and some young women even try to hide it in shame they do not deserve, for they have learned about love from stupid stories that claim such beautiful joy is a state of ending and final reconciliation, and perhaps the man has not quite finished.

But once she has tossed herself over and surrendered completely to that beautiful reward, and you know it for sure, you must grow still on her most secret place, and your best thing to do is to keep a bit of pressure on it and vary the pressure slightly so it just flickers in her mind, but ease off. For as she floats to earth and rests you must abandon it for awhile. For many women it becomes unpleasant if her lover is still touching her in excitement, and she will even reach out her hand to pull the other away.

But you are a smart boy, you know it is happening to her and have planned for it, and as she floats down from her peak you have already taken charge of another unexpected and lovely part of her, and are doing pleasant and wonderful things that keep her attention.

Not the nipples mind you, some like it but for others they become sensitive also. But any part of her you like, which is any part of her. The more strong muscles she has, the more vulnerable she is! For you will be already giving the greatest massage and stroking caresses of some new place that she has ever experienced, and she is glad to receive it, and it will trap her in time as her body relaxes completely, even the sensitive places that give her the hottest fire in love.

And she will submit to it for a while, even if she has already made up her mind to take you and finish you. You must make her greedy for it. And the pleasure of love will still be upon her and your strokes and squeezes will be like little sparks of it, and that is to your advantage.

Do it so well and with surprises of its own and fascinating little journeys, that she remains your prisoner. Her secret place will grow silent and relaxed and she will not even know she is ready to ascend in love again. But you judge this, and the kindling is not as necessary as it was at first. For when she is ready you can approach the secret place in secret and surprise her with it as your other hand is in mid-stroke, and do both together as if she is feeling one hand, and her sudden excitement will become a promise and a new beginning, and she will feel intense love and sweetness as if she had never left it behind. She will surrender again while gazing into your eyes full of admiration for her and clear purpose, as you take her on another long journey of hot love and ascension.

Make sure you are both well rested and very awake and you both pass water before the start. Every time she has climbed a mountain of pleasure and takes flight, when she opens her eyes the first thing she must see is the proud face of her lover offering a drink of water. Only a small drink to replace her efforts, for the passing of water interrupts love. And only with one hand.

Your other hand must be upon her and moving well without stopping as she drinks, for as soon as she lays back again the time of complete massage and gentle relaxation resumes in full, and her mind will say, this is so good and I am so good, I must remain here for awhile before I take him. And in the end you will deceive her, for she will feel something surprising, sudden and delicious with heat and promise, and your smiling eyes are telling her that she will now rise again. And she will, and her heat will be even greater, for that is the most beautiful gift given to women.

And that is how to keep her your prisoner in love.

And his mother smiled at the oldest among them and added, Be sure to have water for yourself also, and put everything where she will not knock it over. For you are going to make her very happy.

——

WANING GIBBOUS

They had loved and slept and loved again into the late afternoon, and she had turned on him and surprised him with many of his own tricks. They rose and took a trip to the stream and steep woods to gather more water and wood to spend another cozy night in the high place. He had found it exciting to round the last corner and see their temporary lodge of sleeping furs among the stones and he said to her, it is so quiet here and so warm by the fire. It feels like a home already. I love this place.

I know what you mean. It is so warm here, she said, kissing him softly.

They dumped the supplies and kindled a new fire as it was almost evening again, and wound through the passages to sit once more in the high place.

She examined his face. Love was transforming them. Emotion is flowing already more easily from him she thought, and there was less of the edge and pensive seriousness that had defined many of his moments. They were already as a couple in love for many comfortable years and their gathering adventure had been filled with easy conversation, taking in the views, brushing caresses and knowing glances.

She felt for the silly and desperate girl she had been. And she loved that girl deeply also, for the buzzing warmth in her body would tolerate no criticism, and everything that had ever happened led directly to this moment.

And he had changed also. Even in her breathless conversation on the day they met, she had seen awe and amazement move across his face, and a stunned expression of happiness had come over him. When he had said he would go catch little fishes, he had been looking down at the ground beaming in a wide smile. He was shy and trying to hide it from me. I really did surprise him.

But so much she had learned of his character, she knew if she asked a strange question he would answer directly and if he wondered why she had asked, he would make that plain also. And he seemed to remember everything. Maybe there is a bright desert in his mind full of me, she thought. I will make it a happy place.

She snuggled against his chest and asked, when you declared you were going to catch little fishes to feed me, you were smiling at the ground. I have never seen a brighter smile. Why?

He tightened his arms around her. That is when I decided at last that you were real, he said. His eyes widened. See? I am deranged also! He laughed easily, and she turned her head to the side and felt him sniff her hair and inhale deeply.

Then they were lost in conversation and discussed the model. She followed it all from before as he had described it, and even took its meaning to a next level on her own.

So the bright one that is always near the... the day-bringer, she said, glancing at the departing sunlight and adopting his custom. So she is a world also with no light of her own, and she circles him, but her circle is much smaller than ours? And she is always moving and her path seems strange to us because our eyes are always moving around her?

He expressed his answer with quiet and enthusiastic affection, and she responded that she understood his answer with affection also.

She looked down at her lap and said, which leaves us with the last part of the mystery, the orange hunter's reversal. It is obvious he would always be somewhere along his circle, seen or unseen by us in day or night. And you say worlds are always in motion and there is no slowing or stopping. So what is the answer to this backwards mystery? She sat up straight and faced him.

Her lips are so beautiful, he thought. She even has a different face for questions! I love that face.

That is a puzzle of circles within circles. Walker might have figured the answer himself, because he posed it to me in such a way that the path to the answer was clear. Maybe that is the usual way people figure things out together, or maybe he knew the answer and just liked to watch me think. So the orange hunter is a world with a larger circle than our own as you saw, right? Circles within circles.

Yes, she said.

And he took her through how circumference of a world circle has many paces to travel in a year, and the orange one has many more paces to travel in his year circle than we do, so we will catch up to him sometimes and outpace him.

He continued, And so what happens when our world faster in its shorter path is approaching him and begins to overtake him?

Wait! she said, holding up her palm and looking down at her lap again.

He stopped.

She continued, He would be forward of us going forward. Then he would look to be slowing as we catch up to him. Then he would be beside us and only appear to stop for a short while. Then he would be behind us moving forward again. But something is not right.

He waited.

Something is not right of course because there is no backward motion in that. But... we are... we are not seeing his true motion with our eyes. We are seeing something else, like the illusion of little circles at the ears of the world... and that is our eyes in motion looking sideways across the world at a star that is not in motion. But there is only one motion in that path of seeing...

Stargazer began to get very excited.

She finally said, Yes! It is the straight path of seeing from our eyes to the hunter and past him to places in the great herd behind that we see, to judge his position. And we judge false, and it tricks us, because we are in motion and he is also in motion, and the herd is not. So that is what overtaking looks like from circles within circles to something behind. There are two motions that are changing our path of seeing! The backwards stroke is... the passing of the slower world. A stick of seeing bridging the two worlds as the inner passes would move backwards against the great herd for a time!

Breeta was astonished by what she had just said. Sticks of seeing and pangolins moving on circles. With such a model in her mind, she could follow!

Her face remained astonished and her lips parted slightly as Stargazer's embrace squeezed the wind out of her with a gasp. He was weeping now.

You... you... he said, unable to gather words. She smiled and stroked his face, and kissed his tears.

Then she whispered in his ear, love me in slow-time again.

And she stood and offered her hand, and once more led him from the high place.

———

JOURNEY'S END

They packed up the lodge and all the furs into a giant roll that was more bulky than heavy, and at the top of the crack he just tossed it over the side. At several places in the steep forest he was stopped short as the shouldered roll spanned two trees.

You will have to help me with this, he said.

She just laughed and let him figure it out.

They descended the stream and set out over the land. After an unusually long silence as they walked, Breeta did a thing she would do often in years to come, something he cherished about her. She moved in front of him and stood still facing him. She looked intently and said, You have stopped talking. What are you thinking right now? Have you been thinking about the same thing for a long time?

Yes it has been a long time. I am thinking about a thing Walker said. He was offering an assumption about our world traveling faster along its circle because of its shorter circle-path. As compared to the orange hunter with a longer path. But what he said exactly was,

It may be possible that all these worlds were started in the same motion by the same hand, or nearly so.

He started walking again, asking, What do you think of this? It seems to have more than one meaning.

She asked him to say it again and thought for awhile and asked, Does 'nearly the same hand' have a meaning?

I guess not, he admitted. Or rather, I cannot think of one. I am not used to thinking of these things with another.

Of course you are! Just think of me as Thing Three with the soft beautiful hands. So we are left with one hand starting all the worlds in the same motion, or one hand starting all the worlds in nearly the same motion, right?

Uhh, okay. You're so funny! And right.

So, she said playfully, did you and Walker discuss worlds traveling in 'other motions' or what I mean is, other than circles? Any other shape or kind of path? 'Nearly the same motion' does not seem to make sense either for paths, it would be one type of path or another type, and he would have described the other he was thinking of.

No, we only discussed circles. But that is an interesting idea, if there is another shape that has no corners yet returns to its start place after smooth motion over time.

That reminds me of a pangolin that hops as it rolls. But Walker could only have meant speed then, she said. You have said as much already. As in worlds pacing along their paths at the 'same speed' or 'nearly the same speed'.

Umm, yes, he admitted.

I am sure it is the hand that is really bothering you, she said finally. And why you are still thinking about it. Otherwise you would have done something like, help I am so confused think-think-think oh he meant nearly same speed think and done!

You are either very funny or very right.

I am both! So the hand that started all the worlds, I guess by giving them a little push or something, was it a scratchy leathery hairy hand or was it a soft, beautiful hand? She flexed them to help him decide.

He stopped and looked at her.

Was the hand attached to anything? Was it walking or hopping around on its fingers? How many fingers did it have? You would only need one finger to start a world. Where is the hand now? Where was it before it started all the worlds? When did this happen? Okay, mister ever-still or forever-in-motion, how does the hand fit in your big picture?

He thought awhile then said while smiling at her, It does not fit. At all. Thinking about the hand has been a waste of my time.

Good. I do not ever want a scratchy hairy hand to come between us.

He lunged for her and again cupped her neck and bottom, and this time lifted her off her feet and spun her round and round.

Conversation began once more as they resumed their journey.

In twilight they reached the bend in the river and crossed again, and headed towards the village.

They ascended the path from the place of bathing and headed across the village, but instead of turning towards his house he led them to the place of fire-watch.

From the doorway several children greeted him on sight.

Two rolled lit torches, please. My love and I wish to set each other on fire.

They shrugged without comment and went to prepare them. Stargazer was older now and this was no more bizarre than anything adults said. Rolled torches were spun in a bowl of animal fat for longer and brighter burning. At last a girl brought two lit torches and handed them to Stargazer and Breeta.

Please don't do it here, the girl said firmly, and it was not clear which possible meaning she was referring to. Probably both, he decided.

Breeta followed behind as he retraced their steps and then, instead of continuing back down the path to the river from which they had come, he unexpectedly veered to the left.

Yet another delicious mystery, she thought.

Let me guess. You want to show me something.

He turned and looked at her, grinning.

It was a trodden path and the grass looked to have been flattened in several places recently. The ground was marked with furrows and scratches. Then the path turned.

A clearing, and in the middle was a standard round dried mud hut with a skin over the doorway. All around it was the raised furrow of a living fence, just young shoots now but they would grow into young trees to be shaped by human hands and bent together until they fused. Around the back was a latrine pit with a shroud over it on a frame of poles. Stargazer approached the doorway and lifted one side of that skin from its peg and stretched it outside and hung it on another peg.

She noticed that the privacy shroud of the latrine pit had a large crescent Moon cut out of it. That's funny! she thought.

He took off his pack and giant roll, and watching him she unburdened also. He beckoned her towards the dark doorway.

Go look inside, he said.

She stepped inside and raised the torch. It was a standard layout for a hut built on a gentle slope, with a central smoke hole sheltered from rain by a small rounded tent on the roof, and a central pole for support. Interlaced branches along the walls to support them knit with smaller ones to provide a foundation for grass and the outer mud covering. Three levels of flat dirt protected from erosion and feet by stone edges, and coarse woven grass mats everywhere but near the hearth.

It was a real hearth edged with flat stones and a wooden frame on each side to support a roasting spit. It was piled with one rack of firewood, with several more off to the side. There were baskets both plain and water-bearing, several small and large water skins. Serving bowls and wood pieces for preparing and serving food.

The sleeping area was large and was the highest dirt level with mats underneath and furs of several types of animal already upon it. There were shelves of wood made from split hollow logs. And there were skin pouches on poles that were for non-perishable foods, some full. And sitting places and logs, the long step facing the hearth with flat stones along the sides and a concave surface for people to sit on lined with mats. And to one side, what was it called? a table-door? stood on end.

And on the ground near her feet, a bowl of salt. Something flickered in her mind at the sight of it, a thought she dismissed before it formed.

But mostly now she felt uncomfortable, there was a feeling that the owner had just stepped out and would return to discover her inside, uninvited. She asked slowly, who... lives here?

From the doorway Stargazer said, you do.

She whirled to face him with mouth open.

This is, and always will be, your house. Almost the whole village has a hand in it, from the digging of the foundation to the laying of branches into a circle and others between them and lots of hewing wood poles and inclining them to the center and anchoring them.

And the small children scrambled up the branches and laid layers of straight grasses on top and draped them over the sides, to receive wet mud. Then we dug a pit, the latrine pit it is now, and tossed loose soil and sand and crushed bones and river mud into it and I jumped in and squeezed it with my hands and feet with a bit of extra water to make sticky-mud. And then we pelted the children with gobs of sticky-mud and scored many direct hits, and the muddy little children patted it into and over the grass from the center outwards. Adults with better reach did the sides under the overhangs, they are tricky! The weavers planted the fence. And so on. And others provided goods you see here. And I helped a great deal, though I could never have done it alone in such a time.

Stargazer said, The village welcomes you with open arms, Breeta, formerly of the lake people.

She could not see him any more through the tears, and the only words she could think of, and the only ones she could manage, was a parody of his own outburst. You... you... and she wiped tears with her free hand.

Stargazer stood in the doorway with the burning torch.

And he asked her, may I?

She was weeping again and she could only stutter through intakes of breath, and it took a while to say it. Yes... always... and... ever...

And he came inside and brought the lodge roll and their packs and set them aside, and walked to the far side of the hearth and held his torch near one side of the racked wood, and looked at her.

She thought Of course! The bonding ceremony! Each lights a side of the hearth and when the flames join they are one. She nodded vigorously through tears and positioned hers at the other end. They gazed at each other smiling and set it alight.

Stargazer busied himself with dousing the torches and rooting through their packs for leftover food and other items, then approached the doorway. He turned.

She had tossed away and stepped out of her clothes and was beckoning him with open arms. Behind her nude silhouette their flames merged.

Come! We must set each other on fire. We promised the children!

I was actually about to close the doorway because of, um, children.

Leave it open! Let them watch, they might learn something.

He embarked on the greatest journey of his life. The phrase is overused, but this one really takes the cake.

—

EPILOGUE

Awe of the universe and desire to understand its true form is no different for any ancient and modern human. His people had migrated North in Africa to where they had been over aeons. They gathered together and told stories about the night sky from the best evidence people could discover. But intuition could be guided by the equator and what can be seen from there.

How many geniuses have there been over the last million years using nothing but Occam's Razor, various talents and pure determination... to infer the true heliocentric nature of the Solar System and a clue about the Universe? I propose that in the equatorial band of Earth at least, all it might take is a child's desire to spin, a few good observations, and perhaps a yen for ball sports.

And a clean-shaven child without a stubble of hairy dogma imposed on them from a young age and carried to adulthood, that might convince them that truth is mainly be found in a process of learning from others, and not pure discovery and inference.

He never glimpsed an actual pole star if there had been one then. It probably always would have been just below his local horizon. Today the North Star we use is Polaris, but the celestial bullseyes of Earth's axis of rotation continue to drift slowly. Stargazer's descendants followed the Nile from its sources in those mountains, leaving more people along the way. Egyptians were far enough North to see a pole star.

They built a great civilization in the Nile Valley with pyramids that align to cardinal directions within 4 minutes of arc. The North-facing entrances of pyramids reveal Egyptians to be not your usual sun worshipers. ~4600 years ago the North polestar was Thuban, thought to be the abode of Osiris. It is still visible in the Northern Hemisphere but Thuban now rises ~25 degrees from true North. One cool theory is that a pyramid was a rocket sled of the spirit to the afterlife. I sent an email to inquire if one Osiris or Khufu is still a resident of Thuban but must wait ~606.6 years for a reply.

Having grown up ~15 degrees North of the equator I feel a sense of kinship to these peoples over deep time. I hope there were a lot of them and none were burned at the stake.

And of course, any lasting remnant of his people with the materials they used is long gone.

Stargazer's full day was ~17 seconds shorter than ours, since the Earth's rotation is slowing from the cumulative effect of ocean tides from the Moon. We know that for certain. You can express it as resting heartbeats if you like.

Stargazer and Breeta live at 101 Bathing Path, North Craft Village. They have four children, two boys and two girls, and none have shown any apparent genetic abnormalities so far aside from an odd sense of humor.

They are the authors of The Heliocentric Day-Bringer System: The World As It Is, now out of print for a million years. The last surviving copy was lost with the Library of Alexandria.